D0286601

MURDER IN THE AFTERNOON

"I'll see you later," said Daisy.

"Can't we come and listen to you?" Belinda asked, disappointed.

"No, it's a talk for grown-ups. You wouldn't find it interesting." *And nor will my audience,* Daisy thought despairingly, crossing the lane. Why had she ever agreed to make a fool of herself, like a monkey in a cage, with everyone staring and wishing she would do something entertaining.

At least she looked professional, she hoped. Peering over her shoulder, she poised first on one leg, then the other, to check that her stocking seams were straight.

She turned down the path to the gate which led to the Parish Hall, her steps lagging as she felt in her handbag for her notes. Had she time to glance over them? She must! She couldn't remember a word. Just for a minute she'd sit down on a tombstone. There must be one nearby.

Glancing around, she saw that the granite angel had fallen flat on its face. Beside it on the grass lay a shabby Panama with a faded tartan band.

And between its head and the top of its wing, a round face with a startled expression stared blindly at the sky . . .

Daisy Dalrymple Mysteries by Carola Dunn

DEATH AT WENTWATER COURT

THE WINTER GARDEN MYSTERY

REQUIEM FOR A MEZZO

MURDER ON THE FLYING SCOTSMAN

DAMSEL IN DISTRESS

DEAD IN THE WATER

STYX AND STONES

RATTLE HIS BONES

TO DAVY JONES BELOW

THE CASE OF THE MURDERED MUCKRAKER

MISTLETOE AND MURDER

DIE LAUGHING

A MOURNING WEDDING

FALL OF A PHILANDERER

Published by Kensington Publishing Corporation

STYX AND STONES

Carola Dunn

KENSINGTON BOOKS
Kensington Publishing Corp.
http://www.kensingtonbooks.com

KENSINGTON BOOKS are published by

mw

Kensington Publishing Corp.
850 Third Avenue
New York, NY 10022

Copyright © 1999 by Carola Dunn

All rights reserved. No part of this book may be reproduced
in any form or by any means without the prior written consent of the Publisher, excepting brief quotes used in reviews.

If you purchased this book without a cover, you should be aware
that this book is stolen property. It was reported as "unsold and
destroyed" to the Publisher and neither the Author nor the Publisher has received any payment for this "stripped book."

All Kensington Titles, Imprints, and Distributed Lines are available at special quantity discounts for bulk purchases for sales
promotion, premiums, fund-raising, and educational or institu-
tional use. Special book excerpts or customized printings can
also be created to fit specific needs. For details, write or phone
the office of the Kensington special sales manager: Kensington
Publishing Corp., 850 Third Avenue, New York, NY 10022,
attn: Special Sales Department, Phone: 1-800-221-2647.

Kensington and the K logo Reg. U.S. Pat. & TM Off.

ISBN 0-7582-1395-6

Published by arrangement with St. Martin's Press
First Kensington mass market Printing: November 2002
10 9 8 7 6 5 4 3 2

Printed in the United States of America

PROLOGUE

The order came when dawn was a mere promise on the eastern horizon. The grumbling men fell silent as they crawled out of the miry, stinking trench, their meagre refuge for the past two days. Bent double, they ran through the mist across no man's land, fixed bayonets aimed at the invisible enemy.

The leaders covered twenty yards before the mine blew. Half the platoon vanished in an eruption of flame, mud, and blood.

Swallowing dry sobs, the chaplain stumbled towards the nearest screams. Private Harvey—'Enry 'Arvey—a Cockney monkey of a man, always a cheerful word for a pal who was down, showing bewildered young recruits the ropes, so proud of his wife in the munitions factory somewhere in the Midlands, his boys, two ever more tattered photographs . . .

Henry Harvey, legless, bleeding to death far from home.

The chaplain dropped to his knees. Beneath him Mother Earth shuddered as the big guns started up. Harvey's limp hand in his, he prayed aloud. Silently, he cursed the Lord.

1

"Darling, I wish I could. But Johnnie's taking me out to lunch and he'll be here any moment."

"Johnnie?" The hint of jealousy in Alec's voice tingled along the wires to Daisy's ear.

With a small, smug smile, she explained: "Johnnie Frobisher—Lord John—my brother-in-law."

"Oh, *Lady John's* Johnnie." His relief was patent, though he was several miles away, at New Scotland Yard.

"Lady John's Johnnie!" Daisy laughed. "I'm sure she asked you to call her Violet, darling. Anyway, he's come up to town for the day and invited me to lunch with him."

"The Ritz, I suppose, or the Savoy," Alec said gloomily. A Detective Chief Inspector's salary did not run to luncheons at the Ritz.

"Darling, you know I'd rather be with you at Lyons' Corner House eating Welsh rarebit, but how could I have guessed you'd be free today? Oh, there's the doorbell, I must run." She turned to call down the stairs to the daily char in the semi-basement kitchen: "I'll get the door, Mrs. Potter! Alec, I'll ring you up at home this evening. Toodle-oo, darling."

Daisy carefully hung up the earpiece of the brand new telephone apparatus she and Lucy had splurged for not a week ago. Lucy had paid the whole cost of the extension to her photography studio in the old mews behind the "bijou" residence they shared, but Daisy's part of the expense was quite steep enough. They were back to living on eggs, cheese, and sardines, so a meal at a good restaurant was jolly welcome.

All the same, and much as she liked Johnnie, she had rather lunch with Detective Chief Inspector Alec Fletcher. She had scarcely set eyes on her fiancé since that glorious weekend in the New Forest.

The memory brought back the small, smug smile as she glanced in the looking-glass over the hall table. She straightened the blue straw cloche garlanded with white rosebuds, which perched on her honey-brown shingled curls. The hat's colour matched her eyes, which Alec was wont, when, annoyed, to describe as "misleadingly guileless," though he spoke in more flattering terms when in a softer mood.

Daisy's linen costume was a darker blue piped with white. Quite smart, she thought, if only her figure were fashionably boyish. The straight lines and hip-level belt could not be said to suit her.

As she wrinkled her nose at the rounded curves Alec considered delightfully cuddlesome, she noticed three freckles. All very well in the country but *not* acceptable in town—she added a quick dab of powder. She had given up trying to hide the little mole at the corner of her mouth, since Alec told her an eighteenth-century face-patch placed in that position was known as the "Kissing."

With a sigh, she wished Johnnie had not happened to invite her to lunch on one of the few days when Alec was able to escape from the Yard at midday.

Pulling on her gloves, she went to the front door. As she opened it, a furnace blast met her. Even here in Chelsea, the August air of the metropolis stank of baking asphalt and petrol fumes.

"An absolute oven, isn't it?" Johnnie greeted her.

Like Alec he was in his mid-thirties and of middling height, but—unlike Alec—slight and fair. He was impeccably dressed in a light grey lounge suit of unmistakable Savile Row cut. Only the sun-browned face gave away that he was a country gentleman come up to town for the day. Against his tanned skin, the white line of a scar slashing from jaw to brow stood out sharply. Otherwise, his most distinctive feature was his nose, passed down in the family from generation to generation.

He fanned himself with the soft hat in his hand. "Whew!"

"Too frightful!" Daisy agreed. "What on earth tore you away from the depths of Kent on a day which must be heavenly among your orchards?"

A hint of colour tinted Johnnie's cheeks. "Oh, 'er, business," he said uneasily, adding hurriedly as he handed Daisy into his maroon Sunbeam touring-car, "I thought we'd go to the Belgravia, it's the closest decent place. Would you like me to put up the hood to keep off the sun?"

"No, thanks. We'd stifle."

Politeness forbade asking what sort of business was making him as jumpy as a grasshopper, but it didn't stop Daisy wondering. She hoped he was not in financial difficulties, as so many farmers seemed to be these days. His eldest brother, the marquis, was immensely wealthy, but Johnnie would hate to have to beg to be bailed out.

Perhaps over lunch he would succumb to the wiles of her guileless eyes and tell her what was wrong. Daisy never quite understood why people, even complete strangers, confided in her, but they did.

As he drove towards the Belgravia Hotel, she enquired after Vi and the boys.

"I thought you talked to her when you had the telephone put in," he said in surprise.

"That was nearly a week ago!" Daisy shook her head at his typically male incomprehension of the female need to communicate. No doubt he heard from his brothers only at births, marriages, and deaths.

"As a matter of fact—promise you won't tell Lady Dalrymple?"

"Cross my heart and hope to die," Daisy said promptly. "I never tell Mother anything unless I absolutely have to."

"Violet doesn't want her to know yet," Johnnie said, his face turning brick-red, "but she's just discovered she's . . . er, she's expecting another baby."

"Spiffing! Congratulations. At least, she's not ill, is she? Is that what's troubling you?"

"No, no, she seems very well at the moment. But it is another reason why . . . Well, that can wait. How is your writing going, Daisy?"

With this suggestion that all was to be revealed, Daisy managed to restrain the curiosity which was her besetting sin. She told Johnnie about the stately home article she had just finished for *Town and Country* magazine, and the London Museum article she was about to begin for her American editor.

Johnnie put in a "Really?" and an "Interesting!" but she suspected he did not hear a word.

"'Twas brillig, and the slithy toves did gyre and gimble in the wabe,'" she said as the Sunbeam turned into Grosvenor Gardens.

"It sounds like fascinating work. Here we are." He drew up in front of the hotel.

What *was* the matter?

Johnnie pulled himself together sufficiently to deal with the commissionaire and maître d'hôtel. They were seated at a quiet table in a corner. The restaurant was not busy, as all those in their right minds who could afford it were out of town.

Glancing vaguely at the bill of fare, Johnnie said,

"What would you like, Daisy? They do very good oysters Rockefeller here. The all-pervading American influence, I suppose."

"August has no 'R' in it," Daisy pointed out. "You *are* distracted."

"Sorry," he apologized meekly.

"Luckily, I don't care much about oysters, anyway. Something cold to start with, please. Melon, perhaps, or do they do consommé Madrilène?"

With a visible effort, Johnnie put his mind to the menu. Daisy refused a cocktail, since they always made her sleepy and she had to get back to work that afternoon. She settled on the chilled consommé, followed by sole Colbert, chicken Mireille, and pêche Melba. Johnnie asked abstractedly for a cut off the joint.

"I shan't need to eat again for a week," said Daisy as the waiter left with their order. "How do you suppose one gets one's name affixed to a dish? Melba was Dame Nellie, of course, but who was Colbert?"

Johnnie blinked at her, bemused.

"Never mind! Though maybe I'll do a spot of research; it might make an amusing article." She leaned forward. "Now, tell me what's wrong, Johnnie."

"Well, it's . . . I . . . No, I don't want to spoil your meal. I'll tell you over coffee. Don't you think most dishes are probably named after the chefs who created them?"

"Probably. Too fearfully dull! But oysters Rockefeller must be after the millionaire, mustn't they? And I think *Madrilène* is from Madrid." Daisy allowed herself to be distracted, though she was beginning to grow anxious about news bad enough to threaten to spoil such a divine lunch.

If Violet was well, was Johnnie ill? Had he been given six months to live, or something ghastly like that? Did he want Daisy to break the news to Vi? Gosh, how simply frightful!

He didn't look ill, only rather careworn. His valiant attempts at conversation tended to lapse into silence, and he toyed with his food. Daisy made herself deliberately savour each delicious mouthful, feeling a need to fortify herself both mentally and physically. Johnnie pushed his roast beef and French beans around the plate. He didn't even taste his pêche Melba, though the peaches and raspberries were fresh, not tinned, and simply too heavenly.

"Will you take coffee in the lounge, sir?"

Johnnie looked at Daisy, who shook her head, deciding it was easier to talk seriously where they were. Unaccustomed as she was to more than a snack for lunch, the food was having the same effect a cocktail would have. She was afraid she might succumb to the comfort of a lounge chair.

The coffee came. The waiter went. "Right-oh," said Daisy, "what's up?"

Shiftily avoiding her eyes, Johnnie said, "Well, after all, I don't think . . ."

"Don't funk it now! You can't leave me in suspense, imagining all sorts of frightful things. You . . . Your business in town wasn't in Harley Street, was it?"

"Harley Street?" Startled, he met her concerned gaze and his resistance crumbled. "No, no doctors, I'm healthy as a horse. Daisy, Violet's been telling me the most extraordinary stories about your detecting murderers right and left, and tracking down kidnappers and such."

"Well," said Daisy cautiously, wide-awake now, "I have given Alec a hand now and then, much as it pains him to admit it."

"I need help," Johnnie blurted out. "Could you come down to Oakhurst for a few days? Violet won't think it at all odd that you want to get away from town. In fact, she'll be delighted to have you come and stay. I'll tell you what, maybe Fletcher would let you bring his little girl with you. She and Derek hit it off like a house on fire at your engagement party. Same age, aren't they? Violet was saying only the other day that it's not good for a child to be stuck in the city in the summer heat." He sat back with an air of triumph.

Daisy brought him remorselessly back to the point. "All very well, and I dare say Belinda would be thrilled, but what sort of help do you need? With some kind of investigation? I'm not a private enquiry agent, you know. Alec's the detective."

"Not the police! It's not a police matter. I'm not even sure if it's a crime, and I certainly don't want anyone else knowing. So . . ."

"Knowing *what?*"

Johnnie tugged on a suddenly too-tight Old Harrovian tie. A dull flush once again crept up his tanned cheeks, showing up the scar, hitherto practically invisible in the diffuse indoor light. "Well, er . . ."

"I have to know what I'm to investigate, Johnnie! Though, actually, I can't possibly spare the time just now, so that's all right, you need not Reveal All." Daisy drank the last drop of coffee in her cup and started to put on her gloves.

"No, please." He reached out a hand across the table. "I must tell someone or I shall go mad, and you are the only person I can bear to tell who might be able to give me practical advice. As a matter of fact, I've been getting perfectly horrible anonymous letters—what I believe our transatlantic cousins call Poison Pen letters."

"Good heavens!" Daisy exclaimed, adding candidly, "I can't imagine you doing anything you could be blackmailed over." Though she was fond of Johnnie, and he suited her sister very well, she had always considered him a bit of a dull dog.

"It's not exactly blackmail. Not yet, anyway, though I suppose it will come to that. No demands as yet, except to repent and sin no more, but one can't very well stop

doing something one did only once, years ago, and repented as soon as it was done."

"Difficult, yes. What was it?"

Johnnie blenched. "Do you really need to know?"

"I take it you want me to try to find out who wrote the
letters. How do you expect me even to begin if I've
never seen them and don't know what they're about?"

"You will come, then?" he asked eagerly.

"I'm not sure. I just might be able to arrange it. But
I'd have to see the letters, so unless you want me to learn
about your evil deeds—sorry, deed—from the Poison
Pen, you had much better tell me yourself."

"Yes." His shoulders slumped. "Yes, you're right. But
not a word to Violet, or to Fletcher. Promise."

"I promise."

"I don't want you to think I'm trying to make ex-
cuses, but let me explain the circumstances."

"Go ahead," said Daisy.

The field hospital was swamped by casualties from the
Third Battle of Ypres—Wipers, as the Other Ranks
wryly called the ruinous remains of the Belgian town.
From snug pill-boxes surrounded by a sea of mud, the
Boches poured forth machine-gun fire and mustard-
gas to wipe out mired British troops by the hundred
thousand.

Exhausted medics stitched and amputated, and evacuated those who survived back behind the lines as fast
as transports were available. No less overtaxed, the hospitals in the rear tidied up the human wreckage sent to
them, and watched helplessly as their patients died in
droves, of infections and gas-corroded lungs.

Naturally, Major Lord John Frobisher received the
best care available. The last scraps of shrapnel were dug
out of his body. Nothing could be done for the crudely
sewn-up wound on his face other than to keep it clean.

He was shipped home to England to recuperate, his cheek still swollen, the gash a lurid purple brand.

"I didn't care much as long as I was with the rest of the fellows," Johnnie told Daisy. "It didn't seem to matter when so many were so much worse off. Then we landed at Dover and everyone else went off on the troop train to London. I took the local to Oakhurst."

"Vi and the baby were in Worcestershire," said Daisy, "at home with us, at Fairacres."

"Yes, but I was very tired and tense, not fit for civilized society. I needed a day or two to put myself straight before I saw Violet. I felt I hardly knew her—we weren't married much more than a year, remember, before I went off to France, and I'd had only one fortnight's leave since then."

"Spent at Fairacres," Daisy recalled, "with Derek afraid of the stranger who claimed to be his Daddy, and Violet having to look after him because half the men were called up so the maids were doing their work. And Mother being Mother."

She exchanged a commiserating glance with Johnnie. Lady Dalrymple, now the Dowager Viscountess, would find something to complain about in Heaven. At the time, Daisy seemed to remember, the burden of her mother's song had been the injustice of her son-in-law's obtaining leave when her son, Gervaise, as yet had not. Gervaise had his fortnight later. He chose to spend half of it in London before returning to Flanders, to his death.

Some of the wounds of war were invisible, and slow to heal.

Daisy shook her head, shook the memories away. "You had to come to Fairacres," she said. "Kent was too dangerous, too close to the Continent, getting bombed regularly. Father wouldn't have let Vi go to Oakhurst."

"By George, no. I don't hold Lord Dalrymple to blame."

"But I understand why you wanted to go home first, after the hospitals and everything."

"I nearly didn't make it that day," Johnnie said. "Three changes, and I kept drowsing off. The trains were practically empty, what with so many women and children having been evacuated. When I reached Rotherden Halt, there was no station fly. Our chauffeur was in the service, of course, but no one was expecting me, anyway. I left my bags in the ticket office and walked into the village. It was just after opening time, so I decided to drop into the Hop-Picker to fortify myself for the slog up to the house."

"A mile from the station if it's an inch, and uphill all the way. A pick-me-up was just what you needed," Daisy agreed.

"The landlord's daughter, Maisy, whom I'd known all my life, screamed when she saw me. She pulled herself together and served me, but she couldn't bear to look at my face. Believe it or not, until that moment I hadn't considered what the effect would be on women. On Violet."

"Oh, Johnnie!"

"I'd only seen nurses, who were used to much worse." He fingered the thin white scar. "It's nothing now, but then it was hideous, loathsome, and I didn't know how it would heal. I finished my whisky pretty quick, glad I'd ordered a double because I didn't have the nerve to ask for another. It was raining, luckily. I more or less slunk through the village without meeting anyone. Then the rain stopped and all at once the sun came out, just as I passed the Vicarage. You remember Rotherden?"

"Yes, of course." Since the War, Daisy had visited often. "The Vicarage is next to the church, which is right across the street from your gates, so you were safe."

"So I imagined."

Opposite the Vicarage, on the other side of the

Oakhurst gates from the lodge, stood a small Queen Anne house, weatherboarded and hung with tile in the local style. A pleasant residence, quite close to the street but with a large garden behind, it had been bought a year or two before the War by a childless widow. Mrs. LeBeau was then about thirty, an attractive and sophisticated woman.

John, newly married, settling down to wedded life and learning to run the estate left him by an uncle, had scarcely noticed her existence.

"She came out of her front door just as I passed. I knew her to pass the time of day—we'd been introduced at someone's house and I think Violet had invited her to morning coffee once or twice. That sort of acquaintance. At any rate, she called a greeting, asked was I home on leave. I couldn't very well ignore her."

He had turned his head to return her greeting. She swallowed a gasp as the westering sun struck full on his face.

"You poor man, you look exhausted," she said. "Are they expecting you up at the house? Lady John isn't there, I know. Come in and have a cup of tea and a biscuit before you go home. I was just going to return this book to Mrs. Molesworth, but it can wait."

After a chocolate bar from a station slot-machine for lunch, and a double whisky drunk much too fast, John felt greatly in need of tea, not to mention sympathy. He went in.

"You'll have guessed by now," he said to Daisy, staring down unhappily at his hands, "that I stayed the night."

Daisy didn't know what to say. Living in Bohemian Chelsea, she was acquainted with any number of people whose marriage vows were more honoured in the breach than the observance. She supposed it didn't matter much as long as neither husband nor wife minded. But it was different when her brother-in-law had been unfaithful to her own sister.

How would quiet, self-contained, self-possessed Violet, always unimpeachably correct, take it if she ever found out?

"Violet mustn't find out!" Johnnie broke into Daisy's silence. He looked at her with a sort of pleading defiance. "Especially now. Yet . . . I told you I repented long since, but it was only half a repentance. I was not Mrs. LeBeau's first lover since she lost her husband, so I'd nothing to reproach myself with there. And she gave me the courage to face Violet."

Unwillingly, Daisy nodded. "Yes, I see that. It was just the once, and you've never told anyone else?"

"Not a soul."

"Then Mrs. LeBeau must have written the letters."

"That was my first assumption, but I can't believe it of her. I've met her quite often in company since the end of the War, and she's never let drop so much as a hint. Not even a sidelong glance. Besides, whatever your opinion of her morals, in other ways she's a lady through and through, well-bred, cultivated. The letters are badly written and spelled, as well as . . . pretty filthy."

"That could be a disguise," Daisy pointed out. "Did you bring them to show me?"

"No. I wouldn't want them found on me if I was knocked down by a bus crossing the street," Johnnie said wryly. "I burnt the first one, but it's difficult to find an excuse to burn things in August. The rest are in a locked drawer in my bureau at home. Will you come?"

Suppose the next letter went straight to Vi? Daisy sighed. "Yes, I'll come. Give me a couple of days to research the London Museum, so that I can write the article at Oakhurst. I must get going, I've an appointment with the curator at three."

"I'll run you there." He pushed back his chair and

came around the table to hold hers. "Er, where is it? I'm not much of a hand at museums."

She laughed. "Lancaster House, right next to St. James's Palace. No distance. I'd rather walk across the parks, thanks all the same. I need a few minutes to get my thoughts on the right track." As they left the restaurant, Daisy asked, "Did you mean it about inviting Belinda to Oakhurst?"

"Certainly. We'll be glad to have her."

"Her grandmother won't approve of 'giving her ideas above her station,' but I'm sure Alec will be pleased. I'll leave it to him to persuade Mrs. Fletcher. I'll telephone when I've settled on a date and train."

"I'll pay the fares, of course," Johnnie said gruffly.

Daisy stopped on the hotel steps and kissed his cheek. "You're a dear, Johnnie. I'll do my best to sort things out for you. Cheerio. See you soon."

"Cheerio, Daisy. Oh, by the way, I don't think I'm the only one getting letters. Something Lomax said made me think he might be another victim."

By the time she turned into Buckingham Palace Road, Daisy realized her folly. She groaned. In the first place, she hadn't the foggiest how to set about finding a Poison Pen. In the second place, if somehow she succeeded, how was she to stop the culprit broadcasting the victims' peccadillos to the world?

Victims, plural. Brigadier Lomax—and how many others?— might prefer not to risk having their persecutor unmasked. Daisy could very well find herself treading on more toes than a centipede's!

2

YOU'RE A STINKING HIPPOCRITT, A
WHITED SEPULKER! YOU'VE GOT A
NERVE, SITTING AS A MAJUSTRATE AND
SENDING POOR FOLK TO PRISON FOR
POACHING, WHEN YOU'VE BEEN CON-
SERTING WITH A WHORE.

FILTHY ADULTORER, YOU BETRAYED
YOUR WIFE. FILANDERERS MUST BE PUN-
ISHED.

FORNYKATION IS A SIN. YOU THINK YOU
GOT AWAY WITH IT, BUT YOU'VE BEEN
CAUGHT OUT AND YOU WILL SUFFER,
YOU FOUL LECHER.

YOUR AFFAIRE IS KNOWN. YOU CAN'T
HIDE FROM JUSTICE. YOU DESERVE TO
BURN IN HELL.

"That's the lot," said Johnnie, "except the first. I
chucked the envelopes, but they were all addressed in
the same writing and postmarked in the village. I'm
sorry to subject you to such beastly stuff. Sometimes I
feel I must have imagined the whole business, and then

I look at them again, and . . ." With a bewildered expression, he glanced around the library.

The crude letters were startlingly out of place in that staid room. Two walls were taken up with bookshelves, crammed with calf-bound volumes collected over the centuries and seldom if ever opened since their purchase. The chairs were similarly aged and leather-covered, but worn to a comfortable shabbiness, as was the faded Turkey carpet on the oak-planked floor. The mahogany and satinwood Sheraton roll-top bureau at which Johnnie sat seemed defiled by the papers strewn on its well-polished surface.

"There's nothing worse than one can find in lots of modern novels, other than the spelling." Daisy shook her head. "And that doesn't ring true."

"What do you mean?"

"Look: Every word with more than two syllables is spelt wrong, yet every apostrophe is correct." She scanned the notes, printed in block capitals with a blunt pencil on cheap notepaper. "In fact, all the punctuation is all right—most unnatural."

"I'm a bit shaky on commas, myself," Johnnie conceded.

"And it's equally unnatural that only long words are misspelled. A girl in my form at school who was a rotten speller hardly ever got long words wrong because she was unsure of them so she looked them up. What tripped her were 'your' and 'you're,' or 'there,' 'their' and 'they're.'"

"Maybe, but someone uneducated might not think to check the spelling, or even own a dictionary."

"No," Daisy agreed, "but he'd get short words wrong as well, things like f-o-w-l for 'foul,' or l-e-t-c-h-e-r for 'lecher.'"

"Or n-o-n-e for 'known,'" said Johnnie, entering into the spirit of the thing. "W-i-t-e-d for 'whited.'"

"Or goodness knows what for 'caught,' which is brief

but frightfully peculiar. It looks to me as if the writer simply stopped whenever he came to a long word and thought up a way to spell it wrong."

"What about 'affaire' with an 'e'?"

"That's the most suspicious of all. What's the odds against misspelling the English 'affair' in such a way it just happens to be right for the French spelling so often used for an *affaire de coeur?* No, I think your Poison Pen wrote that word without thinking, which seems to me to imply a certain degree of sophistication."

"Dash it all, Daisy, I hate to believe one of our sort of people wrote this . . . this *filth,"* Johnnie said gloomily. "I suppose it must be someone I know. How will you set about finding her?"

"Or him."

"Aren't these things usually written by frustrated spinsters? Or him," he added in haste as Daisy frowned. "Do you think you have the slightest chance of . . . ?"

"Daddy! Aunt Daisy!"

Johnnie swiftly scooped the letters into the bureau drawer, shut it, and locked it, as his son and heir bounded into the library. Derek, a wiry nine-year-old with hair bleached to straw by the summer sun, was followed at a more decorous pace by a skinny girl half a head taller, with ginger pigtails. Alec's daughter Belinda came shyly to stand beside Daisy, while Derek skidded to a halt before his father.

"Daddy, Mummy's got up from her rest and she says we can have tea in the summerhouse because Mrs. Osborne's coming, so will you come and have it with us and play cricket afterwards, because you don't like Mrs. Osborne? You can come too, Aunt Daisy. I mean," he corrected himself "we shall be glad of the pleasure of your company. Mrs. Osborne doesn't like children. She pretends to and pats you on the head and calls you a fine little man."

"Frightful!" said Daisy, laughing.

"Well, it is. Po-sit-ively hu-mil-iating." He looked at Belinda, and for some reason they both dissolved in giggles, already sharing a joke which excluded grown-ups. In general, Derek hadn't much time for girls. However, the daughter of a genuine Detective Chief Inspector from Scotland Yard was in a class of her own.

"Derek, you mustn't talk like that about Mrs. Osborne," his father reproved him. "And what makes you think I dislike . . . No, don't tell me. I can't think what children's manners are coming to, these days. Do try for a little discretion!"

"All right, Daddy, but will you come? Please!"

"And you, Miss Dalrymple." Belinda slipped her hand into Daisy's.

"I think not, darling. Mrs. Osborne is the vicar's wife, isn't she?" Who better to know everything going on in the village? "I'm afraid she may be justifiably offended if I make myself scarce."

Belinda's hand tightened. "I'll come with you. May I?"

"Don't you like to play cricket?" Johnnie asked kindly.

"Oh yes, m-my lord," the child stammered, shyly raising eyes a greener shade of grey than Alec's.

"Daddy, she doesn't have to call you 'my lord,' does she?"

"By George, no. Uncle John would seem appropriate in the circumstances," said Johnnie with a teasing glance at Daisy, who felt herself blush, a fearfully Victorian habit she despised but had never managed to control.

Derek added to her confusion. "I suppose," he said consideringly, "you can't call Aunt Daisy 'Mummy' until she's married to your father. You'd better call her Aunt Daisy, like I do. Do come and have tea with Daddy and me. Cricket's more fun with three than two, and Peter doesn't count. You can't help being better than he is, even though you're a girl."

Belinda accepted with equanimity this comparison of her sporting skills with his five-year-old brother's. "All right," she said.

They all went out to the terrace behind the red-brick Jacobean manor house. The heat, so unbearable in London, was a pleasant warmth here, relieved by a slight breeze scented with hops, though the large black dog who thumped her tail in greeting stayed panting in her spot of shade. Violet looked delightfully cool in a simple cotton voile frock and shady hat. She was seated in a white wicker chair, with Peter playing on the Kentish ragstone paving at her feet.

Daisy's younger nephew was a chubby, silent child, quite capable of amusing himself alone for hours. He looked up from the wooden horse and cart he was trundling around the legs of his mother's chair and beamed at Daisy, whom he had not seen since her arrival, but said nothing. Daisy bent down to kiss him.

"I'm bidden to the summerhouse for tea, darling," said Johnnie. "Is that all right?"

"Yes, do go with the children. You won't find it at all amusing here. And take Peter, please. You'd better disappear before Mrs. Osborne arrives."

Her husband glanced back at the house in mock alarm.

"Come on, Belinda, I'll race you!" cried Derek. "Come on, Tinker!"

The big black dog jumped up on hearing her name.

"Maybe I should hold Peter's hand," Belinda said doubtfully, with a slightly nervous glance at Tinker Bell.

"Go on with Derek," said Johnnie. "I'll bring Peter. Come along, old man."

"I'll run too," Peter announced, and he lumbered off across the lawn after the others. Tinker bounded back to him and licked his face before galloping after Derek and Belinda. Johnnie brought up the rear.

"Oh dear," Vi sighed, "poor Peter will never be any

good at sports, I'm afraid. It's such a handicap for a boy."

"Bosh," said Daisy bracingly. "I expect he'll be a brilliant wrestler, or a good, solid batsman, the sort who stays in for hours."

"Perhaps. Belinda's a nice child. Daisy, I hope you won't mind, I asked her to call me Aunt Violet."

"No, why should I mind?"

"Well, if you happened to be having second thoughts . . ."

"None," Daisy averred. "I simply adore Alec, and Bel, too. Mrs. Fletcher's a bit of a fly in the ointment, but we'll come to an accommodation. Did *you?* Have second thoughts, I mean, when you were engaged?"

"Not really, but that was rather different."

Daisy raised her eyebrows. "How so?"

"Oh, I was marrying a suitable man, more or less chosen for me by Mother, amid general congratulations, whereas you're not doing at all what is expected of you."

"You weren't in love with Johnnie?" Daisy demanded, shocked. Fifteen when her sister married, she had believed it the most romantic match conceivable.

"Not then," Vi said softly. "I liked him very much, better than any of my other suitors, and . . ."

"Mrs. Osborne, my lady," announced a footman.

A tall, solid woman of forty or so advanced across the terrace with a determined air more appropriate to the Canadians advancing on Passchendaele. Red-faced, she looked stickily hot in a grey silk frock, too dressy in comparison with Daisy's and Violet's light cottons. Daisy recognized her, having met her once or twice on previous visits.

She recognized Daisy. Having greeted her hostess, she said with heavy whimsy, "A little bird whispered in my ear that you had just arrived in our rural corner of the world, Miss Dalrymple. How d'ye do?"

"It's very pleasant to escape from town in this weather."

"Indeed, London in the summer is unbearable. I try to avoid going up in August. And even worse for children—I heard you brought a little girl with you?"

Obviously, Mrs. Osborne considered it her duty to ferret out every scrap of gossip. Assuming she was equally ready to disgorge the tittle-tattle, she could be useful, so Daisy bit back her annoyance and answered with a smile, "My fiancé's daughter."

Mrs. Osborne returned her smile, revealing tombstone teeth. "Ah yes, we read the announcement of your engagement in *The Times*. Allow me to offer my felicitations. A Mr. Fletcher, I believe. Would that be the Nottinghamshire Fletchers?"

"Not exactly." Daisy threw a mischievous glance at Vi. "The connection with Scotland is closer. And how is your family, Mrs. Osborne? I trust the vicar is well?"

"Very well," said Mrs. Osborne, with an odd emphasis, as if she was trying to persuade herself. "His brother is staying with us for a few weeks during the long vacation. He's at Cambridge, a Professor of the Classics. He and Osbert have such learned discussions, I'm sure I can scarcely follow a word." She produced a rather thin laugh.

"How are the children?" Violet enquired kindly.

"I had a letter from Gwendoline just this morning, Lady John. She's having a marvellous time with her cousins. The Cambridgeshire Osbornes, you know, Miss Dalrymple. My son, Jeremy, is climbing in Austria with a party from his school. A public school, of course, and really quite excellent, though one of the lesser known ones. I'm afraid we couldn't afford Eton or Harrow, but one has a certain position to uphold, does one not, Lady John?"

"Quite," said Vi, whose sons had been entered at Harrow before they were born, automatically and without her having any say in the matter.

"Jeremy and Gwendoline will both be here for the Church Fête, before they go back to school. We hold it at the very end of the month, Miss Dalrymple. So many people seem to go away in August these days," she added disapprovingly, continuing to talk as a pair of parlourmaids unloaded Georgian silver and Royal Doulton onto the wicker table. "What common farmers and shopkeepers want with a day at the seaside I cannot conceive."

"A change and a rest, and a bit of fun for their children, I suppose," said Daisy, trying to keep the tartness from her voice.

"They'd do better saving their money, and so I tell them. Thank you, Lady John, China with lemon, please, and two lumps."

"Indian with milk, please, Vi," Daisy said promptly in a spirit of contradiction, "no sugar. A watercress sandwich, Mrs. Osborne?" She handed a plate of crustless brown-bread triangles.

"From your own stream, Lady John?" The vicar's wife took one and delicately nibbled a corner. "Delicious. I always say it's impossible to buy watercress as good as what is grown at Oakhurst."

"I'll have a bunch sent down to the Vicarage," Violet promised.

"Too kind! To get back to the fête, I was hoping for a word with you on that subject. You won't mind, Miss Dalrymple, if Lady John and I talk a little parish business?"

"Not at all," said Daisy. "Are you opening the fête again this year, Vi?"

"Yes indeed, Lady John is quite indispensable."

"I'm nowhere near as indispensable as you, Mrs. Osborne."

Mrs. Osborne preened herself. "If the church is not to

collapse in ruins, someone must organize these affairs," she said, assuming an air of modesty, "and it usually falls to the lot of the vicar's wife. Nothing would get done if one did not tell people what to do and see that they do it, however helpful they intend to be. However, *some* people one might wish were a trifle less eager to play a part," she added with an ominous frown, "which is what I want to consult you about, Lady John."

"Yes?" Violet asked, looking a trifle dismayed.

"It's Mrs. LeBeau." Her tone was grim. Daisy pricked up her ears, while trying to appear more interested in a scrumptious Banbury tart. Mrs. Osborne went on, "She heard that our usual fortune-teller can't make it this year, and she's offered to take her place."

"I think Mrs. LeBeau would make an admirable fortune-teller," said Vi. "I don't think you've met her, Daisy. She's dark and terrifically magnetic. With a bright scarf over her head, she'll look just like a gypsy."

"You can't have considered, Lady John! To leave her alone in a darkened tent, with the men going in one by one—it's inviting trouble."

"What do you imagine might happen?" Violet was quite angry, considering her usually equable temperament. "What *could* happen, with a queue waiting outside? The fortune-teller's is always one of the most popular booths. What is more, it's women, children, and courting couples who consult her. Men don't seem to find it amusing."

"They will when it's That Woman," muttered Mrs. Osborne not quite under her breath. "I don't think it's wise," she said obstinately, aloud. "If you were to have a word with her . . ."

"I'll do nothing of the kind. It's most generous of Mrs. LeBeau to offer her services in aid of re-leading the church roof. I dare say I shall consult her myself. What else can we anticipate? Tombola, and a white elephant stall, and a bran tub for the children seem to be

staple favourites. Lord John is looking forward to pre-
senting the prizes for the races. I expect you'd like me
to judge the jams and jellies as usual?"

"Speaking of jam," said Daisy, "may I cut you a slice
of this Victoria sandwich? Violet's cook does have a
particularly light hand with a cake, doesn't she? Do you
have a home-made cake stall at the fête?"

Mrs. Osborne's feathers were skillfully smoothed.
Daisy and Violet had a great deal of practice, as the
slightest breath of adversity, real or imagined, was
enough to ruffle their mother's plumage.

After enumerating the prospective delights of the
fête, Mrs. Osborne asked, "May we hope you'll be staying on for our little country jollification, Miss
Dalrymple?"

"I'm not sure." By that time, Daisy thought, she
might have been sent to Coventry by half the population
of Rotherden. "It depends partly on how much I can get
done while I'm down here. This is a working holiday for
me."

"Working!" Mrs. Osborne looked shocked, and avidly
curious. A viscount's daughter working? her expression
said.

"Daisy is a writer," Violet explained. Dear Vi—so
conventional herself, she had always supported Daisy's
desire to be independent. "She does jolly good articles
for *Town and Country,* and for an American magazine."

"Oh, *Town and Country.* For a moment . . . but I
couldn't credit, my dear Miss Dalrymple, that you
would have anything to do with the sort of rubbishy
modern novels written by that most undesirable young
man who has taken Brigadier Lomax's cottage. Piers
Catterick he calls himself."

"I know the name," said Daisy. "He's quite popular."

"Disgraceful! I don't imagine you have met him,
Lady John, but he was shockingly rude when Osbert

called to welcome him to the parish. And when I delivered the parish magazine, he tore it up before my eyes."

"Oh dear," said Violet serenely.

"Naturally I haven't read any of his books, but I believe they are full of . . . You Know What. I spoke to Brigadier Lomax about it—he is a churchwarden, after all, and ought to set an example—but he said the cottage is let on a long lease and there is nothing he can do. I must say, he was quite disagreeable."

"Oh dear," Violet repeated with unimpaired calm. "Another cup of tea?"

"Thank you, so kind, but I really must be going. It's Cook's afternoon off, and Doris is quite hopeless without constant supervision. I dare say she has forgotten to serve tea. Osbert won't mind, very likely won't even notice, but Osmund will crack one of his dreadful jokes and that I cannot *bear!*"

With this final outburst, Mrs. Osborne made her farewells and departed. As soon as she was out of hearing, Daisy succumbed to the laughter she had managed to hold in check.

"What's so funny?" Violet asked resignedly, adding hot water to the pot and pouring them each another cup of tea.

"Oh, Osbert and Osmund Osborne for a start! Poor things, what can their parents have been thinking of?"

"Even worse than Violet and Daisy," Vi conceded, her mouth twitching. "I believe there's a third brother called Oswald."

"Too, too frightful!" said Daisy, awed. "I suppose, once they had two, it wouldn't be fair to change for the third and give him a decent name. I've always thought Gervaise was jolly lucky not to have been christened Narcissus, or Chrysanthemum, or something. But actually, the Osbornes' names were the icing on the cake. What set me off was a vision of Mrs. Osborne tackling the brigadier on the dread subject of S-E-X."

"You Know What," Violet corrected with a chuckle.

"Y-K-W? Ghastly woman. Does she really run the village?"

"She does her best. She's told me her privileged position as vicar's wife makes organizing people a duty, though I think she regards it rather as a pleasure."

"Undoubtedly. She seems well entrenched. Have they been in Rotherden long?"

"Since well before the War, before I came here. He was an Army chaplain during the War, but her uncle was a clergyman and he came out of retirement to take care of the parish, so she stayed on."

Sipping her tea, Daisy wondered whether Mrs. Osborne had seen Johnnie enter Mrs. LeBeau's house that day six years ago. If so, fond as she was of reviling people, she would surely not have kept such a tidbit to herself. Half the population of Rotherden, if not the whole, might be aware of Lord John's misdeed.

"She's a fearful gossip," Daisy observed, reaching for a last Bakewell tart. "Three reputations destroyed at one sitting— Mrs. LeBeau, Brigadier Lomax, and Piers Catterick—besides slanging her maid and her brother-in-law!"

"She certainly *knows* all the gossip," Vi said doubtfully, "but I'm not sure that she passes it on indiscriminately. She once said she felt it was her duty to keep me apprised of what was going on in the village, as though Johnnie or I could do anything about it! She has a rather feudal view of the aristocracy, I'm afraid."

"Not to mention an absolutely Victorian view of You Know What. What was all that about the dissipated Mrs. LeBeau? She lives in the house by your gates, doesn't she? Who is she?"

"Our local Scarlet Woman. She's a widow, and she has a lot of visitors, gentlemen as well as ladies. That's enough to damn her. If there's any more concrete evidence, it has not been passed on to me, thank heaven. I like her. As long as she's discreet, her private life is none of my business. Oh, here come the children. Don't let Derek bully you into playing cricket if you don't want to!"

Derek approached at full speed, his normal mode of progression. Behind him, Belinda had Peter by the hand. Her braids bobbed as she tried to teach him to skip along. From her Clark's sandals, skinny, newly scratched legs rose to grubby knees, and the hem of her white cotton frock was smeared with mud.

Every footstep a squelch, Derek bounced up to the terrace. "I hit the ball into the stream," he announced cheerfully. Retrieving the cart and horse from under Vi's chair, he stood on one foot, the other dripping, and precariously balanced Peter's toy on his head. "It was a *smashing* hit, would've been a six easily. But we couldn't find the ball."

"Po-sit-ively hu-mil-iating," said Belinda, and they both started laughing.

The cart and horse wobbled. "You'll *break* it," wailed Peter.

"No, I shan't. Here, take it. Daddy got fed up and went to write some boring letters or something, so will you come and play with us, Aunt Daisy? We can use an old tennis ball. It really flies!"

"No," said Daisy. "I'm much too full to run after boundary hits. I thought I'd stroll down to the village and buy some postcards. You can come too, if you like."

"Oh yes!" cried Derek. "I've got tuppence. Do you like humbugs, Bel?"

"Not to be eaten before your supper," said Vi. "Go and change your shoes first, and next time do *try* to remember to take them off before you wade. Take Peter up with you. It's time he went back to Nanny."

"I'd like to go with you," Belinda whispered in Daisy's ear, "but I got my frock awfully dirty." She bit her lip.

"You'd better change too, darling, but don't worry, the

mud will brush off when it dries, I expect. I'll tell you
what, we'll see if we can find some cheap shorts and
Aertex shirts in the village. Then you won't have to
bother about staying clean."

"I've only got two shillings. And Granny doesn't approve of shorts for girls."

"Granny isn't here," Daisy pointed out, thankfully,
"and your daddy gave me some money for your ex-
penses. Off you go."

After the vicar's wife, she reflected, the village shopkeeper was usually the person most conversant with
local gossip. Her chief aim, however, was to spy out the
land, to see which houses besides the Vicarage over-
looked Mrs. LeBeau's front door.

Then she'd have to find out who lived in them, how
long they had lived there, and whether they had been
away during the War. Which would be just a basis for investigation, she thought rather despairingly. How long
would it take to get to know her suspects well enough to
guess who might have written those foul letters? And
what if Mrs. Osborne was indeed the source of the
story, so that absolutely anyone might know Johnnie's
secret?

Perhaps he had set Daisy an impossible task. How
much easier it would be to assume the author was Mrs.
LeBeau herself, and just look for proof.

3

Ten minutes later Daisy and her troops set off down the carriage drive, an avenue of ancient oaks winding down the hill with parkland on either side. The verge was bright with pink and white convolvulus and the blue stars of chicory. Derek, Belinda, and Tinker raced ahead, of course. The children stopped now and then, while Derek showed Belinda the best tree to climb, the place where a visitor's motor-car ran into the ditch, and such landmarks. The dog found her own landmarks to investigate.

Daisy walked briskly, wanting to reach the village shop before it closed. As she approached the gates, a high hedge on her left took the place of the oaks. It must be Mrs. LeBeau's. Neatly clipped on top, and presumably on the garden side, it was left to grow wild on the park side.

Derek and Belinda, both already grubby again, had jumped the ditch and found some early blackberries—sour, by the looks on their faces. Daisy caught up with them as Derek handed Bel a green hazelnut.

"Here, try this." He cracked another between his teeth. "They're not ripe yet but they're sort of crunchy."

Belinda turned to Daisy for permission. If she was their mother, Daisy reckoned, no doubt she would worry about tummy-aches, but she wasn't, and she remembered eating the crisp white nutmeats as a child without ill effect.

"Try it," she said, "but come along, or the shop will close."

What time of year had it been when Johnnie came home on medical leave? Could some villager picking berries or nuts have seen him through a sparsely-leaved hedge? The Third Battle of Ypres had gone on for months and months, but Daisy rather thought it was autumn when Johnnie came to Fairacres.

Then there was the lodge. Had it been tenanted during the War? It was a tiny dwelling, but two-storied. From the first floor Mrs. LeBeau's front door might be visible.

At present, the resident was an aged bachelor uncle of Johnnie's, the younger brother of the uncle who had owned Oakhurst. Mr. Paramount bitterly resented the estate being left to his nephew. Refusing to stay at the manor with the family, he had grudgingly moved into the lodge—before the War or after? He seldom set foot outside the little house, where he was looked after by his manservant and a daily woman from the village. Violet's invitations to join the Frobishers for Sunday lunch or a holiday meal were always churlishly rejected.

Daisy had no desire to request permission to look out of the hostile old hermit's upper windows. She hoped it wouldn't come to that, but she must add Mr. Paramount and his servant to her list of suspects.

She smiled, remembering how reluctant Alec always was to cross anyone off his lists.

Directly across from the end of the drive was a tile-roofed lych-gate in a brick and flint wall. Beyond, the ancient stone church rose in the middle of its graveyard, where Daisy noted in passing a figure apparently lost in rapt contemplation of a large stone angel. The square, stubby, seventeenth-century tower gave a fine view of the surrounding area, she knew, including the entire length of Rotherden's main street. Who had access to the tower, and business there on a rainy autumn afternoon?

To the left of the church was the Vicarage. A frill of tall pink hollyhocks made a brave effort to disguise the singularly ugly Victorian building. Grey-stuccoed, it was of a size to accommodate a vast Victorian family. From it, Mrs. Osborne could easily have seen Johnnie enter Mrs. LeBeau's house on the opposite side of the lane. What was more, she would be quite likely to keep a look-out to see how long he stayed.

Daisy passed between the high gates of Oakhurst, now permanently open, bound in place by the bindweed whose white trumpets nodded from the ornate wrought-ironwork. As she turned towards the village, a tall woman came down Mrs. LeBeau's front path.

She wore a tailored linen dress, beige, trimmed with pillar-box red buttons and a matching sash around her slim hips. Unlike Daisy, who was bare-legged, she had on stockings, in the fashionable flesh-coloured tint regarded as immodest by old-fashioned people accustomed to uncompromising black or white. Her broad-brimmed cloche hat was natural straw with a red cockade.

Somehow the Scarlet Woman succeeded in looking both frightfully smart and not overdressed for a village street.

Opening her garden gate, she smiled and nodded to Daisy, who responded, "Good evening." Impulsively she added, "Mrs. LeBeau?"

"Yes, I'm Wanda LeBeau." Her voice was low-pitched, slightly husky. "May I make a guess too? You must be Lady John's sister, Miss Dalrymple. Our village grapevine is efficient, you see."

Daisy laughed. "What village grapevine isn't?"

Close to, the *femme fatale* was obviously older than she looked from a little distance. Perhaps forty, she had a hint of smile-lines around her full mouth and the be-

ginnings of crow's-feet at her dark eyes. She was not the
sort to entirely eschew make-up, as Daisy did on a fine
country afternoon, but it consisted of a mere dusting of
powder on her nose and a lightly tinted lip salve. Her
hair, just visible beneath the hat, was also dark, un-
bobbed. Though she was not classically beautiful, Daisy
thought her very attractive.

"I'm hurrying to the shop," said Mrs. LeBeau. "Are
you going that way? Shall we walk together?"

"I'd like to, but you can't want to walk with two
grubby children and a large—Oh, blast, where have
they got to?" Daisy swung round.

"I rather like children, as a matter of fact," said Mrs.
LeBeau with a throaty chuckle, "but if you don't mind
I'd better get on to the shop before it closes. I hope you
find them in one piece! Do drop in for morning coffee
tomorrow if you're free. Eleven o'clock."

"Thank you, I'd love to," Daisy said sincerely. What
luck, her prime suspect inviting her for elevenses!

But where were the children?

Just as Daisy started back along the lane, Belinda
dashed around the end of the tall hedge, Tinker loping
at her heels, barking. "Miss Dalrymple! Aunt Daisy!
Come quick! Derek climbed the gate and he's stuck. He
was showing off."

Daisy groaned. She reached the end of the carriage
drive, and there was her nephew, hanging onto the top
rail of the tall gate. His fierce expression suggested he
was trying desperately not to cry.

"What's up?" Daisy asked with assumed calm, eye-
ing the ironwork with a devout hope that she was not
going to have to climb it.

"M-my foot slipped and went through the g-gap and
I can't pull it out, and I can't reach to untie my shoe-
laces to take off my shoe."

The dog whined. Belinda hugged her and said with

confidence, "It's all right, Tinker Bell, Aunt Daisy will rescue him."

Daisy had just decided she would have to kilt up her skirts like Leezie Lindsay in the old Scots ballad, when a diffident voice came from behind her.

"May I perhaps be of some assistance, madam?"

A short, portly man was dismounting from an aged bicycle. He wore clerical black, with trouser-clips, and a dog collar. Politely raising an old-fashioned Panama hat circled with a faded tartan ribbon, he revealed thinning black hair, a few strands carefully combed across his involuntary tonsure.

"Mr. Osborne, I don't expect you remember me— Daisy Dalrymple, Derek's aunt. It's kind of you to offer, but I think I'm going to have to climb after him. His foot's caught and he can't take off his shoe."

"Allow me, Miss Dalrymple."

The vicar kicked down his bicycle stand, took off his hat, which he gravely handed to Belinda to hold, and laboriously clambered up the ironwork. A moment later, Derek's shoe fell.

"Gosh, thank you, sir," said Derek, and scrambled down.

Mr. Osborne was descending at a more cautious pace, when a snort of laughter made Daisy turn away from the unlikely spectacle.

A short, portly man was crossing the road from the churchyard. He wore plus-fours in a bright blue and tan check which reminded Daisy of Alec's sergeant, Tom Tring. Above this striking garment floated an academic gown, black with a slight sheen. A face which proclaimed a close relationship to the vicar was topped by a cricket cap a good two sizes too small.

"Ho!" exclaimed the apparition. "A more improbable exponent of Muscular Christianity one can scarcely conceive. D'you need a hand down, Ozzy?"

"Not at all, not at all," said the vicar crossly, glancing

round as he felt with one foot for a toe-hold. "What on earth have you got on your head, Ozzy?"

Ozzy Two reached up, removed his cap, and regarded it with an air of jovial puzzlement. "Good Lord, I believe it must be your Jeremy's. It did seem a trifle tight. I've mislaid my hat again, so I picked up the first which came to hand. And if you're wondering about the gown, madam," he continued to Daisy, "after so many years, I simply feel undressed without it."

As the Reverend Osbert Osborne reached the ground and dusted himself down, a cry of anguish arose.

"Tinker's got my shoe! Grab her, Bel, quick. Tinker, come back here, you rotter. Bad dog!"

But Tinker Bell pranced away up the avenue with her prize. Derek hopped after her, then set socked foot to ground and took off in hot pursuit. Thrusting the Panama hat into the vicar's hands, Belinda sped after them.

The professor chortled. *"Cave canem,"* he observed. "I think I may be permitted that small jest, though I have promised Ozzy not to go about quoting Latin and Greek at people, a habit as difficult to abandon as my gown. My dear sister-in-law, who had not the benefits of a Classical education, finds it distressing. I trust you are not distressed, madam?"

"Not a bit," said Daisy with a smile. She rather liked his archly jocular manner, though she could imagine it might wear thin if one were forced to endure a great deal of it. "'Beware of the dog' is just within my capabilities."

"'*O quanta species . . .*'"

"Miss Dalrymple," the vicar intervened, with an admonitory look, "may I present my brother, Professor Osborne? Lady John's sister, Ozzy."

"How do you do, Professor."

"I do very well indeed, I thank you kindly. Being forced to forage for my own tea, since service in the

Vicarage is quite as ineffectual as the services in my brother's church, ha ha, I found a splendid gingerbread loaf, newly baked."

"For the WI committee's tea tomorrow," said Mr. Osborne gloomily.

"Was it? One must hope the ladies have small appetites. I suppose I shall catch what-for from your missus," the Professor said, with a delighted grin for his own descent into the vernacular. "Cheer up, Ozzy. You missed your tea, that's why you're feeling down in the mouth, I dare say."

"Gresham gave me tea. Oh, *drat!* Ozzy, don't mention to Adelaide that I called on Gresham."

"My dear Ozzy, you are assured of my discretion. Now, if you will excuse me, my dear young lady, I shall continue my stroll. I find a little exercise after a meal extremely beneficial to the digestion." And, raising his absurd cricket cap, he toddled off.

"I do beg your pardon, Miss Dalrymple," said the vicar. "It was very wrong of me to utter an expletive in the presence of a lady. Indeed, a man of the cloth ought not to use such language under any provocation."

"You could hardly have chosen a milder word," Daisy reassured him. "If it's a sin, it's not much of one."

She felt sorry for him, caught between his overbearing wife and his subversive brother. No wonder he was despondent. His round, pink face was the wrong shape for melancholy; the best it could manage was a lugubrious cast difficult to take seriously. How painful to look merely doleful when what one felt was desperation.

For, momentarily, something very like desperation peered like a caged creature from the vicar's eyes.

Had he received one of those beastly anonymous letters? Even a clergyman could have something to hide, especially as the clergy were held to a higher standard of conduct.

If he *was* Johnnie's fellow victim, Daisy wanted to

know. The more letters she read, or at least heard about, the more clues to the identity of the Poison Pen. Even if he was not himself a victim, he could be aware of others. Johnnie had felt he'd go mad if he couldn't tell someone, and had chosen Daisy to confide in. The vicar just might be equally anxious for a confidant.

Daisy could not quite bring herself to ask him outright whether he knew of the letters. She decided to keep him in conversation for a while and hope something useful might emerge. For a start, she was dying of curiosity . . .

"Don't worry," she said encouragingly, "I'll be sure not to mention your call on Gresham—Mr. Gresham, is it?—to Mrs. Osborne."

"I'm afraid you must think it very odd. The fact is, Amos Gresham is an unregenerate atheist."

"But part of your duties, surely, is to attempt to lead straying sheep back to the flock?"

Mr. Osborne shook his head. "No chance of that with Amos. He may be only a tenant farmer, but he is an intelligent man, and his beliefs, or disbeliefs, rather, are the result of deep reflection. Adelaide knows I visit him as a friend, not as a pastor. I would not offend him by trying to persuade him to return to the Church, even if I . . ." He cut himself off, with obvious consternation. "But I am keeping you standing, Miss Dalrymple. I must be on my way."

Abruptly, he raised his hat, and he turned to his bicycle while Daisy was still expressing her thanks for his rescue of her nephew.

Puzzled, her curiosity further aroused instead of satisfied, she watched him wheel the cycle across the lane to the Vicarage. His somewhat rude departure was wholly at odds with his previous courtly manner. He had found himself on the point of disclosing something he had rather keep quiet. What had he been going to say?

Even if he had any hope of succeeding? Perhaps it was rather remiss of a clergyman to relinquish one of his flock without a fight, Daisy thought vaguely, but not bad enough to explain Mr. Osborne's alarm. Surely not enough to warrant a reprimand from the bishop, let alone defrocking!

Even if he received anonymous letters on the subject? A vicar was probably no more immune to Poison Pens than anyone else.

A movement off to her right distracted Daisy from her cogitations. A woman trotted down the steps of the Parish Hall, a high-roofed stucco building of the same vintage as the Vicarage, set well back from the lane on the far side of the churchyard. She passed through a gate in the churchyard wall. As she crossed the burial ground towards the lych-gate, passing behind a row of mausoleums and large monuments, her mudbrown dress and hat vanished at intervals from Daisy's view. The effect was oddly sinister, as if the earth kept swallowing her up and disgorging her.

"Mud to mud and ashes to ashes," Daisy muttered to herself.

But the plump, white-haired old lady who stepped through the lych-gate was very much alive and vigorous, with pink cheeks and bright eyes. These she fixed on Daisy with a querying gaze.

"Good afternoon," she said kindly, "have you lost your way?"

"No," Daisy said in surprise. She was beginning to think all she had to do was stand there and half the inhabitants of Rotherden would come to talk to her.

No doubt she looked as if she was lost, or had lost her wits, she realized. "Oh, no, thank you. I was just waiting for two children and a dog, but I suppose the shop will be shut by the time I get there."

The old lady turned to glance up at the church clock, which promptly began to strike the half hour. "I fear so.

Mrs. Burden has no regard for the convenience of others. Often enough I have seen her lock the door when I was just a few steps away. A selfish woman, alas, as I have upon occasion felt obliged to mention to our dear vicar. You are staying at Oakhurst, then?"

"Yes, I'm Violet's sister, Daisy Dalrymple."

"Ah yes, I had heard you were coming to visit. How delightful for Lady John. I am Mabel Prothero, by the way. I live just two doors down." She gestured.

"Next door to Mrs. LeBeau?" Daisy asked, grasping at another suspect. "I've just met her. I thought her charming."

"All is not gold that glitters," said Miss Prothero darkly. So the kindly, rosy-cheeked old bird had sharp talons, did she? "Much as I dislike speaking ill of my fellow creatures," she continued, "I hope you will not take offence if an old lady advises you not to pursue that acquaintance."

A promising opening, and Daisy quickly jumped in: "Why, what . . . ?"

"Aunt Daisy!" The footsteps galloping down the drive towards her sounded like a herd of elephants, not a mere two children and a dog. "Aunt Daisy, I got my shoe. Now we can go to the shop. Oh, good afternoon, Miss Prothero."

"Hold that dog! I will not have him putting dirty paws on my skirt."

"Her," Derek corrected, grabbing Tinker Bell's collar.

Miss Prothero ignored him. "Children these days are so dreadfully undisciplined, are they not, Miss Dalrymple? A great deal has changed since the War, and not for the better, as I was saying to the dear vicar only the other day. Well, I'd better be getting home. My Puss will be waiting for his fish. Perhaps we shall meet again while you are here."

"I hope so," said Daisy sincerely, or rather purposefully. Miss Prothero was the perfect suspect. As Johnnie had said, Poison Pen letters were practically always written by frustrated spinsters, and by all accounts that description by no means fit Mrs. LeBeau!

Daisy turned to the children, and caught Derek sticking his tongue out at Miss Prothero's retreating back.

"Well, she was rude to me," he said, catching his aunt's admonitory frown.

"Yes, she was," Daisy agreed candidly, "but there's no need to lower yourself to her level. Though, actually, I don't suppose she realized she was being rude. Her generation had a different view of children."

"Pos-it-ively hu-mil-iating." Derek was joined by Belinda on the second word. They looked at each other, but gravely, not laughing. "We're people too," said Derek.

"Our feelings can be hurt too," Bel agreed.

"So can Tinker's," Derek claimed, and now they laughed.

"Sticks and stones may break my bones," chanted Bel, and Derek added his voice to the second line: "But words will never harm me."

"Far less Tinker," Daisy said with a laugh, "who didn't even know she was being insulted. And dirty paw marks wouldn't have shown on that dress anyway. Come along, you two—you three—we might as well go home. The shop is closed now."

"Race you, Bel!" said Derek, and off they ran, hurt feelings forgotten.

Daisy remembered Professor Osborne's Latin tag. *"O quanta species . . ."* wasn't it? The way his brother had cut him off with a frown had made her wonder whether it was insulting. When she reached the house, she asked Johnnie, who hotly denied recalling a word of Latin from his schooldays. He directed her to a dictionary of quotations in the library, which he rather thought might have some scraps of the Classics in it.

With some difficulty, for it was indexed under *species,* not *quanta,* Daisy found it: *"O quanta species cerebrum non habet!"* The translation read, "O that such beauty should be so devoid of understanding!"

Just because she had never been taught any dead languages! Daisy was furious. No wonder Mrs. Osborne disliked her brother-in-law, if she had to put up with such underhanded denigration.

Words were not always harmless, Daisy thought, whatever the old rhyme asserted.

Look at Johnnie's distress over those horrible letters. She was determined to find out who had written them, and she felt she already had a foot in the door. An invitation to morning coffee with Mrs. LeBeau, and acquaintance with the Osbornes and Miss Prothero—not bad going when she had only arrived this afternoon. Surely she could make something of such opportunities.

The door opened wider that evening, just before dinner, when the vicar's wife rang up and asked for Daisy. The speaker for the Women's Institute meeting on Thursday had scratched. Mrs. Osborne wondered whether Miss Dalrymple would be so kind as to stand in. She was sure a lecture on the writing profession would interest members far more than the planned annual lecture on flower-arranging.

Daisy's first impulse was to reject the proposal outright. Let Mrs. Osborne organize her husband's parishioners to her heart's content; Daisy had no intention of being organized.

She hesitated, trying to word her refusal politely. Mrs. Osborne, no doubt adept at assuming that silence gave consent, went on, "That's settled, then. Excellent! Would you care to come to tea at the Vicarage tomorrow to meet the committee members?"

Would she ever!

If anything in the world was guaranteed to be an absolute hotbed of village gossip, a veritable School for Scandal, it was a WI committee meeting combined with a vicarage tea-party.

4

". . . A-and this the burden of his song forever seemed to be-ee," Daisy sang to herself as she went up to her room to put on a hat, "I care for nobody, no not I, and nobody cares for me." Now why on earth should the Miller of Dee be circling irritatingly in her head?

Mrs. Burden at the shop, of course, and Miss Prothero's view of her as disobliging. Daisy did not care for Miss Prothero, and was not at all sure she wouldn't put up the shutters if she saw her coming. The two or three times Daisy had popped into the shop before, for odds and ends, the shopkeeper-postmistress had not struck her as an awkward customer, so to speak.

If Mrs. Burden could be persuaded to violate the sacred confidentiality of the Royal Mail, she might be able to tell who else had received anonymous letters. Johnnie had not kept the envelopes, but he remembered them as all being postmarked in the village and addressed in thick pencil in block capitals. Assuming there had been more than Johnnie's half dozen, Mrs. Burden must have noticed them, even if she could not recall to whom they were addressed.

Hatted, gloved, and stockinged in anticipation of her elevenses with Mrs. LeBeau—luckily the morning was still cool, though the sky was delphinium blue—Daisy collected Derek, Belinda, and Tinker Bell.

"No climbing gates," she commanded as they set out for the shop.

"It's all right, Aunt Daisy," Derek said blithely, yesterday's fright forgotten, "the shop won't close for hours and hours."

"But I have an engagement at eleven. No climbing gates. Or trees. Have you brought a lead for Tinker?"

"Yes, though she doesn't need one." From the capacious pocket of his grey flannel shorts, Derek produced three toffee papers, a grubby hankie with something tied up inside, a pebble, a rabbit's foot and two pennies. "Must be the other side," he muttered, restoring his treasures to their nest. From the other pocket he triumphantly drew a tangle of stout string. "It's a bit knotted."

"I'll untie the knots," Belinda offered. "I'm good at knots. Aunt Daisy, may I get shorts with big pockets?"

"We'll have to see what they have in the shop."

By the time they reached the bottom of the drive, Belinda had reduced the tangle to a useful length of string. Derek tied it to Tinker's collar, much to her disgust, and wrapped the other end around his hand.

While he was thus occupied, Daisy glanced at the lodge. In one of the upper windows a curtain moved. The casement was open a few inches, but there was not the slightest breath of a breeze.

Someone had been watching them. Had the same person watched when Johnnie visited Mrs. LeBeau, all those years ago? If Mr. Paramount was the Poison Pen, his venom was probably directed only at the usurping nephew who had inherited Oakhurst, not at other victims. But why wait so long?

Daisy frowned. The old man might just have grown more and more embittered, or nutty, until something had to give. Yet the letters surely would have at least touched upon his chief grievance—the injustice of his exile from his childhood home— not harped solely on the LeBeau incident. More likely the writer was his servant, either aiming at eventual blackmail or gone round the bend himself after so many years shut up with his dotty master.

Daisy sighed. She would have to try to talk to them, though it was quite possible today's watcher had nothing to do with the letters but simply had his attention drawn by the children's chatter.

As they turned left into the lane, here beginning its transmogrification into Rotherden's main street, Mrs. LeBeau's small front garden caught Daisy's eye and nose. She had been too interested in its owner yesterday to notice the fragrant rambler roses. White, pink, and yellow with deep golden hearts, they filled the garden with sensuous profusion, and a crimson climber draped the front porch.

In startling contrast was the garden next door. Miss Prothero favoured rigid ranks of scarlet salvia and Oxford blue lobelia, as cultivated by a thousand municipal parkkeepers. They grew in rectangular beds surrounding a rectangular lawn where no daisy dared raise its head amidst the short-trimmed grass. The modern bungalow, in a hideous yellow brick, was equally rectangular, with symmetrical windows. The front door, dead centre, was painted the same mud-brown shade as Miss Prothero had worn yesterday.

The whole thing shrieked "repressed old maid" at Daisy.

On the other hand, the bungalow was set back farther from the street than Mrs. LeBeau's house, and was separated from it by a high privet hedge, rigorously clipped. From indoors Miss Prothero could not possibly observe her neighbour's front door. In autumn, she'd be able to see the garden gate and path through the hedge, but probably not clearly enough to recognize a person. Of course, she would have watched Johnnie pass her own gate first before stopping at Mrs. LeBeau's, and then entering.

Yes, Miss Prothero was still a prime suspect. However, for the moment Daisy turned her attention to the houses on the other side beyond the Vicarage, a row of small, two-story cottages opening directly onto the street.

"Who lives next door to the Vicarage?" she asked Derek.

"Sam Basin. He works in Wyndham's Garage in Ashford and he's got a tremendous motor-cycle. It's a Wooler. They're called Flying Bananas, 'cause they're yellow and they have a long petrol tank. He once let me sit on it."

"Not when it was going!"

"No, but all the same, don't tell Mummy. Mr. and Mrs. Basin live there too, and Sam's sister is one of our housemaids at home."

Could those spelling mistakes and the clumsily formed letters be signs of an uneducated writer after all? Daisy would have sworn they were artificial, intended to mislead, but perhaps . . .

"And the next cottage," Derek went on, "that's Mrs. Molesworth-who-came-down-in-the-world."

Aha! Jealousy of those who retained the privileged position she had lost might be a powerful motive.

"What's 'came down in the world'?" Belinda enquired.

Derek explained: "It means she's a lady but she lost all her money so she has to live in a poky little cottage like the common village people."

"Poor lady!" said soft-hearted Belinda.

"It's all right, she's not starving or anything. She's *enormous* and she laughs a lot, and she's always sucking acid drops and she gives them to children, too. Do you like acid drops?"

"Not much. I like Dolly Mixture almost best, besides chocolate."

Daisy ceased to listen as the children compared the joys of various sweets. The cottages they were passing now still had a fair view of Mrs. LeBeau's front gate, but she could not go on interrogating Derek about their inhabitants.

At the end of the row, the village green began on the right, sloping down to the Hop-Picker in the far corner. The people in the houses around the green might have seen Johnnie walking up the hill from the station towards Oakhurst, but they could not have seen more without binoculars. Possible, but unlikely and hard to check, Daisy decided.

On the left side of the street, facing the green, was the police station, or rather the local bobby's house, with a front room devoted to police business. Next to it was the village shop, which included the post office and, in a tiny cubicle walled off from the store-room at the back, the telephone exchange. The letter-box was not a pillar-box but the kind set into the wall, round the farther side of the building, Daisy remembered. A footpath ran down that side, cutting across hop-fields to the main road where the motor-bus to Ashford stopped. Fronting the street beyond the path rose the cone roofs of a pair of oasthouses.

It could not have been better arranged for someone who wanted to post letters without being noticed.

As Daisy and retinue approached the shop, a tall, bulky gentleman arrived from the opposite direction. Clad in brown tweed plus-fours, a shooting jacket of Edwardian vintage, and a tweed cap, he walked stiffly, rigidly upright, stalking along like a crane with the aid of a stout walking-stick. His long face was weather-beaten, with a red tip to his nose, which looked the redder for the bristling white cavalry moustache beneath. With a slight bow, he gestured to Daisy to enter the shop before him.

"No, please do go first," said Daisy. "I have to make sure Derek ties the dog securely. It's Brigadier Lomax, isn't it? We've met, after church one Sunday I believe it was. I'm Daisy Dalrymple, Lady John's sister." *And you are the one other victim Johnnie suspects of having received an anonymous letter!*

"How d'ye do?" As he spoke, gruffly, the brigadier fished with finger and thumb in his waistcoat pocket and pulled out a monocle. Through this he blinked at Daisy, then at the children. "Ah, yes, young Master Frobisher, is it not?"

"Yes, sir, and this is my friend, Miss Fletcher."

"How d'ye do, Miss Fletcher." This time the knobbly hand dived into a trouser-pocket and came up with a shilling. "Here, my boy. Treat the young lady to some sweets."

"Gosh, thanks, sir. Is it all right if we buy a comic paper?"

"Yes, yes, by all means." His duty done by the younger generation, Brigadier Lomax turned back to Daisy. "The wife mentioned you were coming to stay at Oakhurst, Miss Dalrymple. My daughter and son-in-law are staying with us, and my son's fiancée and her brother. There was some talk about getting up a tennis party, I believe, if you should care for it."

"It sounds delightful," Daisy said cordially. She was an absolute duffer at tennis, and could think of a hundred things she'd rather do than run about waving a racquet on a hot afternoon. But she might get a chance to sit in the shade with lemonade, chatting with the brigadier, and who could tell what magic her guileless eyes might work on him?

"I'll tell Rosa," he said, with such gloom she revised the odds of his remaining within a mile of the tennis court. He courteously ushered her between the boxes of plums, pears, potatoes, onions, carrots, runner beans, and peas, and into the shop. There, she once again invited him to go first.

"The children will take ages choosing their sweets and paper," she assured him.

No one else was there except for Mrs. Burden, a thin middle-aged woman with quick, jerky movements. Her daughter's voice could be heard from the telephone exchange cubicle, asking a caller what number he wanted. Daisy congratulated herself on having arrived between the rush of those who considered shopping early a virtue and those who put it off till just before time to get lunch. By sheer luck it was also market day in nearby Ashford, perfect conditions for a good gossip with the shopkeeper.

Brigadier Lomax bought pipe-tobacco and some stamps, and left. Mrs. Burden joined Daisy in the corner of the shop where she had found just what she was looking for. On shelves above the gumboots and plimsolls, among the white lisle stockings, babies' sunbonnets, handkerchiefs, farm-labourers' smocks, and socks of every description, was a pile of white cotton shorts, elastic-waisted.

"Everyone seems to go to the seaside these days," said Mrs. Burden, "at least for the day in a charabanc. These are so much more convenient than a frock for little girls playing in the sand."

"Yes, and in the garden. I'll take a couple of pairs if you have the right size. No shirts? Well, she'll just have to borrow Derek's. Belinda, come and see if these will fit."

Belinda was disappointed with the one small patch pocket considered adequate for girls, but otherwise pleased. She went back to helping Derek decide between *Beano* and *Dandy.* At a counter encumbered by a large yellow cheese and a small display stand of boot polish, Daisy paid for the shorts and half a dozen picture postcards.

"I'll need stamps, too," she said.

"If you wouldn't mind stepping over to the Post Office counter, miss."

"Once you've stuck the stamp on, there's not much space for the address on these postcards, is there?" Daisy said chattily. "A friend of mine has a very long address, and I always have trouble squeezing it in. I expect you get some letters to be sorted with pretty badly written addresses."

"There's some are a real puzzle for sure, miss." Producing a block of penny stamps, Mrs. Burden leaned on the counter, quite ready for a chat. "You wouldn't think they cared if their letters never got where they're going."

"I try to remember to write the town in capital letters. I suppose it would be best to do the whole thing that way. Do you get many like that?"

"Well, miss, to tell the truth, it's mostly those who haven't got much education who write all in capitals, and it stands to reason they don't write many letters."

"I suppose not," Daisy said, trying to think of some more leading yet innocent-appearing questions. "At least, when they do write, the capital letters make it easy for you to read the address."

"You'd think so, wouldn't you?" said Mrs. Burden. "The trouble is, often as not they write in pencil, and it's that hard to make it out, specially by the gaslight. Still, it doesn't happen often. In the general way of things."

Daisy pounced. "In the general way of things?"

"There's been a regular rash of them these past few months." Straightening, she glanced back at the desk where she postmarked the mail, as if some might be lurking there. She looked harried, seeming to regret having spoken, but not knowing what to do other than to rush on to elaborate: "All in bunches, and all written by the same person by the looks of them."

"Do you have trouble deciphering them? It's not so difficult, I suppose, if they're all to people in the village, to addresses you know."

"Well, as a matter of fact, they are," the postmistress admitted, tight-lipped.

"How odd!" Daisy remarked. "Wouldn't you think whoever it is would go to see people instead of wasting the money on postage? You haven't noticed someone suddenly buying a lot of stamps?"

"No, miss." Mrs. Burden spoke quite sharply. "It's not my business to be paying attention to who buys what, nor I shouldn't be gossiping about Post Office business."

"It's my fault," Daisy said with a smile. "I'm a writer, you see, and I'm always interested in the ins and outs of people's jobs. Here's sixpence for my stamps. Thank you."

Winifred Burden had emerged from the telephone exchange a few minutes earlier to serve the children, so they were ready to leave. Daisy was dismayed to see the vast quantity of sweets they had bought for a shilling.

"Don't you dare be sick, you two," she said as they left the shop, "or I shall be in disgrace. Save some for later."

"D'you want a sherbet dab, Aunt Daisy? I bought three."

"No, thanks!"

"Look!" cried Belinda, who had gone straight to Tinker Bell and given her a great hug. "Tinker's chewed through the string, but she just sat there pretending! Isn't she good and clever?"

"I told you she didn't need a lead," said Derek smugly. "Here, Tink, here's an aniseed ball."

Tinker crunched the aniseed ball and followed them up the street with her nose glued to Derek's paper bag.

Daisy felt moderately pleased with herself. Getting names had been too much to hope for, but at least she could be pretty certain Johnnie was not the only victim of the Poison Pen. That cut out Mr. Paramount as a suspect, she thought with relief as they approached the Oakhurst gates. His resentment was aimed specifically at his usurping nephew, so she wouldn't have to beard him in his den.

Of course, Alec would not cross a suspect off his list so easily. The old man never left the lodge and she had never heard that he had any visitors, but his daily woman might provide all the village gossip. General misanthropy could be motive enough for the other letters, or perhaps they were just an attempt to disguise the provenance of Johnnie's.

Alec was right—once someone was on the list, it was difficult to be quite sure one could take them off.

They reached the end of the drive. Daisy glanced at the church clock: ten to eleven. She gave Belinda the shorts. "Here, go and put a pair on right away," she said, "before you dirty that frock. Derek, please tell Nanny I'll be very grateful if she will kindly lend a couple of your shirts to Bel. Straight home, now. I'm going to elevenses with Mrs. LeBeau."

The door was opened by a neat, white-capped maid, not young. Daisy knew as soon as she spoke that she was not local.

"Please to come through, miss. Madam is in the arbour."

What Daisy saw of the house as she passed through left a pleasant impression of light and air. The back garden, rather than sloping up, was terraced on three levels. The lowest was paved. The second was a rose garden, with a shady, rose-grown bower of the kind described by Dickens as a shelter erected by man for the benefit of spiders. Daisy presumed it had been swept clear of eight-legged marauders before its elegant mistress ensconced herself there.

Mrs. LeBeau came to the top of the steps to greet

Daisy. Her dark hair, loosely looped up into a chignon, gleamed in the sun. "You won't object to taking coffee outside, I hope?" she said. "We can easily move indoors if . . ."

"No, no, it's beautiful out here."

"I'm rather fond of roses, as you may have guessed! I spent some years in the grimmer parts of South Africa. Roses grow marvellously in the Cape, but where we were those that survived were generally covered in dust. I used to dream of English rose gardens."

"I have a friend who lived in southern Italy and dreamt of daffodils," said Daisy, sitting down on one of the white-painted wrought-iron chairs, well cushioned, in the arbour. "What took you to Africa?"

"I married a big-game hunter," Mrs. LeBeau said drily, "frightfully handsome and dashing, but without a penny to his name. It was a runaway match and my family cut me off without the proverbial shilling. Shooting lions and buffalo was all Perry knew how to do, so he became a guide, going off into the veldt for weeks while I was left behind in dusty little dorps full of dusty little Dutchmen. With neither shillings nor pennies to our name, we hadn't much choice."

"I suppose not." Daisy regarded with some doubt the expertly cultivated garden and the charming Queen Anne house, in excellent repair.

Mrs. LeBeau laughed. "You're wondering how I managed all this. Sheer luck! A party of prospectors on holiday hired Perry. After the shooting, he went up with them into the Witwatersrand, and they practically fell over a vein of gold. I suspect it was in a drunken celebration they signed over a share to Perry. At any rate, the result was that when a buffalo took revenge on him for all the slaughter, and I came home, I found myself with a comfortable income."

"What luck!" said Daisy, not without a touch of envy. But then, if she had not had to work for her living, she would never have met Alec. "Oh dear, I didn't mean what luck losing your husband. I'm sorry!"

"Oh, as to that, poor old Perry had his points, but as a life's companion . . . Well, let's say my parents weren't far off the mark. I've certainly no desire for a second venture into matrimony. Ah, here's our coffee. Thank you, Alice."

The maid transferred a Wedgewood coffee set and a plate of shortbread from her tray to the wrought-iron table. Mrs. LeBeau dispensed coffee and biscuits.

"Marvellous shortbread," said Daisy after her first bite.

"My cook-housekeeper is Scottish."

"And your maid is from London, isn't she? Not local, anyway."

"I have a flat in London and I spend a good deal of time there. And I don't care for gossiping servants," Mrs. LeBeau admitted with a wry smile. "There is enough talk without a maid who goes home twice a week to report my every move to her family. You live in London, don't you? Lady John mentioned Chelsea, I think."

Daisy accepted the change of subject, for the moment at least. They talked about London and Daisy's work. Mrs. LeBeau kept the conversation steered firmly away from her own concerns, until at last Daisy could not decently prolong her visit.

A fearful waste after such a promising start, she thought as they descended the steps together and went into the house. The police had a great advantage in being able to pose direct questions instead of having to feel around in the dark.

On the way to the front door, Mrs. LeBeau picked up a small pile of letters from the hall table. She opened the door and bade Daisy goodbye. Daisy was half way down the path when she heard an exasperated exclamation behind her.

"Oh no, not another of the wretched things!"

Mrs. LeBeau was leaning against the doorpost, staring at one of the envelopes in her hand with mingled annoyance and apprehension. Perking up, Daisy hurried back to her.

"Is something wrong? Can I help?"

"No, no, it's just . . ." Mrs. LeBeau's voice faded, and she looked searchingly at Daisy, who did her best to appear guilelessly sympathetic. "Actually, it would be a relief to tell someone about it, but I'd hate to shock you."

"I don't think I'm frightfully shockable. Living in Bohemian Chelsea, you know, and then I've helped the police with one or two criminal investigations . . ."

"I wouldn't want the police involved in this," said the Scarlet Woman in alarm.

"Of course not. May I guess? It's an anonymous letter, isn't it? I happen to know you're not the only one to get them."

"No?" Mrs. LeBeau's expression lightened. "Perhaps it's silly, but that does make me feel better. Come back in, won't you?"

She led the way into a drawing room decorated in light blues and greys, with touches of peach, and vases of roses everywhere. A modern, comfortable sofa and easy chairs continued the colour scheme. The rest of the furniture had the simple, elegant lines of traditional Sheraton and Hepplewhite designs, whether antique or reproduction Daisy was not competent to judge. There were two well-filled bookcases, as well as a gramophone with a pile of records, and an expensive wireless set.

"What a lovely room!" A painting hanging over the mantel caught her eye and she went across to study it. A twisted thorn tree to one side framed the foreground of sun-bleached grasses and a range of dark, rocky hills which stood out against a deep blue sky. "And what an interesting picture."

"The Witwatersrand, 'whence cometh my help,' if you'll pardon the blasphemy."

"I'm not very religious. You painted this?" Daisy asked, noticing the initials "W. L." in the corner.

"Yes, I had to keep myself occupied somehow. My friends forgive its deficiencies, and my enemies are not invited into my house. I have enemies, you know, in the village." She took a paperknife from a small writing-table in one corner. Sinking into a chair by the open French windows, she slit the envelope and took out the paper inside. "I thought these letters came from one of them, but if other people are getting them it sounds more like general malice."

Daisy took the other chair. "I know of at least two other recipients," she said, exaggerating a bit since she couldn't be certain of the brigadier. "I'm pretty sure there are more. May I see the envelope?"

The writing was exactly like that of Johnnie's letters. The postmark was earlier that very day. When Mrs. Burden glanced at her desk, this and any similar envelopes must just have left it in the postman's bag.

"I shan't ask who else is being victimized," said Mrs. LeBeau, the unfolded letter in her hand, "though your presence and knowledge lead to certain conjectures. I hope you don't expect to read this."

"No," Daisy said reluctantly. "You've read all of them?"

"Yes. They all say much the same in different variants of foulness. I shall destroy this at once, as I did the rest."

"Forgive me, but may I ask why you go on reading such frightful stuff when you know pretty much what each new one will say?"

"Because, my dear Miss Dalrymple, I'm afraid that sooner or later there will be a demand for money in exchange for silence, and that if I fail to respond . . . Well, my reputation may be already tarnished in Rotherden, but I'm still received in decent houses. It would be painful to lose that. I'd hate to have to move. More important, if word spread beyond this little community, there's someone else who could be badly damaged."

"You mean . . . ?" Daisy ventured.

"My lover," the Merry Widow said flatly. "Despite any conclusion you may have drawn from what you've been told, I'm not wildly promiscuous. I have a satisfactory arrangement with a gentleman of whom I'm very fond. His wife, on the other hand, flits from man to man. Incidentally, she knows about us, and is mildly amused by our faithfulness to each other. His position is such that divorce would ruin him even more surely than exposure of an . . . irregular liaison."

"I see. Does he know about the letters?"

"No. Nor have I any intention of worrying him with them."

Daisy nodded. "Thank you for being so frank. I'll be frank in return. I've been asked to try to find out privately who's writing these beastly things. I don't know if I've any chance of success, but obviously the more information I have the better."

"Rather you than the police," Mrs. LeBeau said irresolutely. "But if you succeed, what next?"

"Frankly, I haven't thought that far ahead. I suppose it would be up to J— to the person who asked me to investigate. He's no keener for publicity than you are. Nor can I see that I need tell him you're another victim."

"Doubtless he suspects. Unless he suspects me of being the writer?"

"No, he told me he couldn't believe you're the Poison Pen."

"Poison Pen!" Mrs. LeBeau shuddered. "What a

dreadful term, but horridly apt. A pen dipped in venom. Let's hope it doesn't lead to worse."

"You mean, that he or she doesn't go on to black-mail?" Daisy asked.

"There's that. But what I was thinking of was that one of the victims may discover the writer before you do, and take violent steps to silence the Poison Pen."

5

Home from the shop, Brigadier Lomax picked up the morning post from the silver salver on the hall table. As usual he grumbled to himself about its lateness: Rotherden was at the end of the rural route. Carrying the letters, he went on to the gun-room. With the house full of his offspring and their hangers-on, it was the only place he could be fairly sure of peace and quiet.

He tossed the letters on the table. Taking from his pockets his tobacco pouch and the tin of tobacco he had just bought, he transferred the contents of one to the other. Gold Flake would have to do until his own blend arrived from Fribourg and Treyer in London.

Dammit, Rosa ought to have sent in the order sooner! Just because he forgot to tell her he was nearly out . . .

He took his favourite pipe down from the wall rack, filled it, and struck a match. His hand trembled as he held the flame to the bowl. What he needed was a stiff peg, but the sun was still below the yardarm.

On the third match the tobacco caught. Puffing, the brigadier turned to the post.

Rosa and the children had already taken any addressed to them. In the old days, when a man was master of his household, no one would have dared to touch the post before the *paterfamilias* had gone through it. Things weren't what they used to be.

Flicking through the pile, his liver-spotted hand—was it really his, that shaky old-man's hand?—stopped on a cheap white envelope crudely addressed in block capitals, in pencil. Another of the confounded things! He ripped it open, tearing the letter inside.

YOU DESGUSTING OLD TOPER, YOU HAD WHISKY ON YOUR BREATH IN CHURCH ON SUNDAY. ONE OF THESE DAYS YOU'LL DROP THE COLLEXION PLATE. YOU'VE GOT A FILTHY TEMPER WHEN YOU'RE DRUNK. EVERYONE KNOWS YOU HIT YOUR WIFE. REPENT!

"Pah!" Brigadier Lomax ripped letter and envelope to shreds and buried them in the waste-paper basket.

He wondered uneasily if it was true everyone knew he had slapped Rosa. She made him furious with her whining. Did he really need another nightcap, indeed! That was for him to decide. Dammit, it was a man's prerogative to keep his womenfolk in order, but one didn't want everyone talking about it.

Besides, he had said he was sorry, hadn't he? She had no need to go running to talk to Osborne about it, devil take it! Someone must have overheard her, the vicar's busybody wife, or their maid, or one of those wretched old women with nothing better to do who always hung about clergymen. That was the sort who wrote anonymous letters, by Jove.

If he could just lay hands on that damned letter writer . . .

Defiantly he reached for the tantalus, poured a good-sized tot of scotch, and swallowed it down. Then he went over to the gun rack and took down a double-barrelled shotgun. His hands steady now, he loaded it, stuffed several cartridges into his pocket, and stalked out through the French doors.

* * *

Sam Basin rode his Wooler motor-cycle home from Ashford for his midday dinner. Setting it up on its stand, the large young man took a clean rag from his pocket and lovingly polished the dust off the bright yellow mudguards and petrol tank.

What a corker! Still as shiny as the day he'd bought her, and running smooth as silk, he made sure of that.

He patted her tank and went into the cottage. Mum had his dinner ready, a nice shepherd's pie, crisp on top and sizzling hot inside, with plenty of gravy. Poor old Dad had to make do with bread and cheese in the hop-fields. Catch Sam getting stuck as a farm labourer—no fear!

Elbows on the kitchen table, he ate hungrily, while his mother pottered around making tea, pouring it into the big, thick mug, taking a plum pie from the Aga.

"Cor, Mum, you done us proud."

"Might as well use the oven while it's hot," she said. "You want a piece now?"

"Nah, save it for tea." Sam swallowed the last of his tea, wiped his mouth on the back of his hand, and stood up. "I got to get back."

"Here, if I wasn't forgetting, a letter come for you. You got yourself a girl in town, our Sam?"

"Nah, I got better things to do with my money than taking girls to the pictures. Give it here, then."

He glanced at the envelope and the shepherd's pie turned to lead in his stomach. Another one of those bloody letters! Well, he bloody well wasn't going to read this one. They all said the same, didn't they?

All right, so he'd done a bit of fiddling, a few jobs on the side. What harm if he charged people a bit less for repairs and pocketed the lot now and then, when the boss was over in Hythe at the new garage? Wyndham was a bloody plutocrat, he'd never miss a few quid.

But Mr. Wyndham wouldn't look at things that way if someone told him. Might even call in the coppers. At the very least, it'd be back to the hop-fields for Sam.

Which of the bloody fools he'd done a favour for was writing the letters? Or was the bugger stupid enough to boast about the deal he'd got, and someone else did the writing? If Sam found out who it was, he'd soon show him which side his bread was buttered!

With a surly grunt, he stuffed the envelope in his pocket and stamped out. Revving the Wooler savagely, he raced off down the village street with the engine roaring.

Piers Catterick whistled tunelessly as his fingers flew over the keys. Words flowed, and the pile of manuscript beside the typewriter grew visibly.

When things went badly, he thought he'd go mad, stuck in this bucolic paradise. When things went well, he knew he had been right to leave town. How could one produce novels of steamy rustic lust stuck in a bed-sitter in Bloomsbury? At least, he never had any trouble getting up steam—the trick was to stay on the right side of the Lord Chamberlain; no use getting one's books banned, like Lawrence's *Rainbow*. But his exile was adding an authentic rural flavour to his writing which was bound to improve already respectable sales.

What was it Lomax called those black and white birds? Magpies, that was it. And the rhyme: ". . . Three for a girl, four for a boy . . ." He could weave that in somewhere, add a nice little touch of primitive super-stition.

Rum old boy, the brigadier. He had been rather shocked when he found out the sort of books Piers wrote, but then some busybody tried to get him to turf out his literary tenant and he dug in his heels.

Piers caught himself staring out of the window at the

chimney-pots of the brigadier's house, visible between the trees. Elms. Be precise.

Turning back to the typewriter, he reread his last paragraph, and picked up a pencil. Rooks in the elms, not black birds in the trees. Vermin, Lomax said. Come to think of it, those distant bangs which had diverted Piers's attention from his work could be the brigadier taking a gun to the rooks or some other pest. Before he came to live in the country, Piers had not realized the extent of the constant slaughter that went on even outside the hunting and shooting seasons. Hares, otters, badgers—all torn to pieces in the name of sport.

A moue of distaste on his long, pale face, he unfolded his long, weedy body from his chair. He had lost his train of thought; time for lunch. Gathering up the pile of discarded manuscript pages to bung in the waste paper basket downstairs, he trotted down, remembering for once to bend his head to dodge the low beam.

Several letters had fluttered through the letter-box an hour ago. With a feeling of conscious virtue for having let them lie unread so long while he wrote, Piers scooped them up from the doormat. A gratifying number of friends wrote regularly: long, self-consciously literary epistles with one eye on possible future publication. Edgbaston and Jill threatened to come down for a few days. Oh Lord, they were arriving in the morning! He couldn't put them up; they'd have to stay at the Hop-Picker. There was something from his editor, and . . .

"Hell, not another of those confounded diatribes! Damnation," he swore again as he gave himself a papercut tearing open the envelope.

Yes, the same stuff again, ". . . FILTHY . . . PERVERTING YOUTH . . . CORRUPTING SOCIETY . . ."

He read no further but dropped letter and envelope in the wpb.

Who was harassing him? Some prude from the Victorian Dark Ages, who didn't understand the need for modern literature to expand its horizons—yet who used pretty vile language in his denunciations. Perhaps the person, unnamed by Brigadier Lomax, who had tried to persuade Piers's landlord to eject him from the cottage?

Piers found himself actually shaking with anger. It was an unfamiliar emotion. His set prided themselves on a cool, sophisticated approach to life, reserving the passions for the imaginary characters in their books. A bad review meant merely that the critic was jealous or deluded—not worth getting hot and bothered about.

But the letters had Piers hot and bothered. Though he did not for a moment repent or regret what he wrote, their vicious nastiness unsettled him and—ultimate sin—made it difficult for him to concentrate on his work. Who in blazes was writing the confounded things, depriving a waiting world of another masterpiece from his pen? He'd like to wring his—or her—unenlightened neck.

Murder . . . there was a thought. Perhaps he should throw in a good juicy murder, a crime of passion. No need to sink to the level of a detective story, ending tritely with a confession and an arrest.

His anti-hero would bump off the prudish old maid who interfered with his seduction of the luscious dairymaid, Piers decided. Now, how to set up the dreadful deed so that he would not be caught?

The usual pre-lunch rush came to an end. Mrs. Burden said to her plump, pasty-faced daughter, "Watch the shop for a minute, Win, I'm going out the back."

"I have to mind the exchange, don't I," Winifred said sullenly.

"It doesn't exactly keep you busy, with so few telephones in the village! If someone rings up, of course you have to help them, but just keep an eye on things in here."

Without waiting for an answer, she went out of the back door. What was the name of those pills she had seen advertised? "Peevish, anaemic girls needed," the advert started. Something about pale, fretful, cross, can't get on with Mother. It sounded just like Win. Dr. Williams' Pink Pills, that was it. She'd get hold of some, put them in Winifred's bedtime cocoa if the girl wouldn't take them.

Still and all, she had worse problems than a surly daughter.

Inside the lean-to W.C. built on behind the shop, she latched the door securely and threw the bolt for good measure. From the pocket of the pink seersucker overall she wore in the shop to keep her frock clean, she took a cheap white envelope.

What had young Master Derek's auntie wanted, asking all those questions? Was she really just interested because she was a writer, or had she guessed something? Several envelopes just like this one had gone to Lord John. Whatever the horrible letters inside said, he surely'd never tell his sister-in-law, but he maybe had let drop a hint by mistake.

Had Mrs. Burden led Miss Dalrymple to suspect she was getting them, too? For just a moment, it would have been that easy to confess, but she'd pulled herself together all right. If anyone found out . . .

Times were hard, and making ends meet was harder. She had a daughter to provide for. Alfie was a fat lot of help, so pleased with himself for making sergeant he stayed on in the regular army when everyone else's husbands got demobbed. He hardly ever sent a penny home.

So what if she did forget to take her thumb off the balance and shaved half an ounce off a pound of cheese now and then? She only ever short-measured them as could afford it. It wasn't as if she got much custom from the Willoughby-Joneses, either, having all their groceries delivered from Ashford.

Anyway, how did Mrs. Willoughby-Jones know her maid hadn't eaten a slice before she weighed the slab and ran tattling to her mistress? Mrs. Willoughby-Jones had a nerve, coming into the shop and making a big song and dance over half a mouthful of Cheddar. Good job no one else was around, but the old battle-axe could've told anyone.

Not that Mrs. Burden had failed to defend herself. She'd cut a wedge, then weighed it, she explained. Her eye was pretty good. If she'd forgotten to mention it had come out just a bit under—well, often enough it was as much over, and the fuss people made if you tried to charge them!

Was it Mrs. Willoughby-Jones writing these letters that made you feel all shaky inside? Or was it someone else? The harridan had had two or three herself, though not today, but that could be a false trail to mislead her vengeful victims. Mrs. Burden stared at the pencilled address on the envelope by the dim light from the high slit windows. She knew most people's writing in the village, but this was unrecognizable.

Without opening it, she ripped up the envelope and its contents. The little pieces fluttered as she dropped them into the toilet bowl. She had to bend down to pick up several which went astray.

Pulling the chain, she watched the damning words swirl and disappear. If only she could flush the writer away so easily!

If she knew who it was, she thought bitterly, if she could only be sure, someone just might find rat poison in their next packet of sugar.

The letters came in bunches, according to Mrs. Burden. Mrs. LeBeau had received one by the morning post. Had Johnnie?

Walking up the drive, slowly because of the hill and

the midday heat, Daisy half hoped poor Johnnie had been spared this time. However, if a new one had come, it might offer some unmistakable clue to the identity of the Poison Pen.

She wondered whether Mrs. Burden had guessed that the illwritten envelopes were the work of an anonymous letter writer. Her manner had been a bit odd. Perhaps it was just the embarrassment of a conscientious post office employee caught revealing more than she ought about the confidential business of the Royal Mail.

Or could Mrs. Burden be victim? In that case, she must be able to recognize the envelopes, so she would know exactly who the other victims were.

Maybe she was the Poison Pen herself, Daisy thought with a flash of excitement. The postmistress was in the perfect position both to hear all the village gossip—her daughter might listen to and report telephone conversations, too—and to insert the letters into the mail with no fear of discovery. But surely she would have guarded her tongue more carefully. More likely she was indeed another victim, one with a better chance than most of discovering the identity of her tormentor.

Still, she had to be added to the list of suspects, which was beginning to grow unmanageably long.

Before her tea at the Vicarage, Daisy had better try to eliminate the old man at the lodge, she decided with a sigh. She would have a shot, though she rather doubted Mr. Paramount would allow her across the threshold, in view of her relationship to his hated nephew.

Johnnie was out for the day, taking the turn of a sick colleague on the Bench. He took his duties as Justice of the Peace very seriously, whatever the Poison Pen's opinion of his qualifications. He had left the house, as had Daisy, before the morning post's late arrival. She saw a pile of letters waiting beside the vase of dahlias on the table as she stepped into the coolness of the hall.

Belinda stood by the table, dressed in shorts and a yellow, short-sleeved shirt. She turned as Daisy came in.

"There's this for you," she said, handing over a folded sheet with "Miss Dalrymple" neatly printed on the outside. Daisy opened it and saw that the butler had taken a telephone message from Lucy. "But not one from Daddy," Bel continued. "He promised he'd write. D'you think it could have got into Uncle John's pile? I didn't like to look."

"We only left town yesterday! Still, I'll sneak a quick peek. You were quite right not to." But it gave Daisy a perfect excuse for checking Johnnie's post. She riffled through the envelopes: blue, buff, white—but not cheap white addressed in capitals in pencil, nor anything in Alec's neat hand. Doubly disappointed, she straightened the pile. "No, I expect there will be one tomorrow, darling. You look very nice in those shorts. Where's Derek?"

"He went upstairs to get his pea-shooter. He said he'd let me have a go with it, but it's hidden in a secret place he doesn't want me to know so I waited here. Here he comes."

The last words were unnecessary, as Derek and Tinker Bell thundered across the landing and down the stairs. They swept up Belinda in their passing and disappeared through the front door.

Daisy started reading the lengthy message from Lucy as she headed for the terrace. There she found her sister talking to a youngish, muscular gentleman in a natty heather-mixture tweed suit. He rose at the sound of her footsteps.

"Daisy, I don't think you've met Dr. Padgett. He kindly drops in once a week to make sure I'm behaving myself. My sister, Daisy Dalrymple, Doctor."

"How do you do, Dr. Padgett." Daisy liked the look

of his open face and charming smile. "I hope Violet obeys your orders."

"Oh yes, Lady John is an excellent patient—not really a patient at all, she's so healthy. I'm here under false pretences. My wife goes up to town every Tuesday, and as I generally have time to spare between my rounds, I'm free to cadge a good meal where I may."

Daisy laughed.

"No joke," he said with a comic grimace. "It's Cook's day off."

"Dr. Padgett will lunch with us, Daisy," said Violet, smiling. "Since he has that prospect of your company, I don't suppose he'll mind if you read your note. Since Lucy telephoned, I expect it's important."

"If you'll excuse me," Daisy said apologetically. "It's a message from my American editor."

"Editor?" queried the doctor in surprise. "You write, Miss Dalrymple?"

"As a way to pay the bills, it's more fun than digging ditches."

"You mean you work for a living?" His tone was disapproving.

Daisy suppressed a sigh. "I do. So if you don't mind, in case it's urgent . . ." She moved away to lean against the stone balustrade, her back to the terrace, and finished reading the note. It reported the lengthy text of a telegram from Mr. Thorwald, which Lucy had forwarded by telephone. "Oh *bother!*"

"What is it, Daisy?"

"He wants a potted biography of the Duke of Gloucester to go with my article about the Henley regatta. I told you I met him there."

"You met Prince Henry?" Dr. Padgett was all agog.

"Yes, but all I know about him is that he's a soldier. Mr. Thorwald wants a bit more than that, and he wants me to telegraph it! At least he says he'll pay for the cable. But I'll have to do some telephoning, Vi."

"After lunch," said Violet firmly. "An hour won't make any odds. Sit down and relax, darling."

Daisy obeyed, but after lunch she went back out to the terrace with them only to collect a cup of coffee to take to the library with her. Derek and Belinda were outside already, playing a quiet game of draughts after their nursery meal, Tinker Bell sprawled at their feet, while Peter took his nap upstairs.

Tinker came to greet the new arrivals, bestowing lavish licks on Vi's and Daisy's hands. Daisy noticed that the doctor hastily put his hands behind his back when the dog approached him, perhaps from motives of hygiene; but she thought he looked as if he didn't much like dogs. Another flaw in the charm!

At the telephone in the library, when Mrs. Burden's daughter came on the line, Daisy asked for her own Chelsea number. Lucy, the granddaughter of an earl, was far more mindful than Daisy of her aristocratic background, though she too worked for her living. If she was in, she could probably produce enough information about His Royal Highness to fill the necessary three or four paragraphs.

The trunk connection went through unusually quickly, and Lucy's clear soprano voice said, "Hello?"

"Darling, it's me, Daisy."

"Darling! You got the message? Oh, by the way, your copper rang up not half an hour ago."

"Alec 'phoned *you?* What's wrong?" Daisy asked in alarm.

"He'd mislaid a shirt-stud and wondered if he'd lost it here. I searched your room, and lo and behold . . ."

"Alec never set foot in my room!" Daisy said vehemently.

"Keep your hair on, darling," came Lucy's amused drawl. "Your study, not your bedroom. Still, one can't help wondering just what was going on to loosen a shirt-stud." She paused invitingly.

"Nothing! There's no room in my study for anything to 'go on.' Never mind that, Lucy, I don't want to run up Johnnie's telephone bill for nothing. Tell me, what do you know about the Duke of Gloucester?"

As expected, Lucy had loads of information at her fingertips. Daisy scribbled notes in her own idiosyncratic version of Pitman's shorthand.

"Thanks, darling, that's plenty. I'm not writing a book on the subject, thank heaven."

"Just as well. He's too young and—dare I say it?—dull for a biography. *Lèse majesté!*

"I shan't report it. Toodle-oo, then, Lucy."

"Pip pip, darling. Oh, I nearly forgot, Alec mentioned he was going to phone you this evening."

"Spiffing!" said Daisy, and hung up the earpiece. She sat for a moment in happy contemplation of talking to Alec this evening. It was amazing how much she missed him just because he was sixty miles away, though she very likely would not see him if she were in London. A Metropolitan Police detective's hours were irregular, to put it mildly.

She went up to her room to turn her notes into a couple of print-worthy paragraphs, using the portable typewriter now on semipermanent loan from her English editor. Then she went to see if Belinda and Derek wanted to walk down to the shop with her to send the telegram. She didn't want to risk phoning in such a long cable, in case something got mixed up or omitted even before its transatlantic transit.

The children, with dog, had gone off to dam the stream. "Because," Violet explained, "now that Belinda has shorts which it doesn't matter if she gets dirty, they might as well make sure they're not wasted."

"So says Derek?" Daisy laughed. "I'm off to the Post Office, and I may not be back till after my tea at the Vicarage, depending."

"I was just about to leave," said Dr. Padgett. "May I offer you a lift, Miss Dalrymple? It's hot for walking."

Daisy accepted. They went through the house to the carriage sweep at the front, where his dark blue Humber was parked off to one side in the shade of a sycamore. Not an economy motor-car; his practice must be doing well.

"Shall I put the hood down?" the doctor asked, opening the door for Daisy. "It won't take a minute. I was driving along dusty country lanes this morning, but just motoring down to the village, you shouldn't get too blown about for Vicarage tea."

"Yes, please," said Daisy. "I'll move your bag to the back seat, shall I?"

"Sorry, forgot it was there. Yes, just bung it over—gently, please!"

The black medical bag had been holding down a sheaf of papers. As Daisy scooped them up to deposit them in the back, a couple of envelopes slipped out. One looked unpleasantly familiar. With a shock of recognition, Daisy stared at the pencilled words: DR R S PADGETT, OLD WELL HOUSE, ROTHERDEN, KENT.

Her first impulse was to tax him with it. Reaching for it, she had actually opened her mouth to speak when a second thought struck.

What had the doctor done to make himself a target?

A medical man was in a peculiarly sensitive position. The least whiff of scandal might send patients fleeing in droves. A botched diagnosis, a wrongly dispensed prescription, even a rumour of an affair with a patient could destroy his livelihood. Faced with ruin, Dr. Padgett would not take kindly to Daisy's discovery that he was the victim of a Poison Pen.

Maybe it was worse than an affair or a fatal mistake. Perhaps he had performed an illegal abortion; perhaps some grateful old lady who had left him money had died under mysterious circumstances. Doctors had undetectable ways to bump people off. In that innocent black bag . . .

The hood folded back, exposing Daisy to Dr. Padgett's view. Hastily she shoved the tell-tale envelope in among the rest of the papers and tucked the sheaf under the black bag on the back seat.

Had he seen her staring at it? Surely only a few seconds had passed while he unfastened the hood at the front.

"There, at least we'll have some air," he said with his personable smile.

Silently Hamlet reminded her, "One may smile, and smile, and be a villain."

"I can't remember when we last had such a hot summer" she said as he sat down beside her and pressed the self-starter. Nervously anxious to distract him from her nervous anxiety, she seized the first topic that came to mind. "Violet's finding the heat rather trying, I think. Is she really as healthy as a horse? Johnnie seems a bit over solicitous. I have friends who dance and play tennis, everything but ride."

"Lady John has had two miscarriages since Peter's birth."

"Oh, poor Vi! I didn't know."

"And I ought not to have told you, but I didn't want you to be urging her to exert herself. I hope you won't give me away."

"I shouldn't dream of it," Daisy said with fervour.

6

Cabling the article to Mr. Thorwald took some time. Mrs. Burden practically bent over backwards to be helpful, but she got flustered when she couldn't lay her hands on the transatlantic telegraph rates.

"I'm so sorry, Miss Dalrymple," she said, scrabbling frantically through the drawer. "We don't get much call for them—I don't know that I've ever been asked before—but I know it's in here somewhere."

Daisy hadn't the heart to upset her further by trying to extract more information about the anonymous letters. Besides, she hadn't yet come up with an indirect way to find out who had received them, let alone whether the postmistress herself was a victim. A direct question was hardly likely to get a useful response, and it would give away Daisy's interest, which might be disastrous if Mrs. Burden was in fact the writer.

It was madly frustrating not being able to question people. Alec, or Sergeant Tring, would wring the truth from her in no time, Daisy was sure. Even the village bobby could demand answers. But no one had reported the epistolary persecution to the police. Apparently all the victims were as reluctant to risk seeing their secrets revealed as were Johnnie and Mrs. LeBeau.

Which suggested that they all had secrets. The Poison Pen was not spraying venom more or less at random, but injecting it into carefully chosen subjects. Someone had an excellent source of information—though out of date in Johnnie's case.

Wasn't it?

"Oh, *here* it is," said Mrs. Burden in relief, disinterring a sheet of paper from a cache tucked away behind her parcel scales. "It won't take a moment now, Miss Dalrymple. I'll be with you in just a minute, Miss Hendricks."

While she searched and Daisy ruminated, several customers had come into the shop. Winifred Burden had slouched through from the exchange to wait on the first, someone's cook-maid with a long list. A pale, thin woman in a badly tailored bottle-green costume stood by the counter, clutching her purse.

From the far side of the shop came an irate voice: "I'm next!" A well-dressed, hard-faced woman surged forward. "I've been waiting for ages. I can't think why you don't hire a girl to help, Mrs. Burden. I'm sure you can afford it, the prices you charge."

Mrs. Burden quailed, burying her nose in the rate list.

"Village shops have to charge more than town shops," the fourth customer intervened pacifically. A stout woman with several chins and a lovely pink and white complexion, she had large, rather cow-like brown eyes, with an un-cow-like twinkle. Her frock was a cotton crêpe tent in a cheerful cherry and white stripe, obviously designed for comfort. "They pay extra carriage, Mrs. Willoughby-Jones," she continued in her deep voice, "besides having fewer customers to rely on."

"Nonsense, Mrs. Molesworth, it's sheer thievery," snapped Mrs. Willoughby-Jones. "I don't know why I put up with it."

"Because Mr. Willoughby-Jones drives your motorcar to his office, and Mrs. Burden's shop is much more convenient than taking the bus into Ashford." Mrs. Molesworth smiled warmly at the cringing shopkeeper. "I don't know how we'd manage without her."

"I wish I had a motor-car," Miss Hendricks complained in a discontented voice, "but of course I could never afford to employ a chauffeur."

"If you can afford to buy a motor-car, learn to drive it yourself," Mrs. Molesworth suggested genially.

"Oh, I couldn't! And you're right, I can't afford to buy one anyway."

"Buy a bicycle."

"I'm afraid I'm not strong enough," Miss Hendricks sighed.

"Don't be so feeble," Mrs. Willoughby-Jones exhorted her.

Miss Hendricks bridled, her pale cheeks flushing. "I assure you, Mrs. Willoughby-Jones, I deeply regret my frail constitution and envy those who enjoy robust health."

"Nonsense! It's all in your mind, and if you would just . . ."

"I can help you now, madam," Mrs. Burden intervened, having completed Daisy's business and gone round to the shop counter.

"About time too!" Mrs. Willoughby-Jones declared.

Lingering by the Post Office counter, Daisy pretended to read an official notice about the air-mail service to Paris. How long before air-mail to America became commonplace? she wondered idly, but her attention was on the muted voices behind her.

"I'm sure I was here first," Miss Hendricks muttered to Mrs. Molesworth. "I'm not one to complain, but no one ever pays any attention to me. I must say, Mrs. Willoughby-Jones was positively rude!"

"To me as well," Mrs. Molesworth soothed her. "It's best to pay no attention to *her.*"

"I do believe she deliberately tries to pick quarrels."

"Anything for a little excitement. Think how boring her life must be, married to a dull dog like Willoughby-Jones."

"My life is dull, too," Miss Hendricks said with some heat, "but I don't go about starting fights."

Mrs. Molesworth's laugh rumbled out. "No, thank heaven."

"One day she will pick on someone who strikes back. I think someone should ask Mr. Osborne to have a word with her."

"Poor Vicar! I'm afraid he probably spends a great deal of time listening to his parishioners complain about each other."

"Well, if that's how you feel," said Miss Hendricks, her tone offended, "I'm sorry I spoke, I'm sure."

Daisy turned, to see Mrs. Molesworth shaking her head in regret as Miss Hendricks moved away with her nose in the air. Excusing herself with a smile, Daisy threaded her way between the fat woman and a pyramid of tinned soup.

Two more possible villains, she thought as she left the shop. Mrs. Molesworth, "come down in the world" or not, was far too good-natured to be the Poison Pen. However, Miss Hendricks was the sort of frustrated spinster Johnnie had automatically suspected, while Mrs. Willoughby-Jones might have written the letters just to stir up a bit of excitement. She would very likely have signed them, though, not being shy of insulting people to their faces.

Two more *female* suspects. Too, too maddening if Johnnie proved right! Daisy decided to go and see Mr. Paramount.

While she was in the shop, the pleasant afternoon breeze had strengthened to a gusty wind, raising swirls of dust from the village street. Between gusts, the air felt muggier than ever. A thin haze of cloud dulled the blue of the sky.

"Afternoon, miss," said one of two women with string bags who stood chatting near the door, stepping aside with a friendly nod to let Daisy pass. "Rain by termorrer, I shouldn't wonder, and we can do with it."

Daisy recognized an Oakhurst maid who had married and left service. "Good afternoon," she responded with a smile. "I just hope it holds off till I get back to the house."

"Not to worry, miss." Turning back to her older companion as Daisy walked on, she asked, "Now what was you saying, Mrs. Basin, about your Sam?"

"Got a letter, he did, made him mad as hops without he even opened it. Di'n't look like a bill, neither, but I dunno . . ."

Moving—regretfully—out of earshot, Daisy wondered if Sam Basin was another victim. What had he done to attract the malice of the Poison Pen? Derek said he worked at a garage in Ashford and rode a motorbicycle. Dangerous driving, perhaps, though if he made a habit of it, it would be no secret.

For the present she dismissed young Basin from her mind, to concentrate on inventing an excuse to speak to Mr. Paramount. An invitation to lunch at the big house would do. In the extremely unlikely event of his accepting, Vi would not leave Daisy in the lurch by denying it.

The lodge's blue front door boasted a knocker in the form of a black cast-iron oak tree. Daisy rapped twice and listened for footsteps.

Silence within. She raised her hand to bang again. Before she touched the knocker, the door swung open.

"Shush, do! 'E's just nodded off." The admonition came from a diminutive woman with the small, pointed face and twitching nose of a dormouse. She wore a buttercup-yellow overall and house-slippers, and wielded a mop. "Begging your pardon, miss, I'm sure," she added, taking in at a glance the unexpected caller's quality.

"No, I'm sorry, I don't want to disturb Mr. Paramount. I'd hoped for a word with him. I'm Lady John's sister, Miss Dalrymple. And you're . . . ?"

"Wotherspoon's the name. Mrs. I obliges Mr. Paramount mornings, but Tuesdays being Mr. Popper's day off, I stays all day. 'Is man, that is. You'd best step in, miss, if you don't mind the kitchen, for 'e might wake up agin any minute and call for 'is tea, and I could ask 'im, will 'e see you."

"I don't mind the kitchen," Daisy assured her, stepping in.

By the look of the place, the ground floor had once been one large room. Partitions now divided the narrow, windowless hall from Mr. Paramount's room, indicated by Mrs. Wotherspoon with a finger to her lips, and from the kitchen on the other side.

For the old man, it was a frightful come-down from his life at the big house. Daisy reminded herself that Johnnie had invited—in fact, expected—his uncle to remain in residence with the family. Nonetheless, she empathized with Mr. Paramount's reluctance to hang on as his nephew's dependent after his brother's death. She felt exactly the same about her cousin Edgar, after all, and she had never expected to inherit Fairacres.

Still, she didn't blame and ostracize Edgar as Mr. Paramount did Johnnie and Vi. "I've brought an invitation," she said, following Mrs. Wotherspoon into a small but well-appointed and spotless kitchen. It looked as if it had been modernized, with gas stove and hot-water geyser, when the old gentleman moved in. "Lady John would like Mr. Paramount to come to lunch one day this week."

"Bless 'er 'eart, 'e don't go nowheres, miss. Sit down, do. You'll take a glass of lemonade? It's 'omemade, not that stuff in bottles."

"Thank you, I'd love some. Mr. Paramount never leaves the house?" Daisy asked, as the daily turned to the larder.

"'E don't 'ardly walk no more, miss." Mrs. Wotherspoon emerged with a bedewed pitcher. "Not but what I expect 'is lordship'd send a car?" Looking rather anxiously at Daisy, she leaned back against the sink, jug in hand.

"Of course."

"And a couple of men to carry 'im? Though it wouldn't take more'n one, so little and frail as 'e's got. But 'e wouldn't go, miss, not the way 'e goes on writing them letters."

Daisy perked up. "Letters?"

"To the lawyer, miss, and the courts, and Mr. Nesbitt that's our Member, and even the papers, the which hasn't printed 'em in more years'n I can tell. Two or three times a week, Mr. Popper pops down to the post with a bunch, har har my little joke. Nor nobody but the lawyer don't answer 'im no more, but 'e goes on a-writing for all that, and 'oping for to get the 'ouse back. Truth is, miss, 'e's a lonely, bitter old gentleman." The phrase was pronounced as if she had heard it somewhere and stored it up.

"I'm sorry to hear it," Daisy said gently, touched by her obvious solicitude.

"Yes, well, I does me bit to keep 'im entertained. 'As a little gossip, we does, when I goes and does 'is room. 'E's still interested in the goings on in the village, 'e is and it gives 'im a break from holding that pen. 'Is hand gets that tired. Shakes something awful it does sometimes, and ink all over the place and you should just 'ear the laundry-woman complaining. I don't do laundry," declared Mrs. Wotherspoon, suddenly sternly on her dignity.

"I don't blame you. Has Mr. Paramount thought of writing in pencil?"

"Oh, 'e does, miss, for what 'e calls 'is rough drafts, whatever they may be when they're at 'ome. The paper that gets thrown away in this house, it's a scandal. 'Well, Mrs. W,' 'e says to me, 'I might as well 'ave wrote a book for all the good it's done me.' But 'e won't give in, 'e won't, not if it was ever so."

With this obscure but triumphant pronouncement, Mrs. Wotherspoon handed Daisy her glass of lemonade, folded her arms, and watched with grim satisfaction as the cooling liquid disappeared.

"Thank you, that was delicious and most refreshing." Daisy set the glass down on the table and stood up. "Well, I don't suppose it's any good waiting to see Mr. Paramount. It doesn't sound as if he's likely to relent towards my sister and Lord John."

Mrs. Wotherspoon shook her head mournfully. "Bitter, 'e is, like what I said. I'll tell 'im you come by, though, miss, and maybe it'll soften 'is 'eart." She ushered Daisy out.

It was still too early to put in an appearance at the Vicarage, but Daisy did not want to slog up the hill to the house only to turn round and come back down. She crossed the lane, intending to sit for a few minutes in the ancient stone coolness of the church.

Mr. Paramount was definitely a suspect, she thought, passing through the lych-gate. He was bitter, he knew the village gossip, and he wrote letters by the dozen. His manservant, Popper, might know the truth, and he might even be glad of a sympathetic ear to pour his worries into. The sympathetic ear was a role Daisy filled with ease. But how . . . ?

"Miss Dalrymple!"

She looked around. The vicar—no, it was the professor who stood among the tombstones, waving vigorously. His academic gown was easily mistaken for a clergyman's cassock. What was more, today he had on his head a shovel-hat of the sort favoured by Victorian churchmen, which had probably lain around the Vicarage unworn for decades until he absentmindedly picked it up. Daisy could not imagine the diffident Osbert Osborne wearing such conspicuous headgear.

The vicar did not affect a cassock outside the church either, come to that; fortunately, for it would have cramped his gateclimbing style.

Though Daisy was still annoyed with the professor over his insulting Latin tag, she strolled along the path towards him. He did not come to meet her, but kept his place facing a large angel of pinkish polished granite.

Daisy couldn't see anything very fascinating about the angel. It was about three-quarters lifesize (if the word could apply to a mythical being), with spread wings and what looked like a beret on its head—presumably a halo. Its back turned to the path and the church, it perched on a pedestal about eighteen inches high. Both angel and pedestal looked relatively unweathered, quite new by country churchyard standards.

"Look!" crowed the professor gleefully. "This almost restores my faith in human nature. I do believe, my dear young lady, that you are capable of comprehending the humour."

Blasted cheek, Daisy thought, after condemning her as lacking understanding. "Humour?" she asked. "It seems to me a singularly frightful object."

"Yes, indeed, the angel is the epitome of Victorian sentimentality. But come and read the epitaph—*nil desperandum,* it is in English, not Latin. Regular contemplation thereof does as much for my digestion as my little walks."

Intrigued, Daisy stepped off the gravel path and joined him. Though the gilt was wearing off, the letters engraved upon the pedestal were easy enough to read:

James Absalom Paramount
1815–1886
Life's a Jest,
And all things show it.
I thought so once,
But now I know it.

"Amusing," said Daisy politely, quite unable to comprehend the chortles now emanating from Professor Osborne.

Producing a handkerchief from somewhere in the

depths of his gown, he wiped his eyes, still chuckling. "Excuse me, my dear Miss Dalrymple," he said. "I dare say further information will be of assistance in appreciating the full flavour of the jest. Allow me to enlighten you."

"Please do."

"James Paramount—the father, I believe, of the present old gentleman of that name—was a progressive man for his time. He was one of the first Englishmen to be cremated upon his demise, a disposition he insisted on in his will, much to the distress of his wife, who feared he would be unable to rise at the Last Trump."

"Good heavens!"

"On the contrary, ha ha!" cackled the professor. "To continue: The incumbent of that period, of a like mind, refused to permit interment of the ashes within the church, alongside generations of ancestors. Paramount, I hasten to point out, would have been profoundly indifferent to such a fate, being a free-thinker. However, Mrs. Paramount's pleas softened the reverend gentleman to the extent of consenting to a small cinerarium, designed by the deceased, to be placed in the churchyard."

"The pedestal?" Daisy guessed.

"Precisely. The verse, I need hardly add, was enjoined by Paramount's will, encompassing, as it did, his view of existence."

"He wouldn't have wanted an angel, though."

"How right you are! For a number of years his widow respected his wishes, but at length the impropriety of the entire lack of religious sentiment associated with his tomb overcame her sensibilities. Arguing that the angel was an addition, not an alteration, to his requirements, she caused that monstrosity to be erected in the hope of placating the Almighty. Soon thereafter she went to her own demise, trusting in a merciful God to reunite her with her husband in the Paradise in which he did not believe."

"I wonder if the late Mr. Paramount now regards the Afterlife as a jest, too," said Daisy, smiling.

"I knew it," cried Professor Osborne in delight. "I knew you would appreciate the irony, though you are, no doubt, a church-goer."

"Occasional, I'm afraid," she confessed. "Mostly when I'm staying with people who assume one will go."

"Afraid? My dear young lady, why afraid? Do you fear the thunderbolt of an angry Deity? It is perfectly rational to regard a religious service as an occasional social obligation. Why, I frequently attend chapel in my college. It is expected, but *ceteris paribus,* one might as well celebrate the rites of Zeus or Jove. Better yet, of Athena/Minerva, Goddess of Wisdom. She would be worthy of enthusiastic worship, did she but exist!"

"So you don't share your brother's faith, Professor?" Daisy said ironically.

The professor guffawed. Speechless with laughter, he had to take out his handkerchief again to mop away the tears. At first rather flattered by her success in amusing him, Daisy became irritated. He was, after all, too easily amused.

The church clock came to her rescue, striking four. "I'm expected at the Vicarage for tea," she said. "Are you coming?"

"I shall follow shortly. Pray don't take it personally if I say that my intention is to avoid the drawing room this afternoon, *nam multum loquaces merito omnes* . . . I shall take my tea in Ozzy's study."

One didn't have to be a Latin scholar to put *loquaces* and *omnes* together and come up with a sweeping generalization on the loquacity of all women. Professor Osborne was a fine one to talk, Daisy fumed, when he had just blathered on at quite unnecessary length to tell a mildly entertaining story.

As she took the path to the gate leading directly from the churchyard into the Vicarage garden, again she found herself sympathizing with Mrs. Osborne. The professor must be a trying guest. Hard on the vicar, also, to have to play host to a brother who was an outspoken atheist. Or not too hard, perhaps—Daisy recalled his friendship with Amos Gresham, the atheistic farmer.

Mrs. Osborne had complained about the vicar and his brother holding such learned discussions she could scarcely understand a word. Perhaps they argued their respective views on religion. Though the vicar had given up on Gresham, he might feel an obligation to call his brother back to the Church, while the professor doubtless found it amusing to undermine a clergyman's faith.

Would he also find it amusing to write anonymous letters?

He bemoaned female garrulity: How much village gossip had he absorbed while staying at the Vicarage? How long had he been there? When had Johnnie received the first letter?

Yet another suspect, Daisy groaned silently, knocking on the Vicarage front door.

7

The maid who answered Daisy's knock was a sturdy young woman with a pudgy, sulky face. She looked like the sort of servant who might forget to serve tea to the gentlemen when neither her mistress nor the cook was there to chivvy her. Dora, was it? No, Doris.

"Thank you, Doris," Daisy said with a smile as the maid opened the drawing-room door to show her in. One never could tell, she might be a useful source of information sometime. She appeared old enough to have been in service at the Vicarage during at least the latter part of the War, when Johnnie had been spied on.

Doris didn't breach etiquette—or her own sullen nature—so far as to smile in response, but she gave Daisy a look that was almost cordial. "Miss Dalrymple, ma'am," she announced.

The room, like the house, was of a size to fit a Victorian family. It was probably frightfully draughty in winter, and even on this summer day it was gloomy, with its dark, heavy furniture and sombre wallpaper. The tea-table was set up on the far side, near the open windows. Four ladies were in attendance.

A slight, faded woman in blue started up from her seat and fluttered to meet Daisy. "So kind," she faltered breathlessly. "I don't expect you remember . . ."

Fortunately, Daisy did. "Of course, Mrs. Lomax," she

assured the brigadier's wife. "How nice to see you again."

"So kind . . ."

Seated behind the tea-table, Mrs. Osborne intervened. "Mrs. Lomax is our chairman this year, Miss Dalrymple," she announced with a severe glance at that flustered lady, who promptly retreated to her chair. "The rest of the committee is delighted to second my invitation to you to speak to our members tomorrow."

Daisy was not pleased to learn that the request for her services had not been agreed upon beforehand by all those involved. Still, whoever was chairman, the committee was obviously controlled by the vicar's wife, and she had presumably taken the concurrence of the others for granted.

She poured Daisy a cup of tea. "Ceylon, in your honour," she said with a heavy-handed playfulness. "You see, I noted your preference."

Though she really did prefer Indian, Daisy was tempted to express a craving for Oolong. She murmured something polite, accepted a piece of gingerbread—presented already sliced, she noted, after the professor's depradations—and took a seat.

"You are acquainted with Miss Prothero, I understand," Mrs. Osborne went on.

"Not properly introduced, I fear," the white-haired old lady tittered. "How do you do, Miss Dalrymple. We all anticipate your lecture with the greatest pleasure."

"Thank you," Daisy said, with a sudden qualm. Having accepted the invitation thinking only of her quest, without the foggiest idea what she was going to talk about, she hoped no one would ask. Hastily she turned to the fourth member of the committee. "I don't believe we've met?"

"Mrs. Gresham." Mrs. Osborne's tone was dismissive.

Farmer Gresham's wife? She was a dark, pretty

woman, a few years older than Daisy, dressed in a neat, unpretentious navy frock. Her Sunday best, perhaps—except that her husband was an atheist, so possibly Sunday was just another day of the week.

"How do you do, Miss Dalrymple," she said composedly, in a soft voice with a slight but definite Kent accent. "I know our members will be grateful to hear about something different for a change."

"I hope I'll manage to interest them," Daisy said with a friendly smile.

Mrs. Gresham's answering smile was quizzical. With a glance half challenging, half mocking at the vicar's wife, she said, "I shouldn't worry. For most of them, the meetings are an excuse to get out of the house. They will even sit still for a lecture on flower-arranging, a genteel occupation few have the leisure to indulge in."

Daisy laughed. "What a relief! How long am I expected to blather on?"

Mrs. Osborne firmly retrieved the reins of the conversation. "Half an hour is the usual. We have a general meeting first, and tea afterwards—urn tea, I'm afraid—so if you can be at the Parish Hall by three, Miss Dalrymple, that will give me time to introduce you and—You don't want to do the introduction, do you, Mrs. Lomax?"

"Oh no, you're much better at it, Mrs. Osborne," the brigadier's wife yielded, rather regretfully. "I'm always afraid of muddling things when I can't take my time."

"Speaking of time," said Mrs. Gresham rising, "it's time I was on my way home to get my husband's tea. High tea, that is, or supper, as I dare say you'd call it, *ladies.* Excuse me, please. Miss Dalrymple, I look forward to hearing you tomorrow."

"And I look forward to seeing you again."

"Don't trouble to see me out, Mrs. Osborne," said the farmer's wife, unnecessarily, as Mrs. Osborne showed no sign of budging. "I know my own way."

Silence reigned until the door closed behind her.

"Impertinent creature!" snorted the vicar's wife.

"Educated above her station." Miss Prothero nodded wisely. "It never does."

"We invited her to join the committee," Mrs. Osborne explained to Daisy, "because the Women's Institute was, after all, founded for the edification of that class of person."

"And it is not affiliated with the Church," put in Miss Prothero. "Mrs. Gresham does not attend Church."

"Nor even one of the dissenting chapels," said Mrs. Lomax, her indeterminate face tight-lipped with disapproval. Daisy wondered whether, ineffective as she seemed, she could be writing anonymous letters to her husband and the others.

Mrs. Osborne took up the tale: "I decided . . . *we* decided it would look better to have an outsider on the committee, and to pick a Baptist would offend the Methodists, and vice versa. Disgracefully quarrelsome, these nonconformist sects! So I . . . we chose Mrs. Gresham as the least of a multitude of evils."

"A mistake!" Miss Prothero declared, a glint in her bright brown eyes as she dissociated herself from the choice. "I always said she would not be properly appreciative of the honour."

"As you heard, my dear Miss Dalrymple," said Mrs. Lomax, almost breathless with indignation, "she has the *impudence* to imagine she knows better than we do what speakers will appeal to our members."

"But isn't that why . . . ?" Daisy stopped as the vicar came into the drawing room.

"Good afternoon, ladies," he said with a smile.

"You remember Miss Dalrymple, Osbert."

"Yes, indeed."

"We renewed our acquaintance yesterday," said Daisy. Catching his look of dismay, she swallowed the story of the gate rescue.

As his wife poured him a cup of tea, Miss Prothero remarked, "We were just talking about Mrs. Gresham, Vicar."

"A charming woman," Mr. Osborne observed, helping himself to two watercress sandwiches and a slice of gingerbread.

"I'm afraid you are far too charitable," said Miss Prothero firmly.

"A trouble-maker," said Mrs. Osborne with a decided nod.

"They say," Mrs. Lomax half whispered the shocking revelation, "that her husband is an *atheist!*"

The vicar's defence of his friend was ambiguous: "Amos Gresham is a highly intelligent fellow." He sat down next to Daisy.

"I'm sure you exaggerate his intelligence, Osbert," said Mrs. Osborne, unwontedly perturbed. "And I'm sure you exaggerate his lack of faith, Mrs. Lomax. Not all the world belongs to the Anglican communion, alas." She displayed her horsey teeth in an unconvincing laugh.

"No smoke without a fire," Miss Prothero reminded her. "Which reminds me, Mrs. Lomax, I heard the dear brigadier firing away earlier, quite wildly."

"Maurice knows what he's doing with a gun," said Mrs. Lomax defensively—and slightly uncertainly? "He was a soldier, after all, and he spends *hours* in his gun-room. He's just after rabbits and rooks and pigeons. They eat the crops, you know."

"It's a pity he doesn't go after that young wastrel who's renting your cottage. Do you know what I just heard?"

Mrs. Osborne and Mrs. Lomax leaned forward eagerly. Daisy hoped she was going to learn something useful. The vicar said in gentle admonishment, "My dear Miss Prothero, 'Thou shalt not bear false witness . . .'"

"I assure you, Vicar," Miss Prothero interrupted, affronted, "I have every reason to believe this story is true, or naturally I should not repeat it."

"'Uncharitableness,'" Mr. Osborne muttered feebly.

Miss Prothero started, and gave him an oddly searching look.

"Osbert, it's your duty to know what your parishioners are up to. What did you hear, Miss Prothero?" Mrs. Osborne demanded.

Dismissing whatever momentary qualms she may have felt, the elderly cherub announced, "London friends of Mr. Catterick have come to visit him. He has no room to put them up, of course, so they are staying at the Hop-Picker. Sharing a room—and one is a young woman!" she ended triumphantly.

"Good gracious!" Mrs. Lomax exclaimed.

"Disgraceful," said Mrs. Osborne. "Of course, it's only what one might have expected, considering the kind of books Piers Catterick writes. We can't have him importing that sort of thing into the village. A shocking example! Osbert, you must have a word with Jellaby."

"As to that," Miss Prothero said, "I don't suppose the landlord can do anything about it. The precious pair claim to be man and wife."

"Perhaps they are," suggested Daisy.

The three ladies stared at her, identically incredulous.

"My dear," said Mrs. Osborne in a soothing voice, "you are too young to realize the full wickedness of the world. The young do tend to think the best of people, and very proper, too, though I'm afraid you are in for a sad disillusionment. Osbert, you had better confront them . . ."

"No!" cried the vicar. "Two visitors from London cannot possibly be construed as any responsibility of mine. I do my poor best to guide my parishioners. I'm even willing to make an attempt to persuade Piers Catterick of the error of his ways, but his friends are beyond my purview. Excuse me, my dear; excuse me, please, ladies. I have one or two things to see to before evensong."

As he stood up, Daisy also rose. "I must be getting along, too," she said.

She did not feel she was gaining any helpful information. Either Miss Prothero or Mrs. Lomax could be the Poison Pen, or even Mrs. Osborne, though surely a clergyman's wife, like Caesar's, ought to be above suspicion. At any rate, between running the village and interfering in her husband's pastoral duties, Mrs. Osborne had plenty of public outlets for censure, without resorting to anonymous letters.

Daisy thanked her hostess for the tea and promised to be at the Parish Hall by three next day. She and Mr. Osborne left the room together.

"If you wouldn't mind waiting just a moment," said the vicar diffidently, "I'll walk a short way with you. I could do with some fresh air."

"Of course."

He ducked into a cloakroom and reemerged Panama in hand. When he opened the front door, however, they discovered that the sky had clouded over and a few drops of rain were spitting down. "You must borrow an umbrella," he said, reaching to take one from the stand just inside the door.

"Thank you." Daisy opened the brolly, a newish black one. "It looks as if it may pour any minute. You won't want to come out, after all."

"I do." The vicar hung a second umbrella over his arm and absently put on his summery hat, now thoroughly inappropriate. "I want to ask you," he said anxiously as she preceded him down the path to the front gate, "not to judge Mrs. Gresham too harshly."

"I shouldn't dream of it. She didn't stay long after I arrived, but I liked what I saw of her. I'd like to know her better."

"Her husband, as I believe I mentioned yesterday, is a good friend of mine, and she has been kind to me. I'm afraid country-bred ladies tend to be rather too . . . quick to judge. Also, my wife has a good deal on her mind at present."

"Oh?" Daisy said encouragingly. Perhaps Mrs. Osborne had received, not written, anonymous letters. There must be lots of people who resented her managing ways—Mrs. Lomax for one.

They crossed the lane and started up the avenue before the vicar responded. "You see, I've been offered a position as a canon at the Cathedral. At Canterbury, that is. Adelaide is having some difficulty making up her mind whether she wants to go or not."

Big fish in a small pond or small fish in a big pond, Daisy thought. Mrs. Osborne would find more scope for her organizing talents in a cathedral city, but also more competition. "What about you?" she asked. "What do you want?"

"Oh, I can't possibly accept!" Mr. Osborne's voice trembled with agitation. "I can't! It's hard enough here. I could never keep it secret in a Cathedral precinct, constantly surrounded by clergymen and Church officials. As it is, since Ozzy—my brother—came to stay, Adelaide has begun to suspect. All these years I've kept it from her, from everyone, but I can't go on much longer!"

Surely Mr. Osborne couldn't have been getting poison-pen letters from his *brother!* The professor's visit must be coincidental. But who *would* write horrible accusations to the inoffensive, kindly vicar? And accusing him of what?

"What, exactly, does Mrs. Osborne suspect?" Daisy asked cautiously.

"She's afraid Ozzy and Gresham between them are subverting my faith. Sooner or later she'll realize I've none to be threatened. I lost it in the trenches."

"You're an atheist?" Daisy breathed, stunned, yet feeling she ought to have guessed. "An unbelieving vicar?"

Stopping short, he looked at her, his round face wild. The rain was beginning to fall in earnest now, damping the absurd Panama and the shoulders of his black jacket. He was oblivious. Daisy took the umbrella from his arm, managed to open it while holding on to her own, and put it in his hand.

"I can't go on." He swung round and started up the hill again, his tread heavy, effortful. "I don't know why I'm telling you, except that I must tell someone and you look sympathetic. Ozzy doesn't understand. Even Gresham . . . They've both rejected religion on logical grounds. They feel no conflict. My revolt is emotional, I know it. I don't *want* to believe in a God who permits young, hale, well-meaning men to be tortured, crippled, slaughtered by the hundred thousand!"

"I know what you mean," Daisy said soberly. "I wasn't there, of course, but I lost my brother and my fiancé."

The vicar seemed not to hear her. His bitter, passionate words flowed on: "Nearly five years since the War ended, yet it seems like yesterday. The stench of blood . . . but the Church was founded in blood. How can I bear to hold services of praise and thanksgiving for a God who demanded a human sacrifice before he'd grant forgiveness for our petty sins? I've tried. I've preached countless sermons, hoping at least to alter people's behaviour for the better though I can't sincerely offer them rewards in Heaven. No one changes. And they call themselves Christians! I can't go on, I can't go on."

"Why should you? I should think you'd better leave the Church. Couldn't you teach or something?"

"What I'd like to do is join one of the secular groups working to educate the poor, in the East End slums of London, or Birmingham, Manchester . . . anywhere."

Mr. Osborne sounded quite enthusiastic, but then he groaned. "Can you imagine my wife leading such a life? Even a school, if any respectable school was willing to hire an atheist, she would regard as a bitter pill after . . ." He turned and waved his free hand at the red tile roofs of the village, straggling across the hillside below.

"After being monarch of all she surveys?" Daisy suggested.

He gave her a rueful smile. "I'm being grandiloquent, am I not? But all the same, my dear Miss Dalrymple, I can't do it to her. I have a duty to her. I married Adelaide for better or worse, and though I no longer believe in the God before whom I plighted my troth, still, I promised to comfort, honour, and keep her."

"And your children."

"Yes, the children, too, with their future ahead of them. So I struggle on, mired in hypocrisy, no better than those I . . . rebuke. I must be off," the vicar added hastily, suddenly in a hurry to get away, as if he regretted his confession. "Forgive me for burdening you with my troubles."

"I shan't tell anyone."

"Oh, but half of me wishes you would. Then the decision would be out of my hands. Good-bye, Miss Dalrymple." He set off down the hill at a near trot.

Frowning, Daisy watched him go. Whatever his mixed feelings, of course she would not give away his secret. It ought to be safe with his brother and his friends, the Greshams—but either one of them was the Poison Pen, or someone else had discovered or guessed the vicar's loss of faith.

That was assuming he had received one or more anonymous letters. Continuing up the hill, Daisy wished she had asked him outright. He might turn out to be an ally in her investigation. As it was, she had not even got around to finding out how long Professor Osborne had been staying at the Vicarage.

This evening she'd ask Johnnie when the first letter had been delivered. Tomorrow, chatting over "urn tea," it shouldn't be difficult to inveigle Mrs. Osborne into putting a date on her brother-in-law's arrival in Rotherden. Come to that, any of the village busybodies at the WI meeting would probably remember not only the date but which train the professor had come down on from town.

Oh gosh, the WI meeting! What the dickens was she going to talk about?

Daisy had no opportunity that evening for a private word with Johnnie. He had telephoned to say he was bringing one of his colleagues on the Bench home for dinner as they had business to discuss. After dinner, they disappeared into the library.

Vi professed herself perfectly happy to listen to a concert on the wireless. Daisy still had no brilliant ideas of what to say to the WI, so she fetched her London Museum notes from her room and settled down to put them in order, to the pastoral strains of Beethoven's Sixth.

When the last notes of the "Shepherds' Thanksgiving After the Storm" had died away, Violet stretched and said, "I'm for bed. Are you coming up? Shall I turn the wireless off?"

"In a few minutes, and yes, please. Oh, Vi, what *am* I going to talk to those women about?"

"Why not explain what you're doing now? It's a sort of magic, reducing chaos to order. I mean, I wouldn't know where to begin turning a sheaf of notes into an interesting article. Maybe you'll get them all started writing 'A Day in the Life of a Farmer's Wife.'"

"Heaven forbid!" Daisy laughed. "That's a starting point, though. I'll see what I can come up with. Thanks, darling, and good night."

After her active day, Daisy slept soundly. She only

half roused when a maid brought her early-morning tea. A few minutes later, a tap on the door brought her the rest of the way to wakefulness. "Come in."

Belinda was already dressed—in her shorts, although her first, tragic words were, "It's still *raining,* Aunt Daisy."

"I'm sure you and Derek will find plenty to do indoors."

"He wants to play with Meccano."

"And you don't?"

"It's for boys."

"Why?"

"Gran says . . . You mean I can build stuff, too?" Bel asked in wonder.

"Of course, silly." Another source of strife with Mrs. Fletcher, Daisy groaned silently. Having been coerced in the past into assisting her nephew, she added, "I bet your fingers are better at those beastly little nuts and bolts than Derek's."

"I'll make a house. He's got *loads."* She dashed off, full of enthusiasm.

Sipping her cooling tea, Daisy wished she could summon up equal enthusiasm for this afternoon's lecture. At least the rain made it easier to devote the morning to preparation. This she did, with a break in the middle to start typing her London Museum article, a boring task which was positive bliss in comparison. She had frightful visions of droning on while her audience fell asleep one by one—Mrs. Osborne would never let them abscond.

By lunchtime the rainclouds were blowing over, and by the time Daisy had to leave for the Parish Hall, the sun shone on a refreshed, sparkling world.

Violet told her bracingly that she looked very smart in her dark blue costume and a pale blue blouse, with silk stockings, hat, and gloves.

"Well, at least I shan't look like a chump, even if I

sound like one," Daisy said glumly. "Why did I ever let myself in for this?"

Afraid that, left to her own devices, she would turn tail and flee in panic, she invited Belinda and Derek to walk down the drive with her. Gumbooted, at Nanny's command, they skipped and hopped on either side of her, telling her about the lion's cage they had constructed around Peter while he lay on the floor drawing.

"It had a real gate, with hinges and everything," Belinda reported.

"When it was all built, we made Tinker go inside with Peter, only she jumped out," Derek said admiringly. "I didn't know she could jump so high."

Tinker Bell apparently bore no resentment. Naturally she had come along. She dashed hither and thither, exploring smells enhanced by the rain.

"She spoiled Peter's picture," Bel said, "so I helped him do another one. I drew a lion in a cage, but he coloured it green and it just looked like a bush behind a fence. He's never seen a real lion, Aunt Daisy. Can we take him to the zoo, one day?"

"Me too," Derek begged. "I've only been once."

"I've been lots of times, 'cause I live very near. Sometimes I can hear the lions roaring in the night."

"Lucky thing!"

"We'll all go, Daddy too, if he can. We'll see the sea-lions getting fed, and go for a ride on an elephant, and watch them having their baths . . ." Belinda was still enumerating the wonders of the zoo when they reached the gates.

"I'll see you later," said Daisy.

"Can't we come and listen to you?" Belinda asked, disappointed.

"No, it's a talk for grown-ups. You wouldn't find it interesting." *And nor will my audience,* Daisy thought despairingly, crossing the lane to the lych-gate. Why had she ever agreed to make a fool of herself, like a monkey in a cage, with everyone staring and wishing she would do something entertaining.

At least she looked professional, she hoped. Peering over her shoulder, she poised first on one leg, then the other, to check that her stocking seams were straight.

She turned down the path to the gate which led to the Parish Hall, her steps lagging as she felt in her handbag for her notes. Had she time to glance over them? She must! She couldn't remember a word. Just for a minute she'd sit down on a tombstone. There must be a sittable one nearby.

Glancing around, she saw that the granite angel had fallen flat on its face. Beside it on the grass lay a shabby Panama with a faded tartan band.

And between its head and the top of its wing, a round face with a startled expression stared blindly at the sky.

8

The vicar couldn't possibly be alive, with his head at that angle, and the glassy look of his eyes, and his body pinned by the ironic—avenging?—angel.

Nonetheless, Daisy had to make sure. Feeling sick, she approached the horrible spot. His arms were hidden by the angel's wings, so she couldn't try for a pulse. What else was hidden by the granite mass, she didn't care to think. She knelt on the wet grass, dug her vanity mirror out of her handbag, and held it to the vicar's mouth and nose.

No sign of condensation. Daisy pulled off her gloves and steeled herself to lay her hand on his cheek. Still warm. Of course, the accident must be very recent or the women going to the Parish Hall would have seen him lying there.

Accident? The angel had stood stable on its cinerarium pedestal for decades. Yesterday's gusty wind had died hours ago, and in any case it had not been particularly strong. Certainly not strong enough to shift a granite monument which must weigh several hundredweight. Yet would the angel be any more easily pushed over than blown over?

And who would want to murder the vicar? Had he discovered who was writing the anonymous letters? He was—had been—in a good position to do so. Could the Poison Pen have killed to protect his identity? Did she know Daisy was on her trail? Was he lurking now behind a tombstone, waiting to pounce?

With a shiver, Daisy looked around. She ought not to have embarked on this frightful investigation alone without Alec's support! Standing up for a better view, she wished more people over the centuries had been satisfied with small, modest gravemarkers. No one in sight.

It *must* be an accident, she tried to persuade herself.

Accident or murder, it was sudden, violent death. The police and a doctor must be summoned. The body ought not to be left unattended. Daisy was due at the WI meeting. Suppose someone came to look for her and found the dead vicar: In no time there would be a gaggle of nosy women trampling all over any clues. For the same reason she could not go to the Parish Hall for help. Yet she must not be away more than a few moments.

Not the Vicarage. Mrs. Osborne was not there, and Daisy decided with a hysterical giggle that she didn't feel capable of announcing to the professor that his brother had been squashed by an angel.

Mrs. LeBeau, just the other side of the lane, would be calm and capable, and surely had a telephone.

Daisy glanced up at the church clock. Only five to three. In her anxiety she had arrived early, anxiety which now seemed appallingly trivial. She had a few minutes' grace before she was missed.

Involuntarily, her gaze returned to the ghastly eyes. She found her handkerchief and stooped to cover the vicar's face with the small, inadequate square. As she straightened, a corner of black cloth, protruding from beneath the angel's wing, caught her attention. Black cloth with a slight sheen in the sunshine—black poplin. An academic gown.

The professor?

The Poison Pen had mistaken Professor Osborne, in his brother's Panama, for the vicar. Daisy was shocked by the relief which flooded through her. She liked the vicar; she had not liked the professor. But neither deserved so horrible a death.

The clock struck three. She was wasting time. Trying to step in the spots where her tread had already crushed the grass and dented the rain-softened ground, she returned to the path, then hurried along it and through the lych-gate.

"Aunt Daisy!"

Both the children were high up on the gate. The dog, sitting at the bottom, watched them with a solicitous, reproving eye, as if she was named for Nana in *Peter Pan,* not Tinker Bell. The tip of her tail swished back and forth as Daisy crossed the lane.

"We took our gumboots off. We won't get stuck," Belinda assured her.

"What were you looking at in the graveyard?" Derek asked curiously. "We saw you from up here, but we couldn't make it out."

Thank heaven! "There's been an accident, darlings. Come down quickly, both of you—and carefully!" Daisy added as they swarmed down the wrought-iron curlicues. Mrs. LeBeau might be out, she thought. Faster to dispatch the children for help. "I want you to run up to the house and send for the police and the doctor. You understand?"

"Gosh, yes, Aunt Daisy."

As they pulled on their boots, Daisy impressed upon them, "Hurry. And stay up there, don't come back."

"Why not?" said Derek. "Oh, all right. Come on, Bel. Come, Tinker."

Belinda, her grey-green eyes wide with alarm, dashed over to Daisy and gave her a quick, silent hug, then sped after Derek and Tinker Bell.

Daisy returned to the churchyard. Now that she had nothing to do but wait for the police and the doctor, she felt rather sick. Actually, she felt altogether pretty wishy-washy. Though, being a modern woman, she naturally was not going to faint, she thought it might be quite a good idea if she sat down. Soon.

Failing all else, she subsided on a sort of marble kerb outlining a grave just beyond the lych-gate. Her head soon stopped whirling when she stuck it between her knees.

As long as she didn't think about what was beneath the fallen angel, she'd be all right. She did have something to do, she remembered. Any minute someone would come out of the Parish Hall to see where she had got to. She had to stop them approaching the body . . . which she was *not* going to think about. To do that, she needed to be beyond it.

A gravel path recently trodden by a horde of women seemed unlikely to provide much in the way of evidence, but just in case, Daisy circled round on the grass, among the tombstones. That route took her further, too, from the—from what she wasn't thinking about.

By the time she rejoined the path, her good shoes were sopping, to match the hem of her skirt. Her stockings also were wet and uncomfortable down the front, from kneeling by—from kneeling. She glanced down to see if they were laddered, and was relieved to see them undamaged, though it seemed heartlessly petty when the professor . . .

Oh *blast!* She was feeling wobbly again. Nowhere nearby to sit, so she leaned against the nearest upright stone slab. When she died, Daisy vowed, she would have a bench for a tombstone.

It was odd that no one from the WI was looking for her yet. The Parish Hall's windows were the high, narrow kind meant for illumination, not an exterior view, so no one could see her. She checked the time by the clock on the tower again. Ten past three. Perhaps Mrs. Osborne thought she had funked it. No doubt the vicar's wife had a fund of rhetoric to fill in with when a speaker didn't turn up.

And how long was she going to have to wait for the doctor and the constable? Eleven minutes past three. It seemed like forever since she had sent the children off, but they had probably only just reached the telephone.

Detective Sergeant Tom Tring turned back from the filing cabinet and regarded his empty desk with satisfaction. "That's the last of the Islington arsonists, Chief," he said. "Reckon you might get away for a day or two after all."

Alec quickly touched wood. "Don't tempt fate, Tom. Saying something like that is an incitement to every crook in the Metropolitan area to—"

The telephone shrilled. As Tom's burly arm, chequered in robin's-egg-blue and white, reached out for the apparatus on his desk, Alec groaned. He'd known a couple of days in Kent with Daisy and Bel was too much to hope for.

"Who?" The sergeant's luxuriant moustache quivered with astonishment, and his eyebrows climbed his boundless brow. "Yes, of course, put her through. It's Miss Belinda, Chief. She *never* phones you at the Yard!"

"She'd better have a good reason for doing it now," said Alec ominously, reaching for his telephone as Tom pressed the button to transfer the call. "Hello? Bel?"

"Daddy! I'm awfully sorry to disturb you, but we didn't know what else to do."

"We?"

"Me and Derek. Derek and I," Belinda amended scrupulously. "You see, there's a body in the churchyard and . . ."

"I imagine there are lots. Belinda, are you having me on? Because if Derek has put you up to—"

"Daddy, *listen!* Aunt Daisy's found a *body* in the churchyard."

"I don't believe it," Alec said flatly. It could not be true. Not another one!

"Well, we're not *absolutely* certain," his daughter wavered, "but she said there'd been an accident, and she told us to get a doctor and the police, like on the train, 'member? When I found—"

"I remember only too clearly."

"So we think—'cause I told Derek all about the train—we think it's another murder. She did say police first, after all. And he rang up the doctor and he's coming but the village bobby's not at home and we didn't know what to do. 'Cause Uncle Johnnie's out riding and Aunt Violet's asleep, and Aunt Daisy sounded urgent. She looked *frightfully* pale."

Alec's heart twisted in his chest. The two beings he loved best in all the world mixed up with a murderer on the loose, and he was too far away to protect them.

If Bel hadn't misunderstood. She would not make up such a story, but she had a vivid imagination.

He could not risk it. "All right, Bel, you were quite right to ring me. Ask Derek what's the nearest town."

Over the wire came the faint sound of the question being passed on. Then, "He says Ashford, Daddy."

"Hang on." Alec put his hand over the mouthpiece and said to his sergeant, "Get hold of the police in Ashford, Kent, Tom. Criminal investigation, if they have such a thing."

"Right, Chief."

"Belinda, we'll have a policeman on his way right away, but it may take a little while." He felt helpless, knowing so little of the situation. "Let me talk to Derek, now, love."

An agitated colloquy, far away, mingled with Tom's voice on the other telephone. Then a scared young voice, "This is Derek, sir."

"Derek, I need your advice and help."

"Yes, sir!" The voice swelled with pride.

"Someone must take a message to your aunt."

"I'll go." Excitement, and more than a touch of trepidation.

"No, absolutely not. You are not to go anywhere near the churchyard, nor to allow Belinda to go, understand?"

"Yes, sir." Disappointment and relief. "Shall I send a servant?"

"A manservant, not a maid. Do you have footmen?"

"Just one. Arthur."

"Is he a sensible chap, Derek? And will he do what you say?"

"Oh yes, sir, pretty much. Both, I mean."

"All right." Catching Tom's eye, Alec held up a finger and mouthed, "Just a minute."

He heard Tom saying, "This is Scotland Yard, sir. Detective Chief Inspector Fletcher wishes to speak to . . ."

"Derek, tell the footman to tell Daisy the Ashford police will be there as soon as possible." Alec hoped it was true. "And he's to stay with her and help her in any way she asks. Got that?"

"Yes, sir. Bel, ring that bell over there. That's right. Arthur should come right away, sir."

"Good man. Remember, you and Belinda are absolutely not to go near the churchyard. Everything is under control. I must go now, Derek. Give Bel my love." Feeling as if he were casting his daughter adrift in a storm, Alec pressed the hook to cut the connection. When he let it up again, Ashford was on the line.

"Inspector Flagg, Chief," Tom advised in an undertone. He listened in on his apparatus.

"Inspector Flagg, this is Fletcher. We have received a report of . . ." Of what, for heaven's sake? A body in a graveyard! ". . . Of a sudden death, possibly by violence, in the village of Rotherden. That's in your district?"

"That it is," said the Ashford inspector suspiciously,

with a strong country accent. "Might I enquire, sir, why it was Scotland Yard was informed?"

Alec couldn't say the news had come from two nine-year-olds, one of them his daughter, who hadn't even seen the body. "I gather the person who rang us up had tried to get hold of your local constable. He was out, and the informant apparently didn't think to telephone Ashford. I thought less time would be wasted if I got in touch with you myself."

"You think it's an urgent matter, then, sir?" Flagg sounded dubious in the extreme.

"I think someone official ought to get there soon," Alec said, trying to keep the irritation from his voice, "before half the village tramps over the scene of the crime. If any." Which, knowing Daisy's penchant for stumbling upon murder, was inevitable. "I understand a doctor is on the way already."

"Which doctor would that be, sir?"

"I haven't the first idea, Inspector! I suggest you take a police surgeon with you."

"Have you any idea, sir, whereabouts in the village I'd be taking him? Rotherden may not be a big city like London, but it's spread out over a fair bit of countryside, so—"

"The churchyard," Alec interrupted. "Do you think you can find it?" He immediately regretted his sarcasm. If the man's back was set up, Daisy and Belinda might suffer for it. He decided to come clean. "I beg your pardon, Inspector, that was uncalled for. The fact is, it was my fiancée who found the body, and my little girl who telephoned. I'm worried about them."

"Your little girl, eh? I've two myself. I'll get over there right away, Chief Inspector."

Hanging up after telling what little else he knew, Alec sighed. "I wish I'd mentioned Belinda right away. I was afraid he'd take the report even less seriously."

"Never can tell, Chief," Tom said soothingly. "Better

get moving right away, afore something crops up here to keep you."

"What makes you think . . . Oh, all right, Tom! I *am* due a couple of days off."

"Make it official, and we'll be down to join you on the next train, young Piper and me."

"That depends, at least initially, on Inspector Flagg, and I don't think he's keen on the Met butting in on his patch."

"He softened in the end there, Chief. Now off you go and soften up the Super while I check there's nothing in that bumf on your desk can't wait till Monday for a signature."

"Thanks, Tom." Alec went off to tackle Superintendent Crane, secure in the certainty that the mere possibility of Daisy's meddling in another criminal investigation would have his superiors rushing him down to Kent.

Running footsteps crunched on gravel.

"Stop!" Daisy cried.

The Frobishers' young footman skidded to a halt a couple of yards short of the fallen angel. "Master Derek said to tell you, miss," he panted, "as Dr. Padgett's on his way and there's a copper coming right away from Ashford acos our local chap's not home, and I'm to do whatever you says. Golly, is that . . . ?" Goggle-eyed, he pointed.

"I'm pretty sure it's the vicar's brother. We must keep people away until the police and the doctor arrive." Daisy reflected for a moment. "You had better come over here, Arthur—*No!* Not by the path! That's right, go round."

"Clues," said the footman sagely as he tramped around through the grass. "I read detective stories, miss."

"Good for you. It's probably an accident, but just in

case, we mustn't let anyone near. The WI's meeting in the Hall, unfortunately. There's another way into the lane, isn't there?"

"Yes, miss. Them as comes from the village generally cuts the corner coming along this here path, but them as lives out thataway just goes straight in."

"I thought so. Right-oh, I want you to stand here by the gate and stop anyone coming through. Tell them there's been an accident. Oh, I suppose you'd better call me when Mrs. Osborne turns up." The vicar's wife had disliked the professor and presumably wouldn't be devastated by his death, but after all, she was his sister-in-law and the best person to break the news to his brother. "Don't allow her through, though."

"Mrs. Osborne?" Arthur blenched. "I'll do me best, miss."

Daisy picked her way back in a wide circle. As she stepped onto the path near the lych-gate, the doctor's blue Humber pulled up in the lane and Dr. Padgett jumped out. He turned and reached in for his black bag, then strode through the gate.

"Miss Dalrymple! I came as quick as I could. I was napping," he said with a wry grimace. He looked a bit rumpled. "One of my patients had a seizure at two o'clock this morning. An accident, young Derek said?"

"I couldn't tell the children, but he's dead. I'm sure of it. Over there." She waved, and Dr. Padgett started past her. She caught his sleeve. "Careful! It. . . . it may not be an accident."

"Suicide?"

"No." Daisy shook her head. "Impossible."

He stared at her. "You're not suggesting . . . *murder?*"

"I don't know!" She didn't want him to find out she was aware of the anonymous letters, so she couldn't tell him she suspected a link between the death and the Poison Pen. "But I do know the police will want to look for footprints on the path."

"I'll go around. Where am I going? Over there?" Dr. Padgett gazed in the direction she had waved. "And who—? That hat! Oh lord, not Osborne?" He sounded horrified, but Daisy couldn't see his face as he stepped onto the grass.

"Professor Osborne," she informed his retreating back. "At least, I saw a bit of what seems to be an academic gown, and he was awfully absentminded about taking the first hat that comes to mind. Don't touch or move anything you don't have to."

"I'll just make quite sure he's beyond help, poor chap."

The doctor's words struck Daisy with a sinister ring. Suppose the professor had been the Poison Pen, and Dr. Padgett had guessed. He might have pushed the angel over, then fled before he was sure his tormenter was dead. Now she had given him the perfect opportunity to finish him off.

But the professor was already quite dead, she assured herself. The worst the doctor could do was destroy evidence. But he could have muddled any traces of his earlier presence just by continuing along the path against her advice, and he had not.

All the same, Daisy was glad to see a policeman's helmeted head and blue-clad shoulders sailing along above the churchyard wall towards the village. She ran to the lych-gate.

"Officer!"

"Yes, miss?" The Rotherden bobby descended ponderously from his bicycle and lumbered towards her, pushing it. He was a large young man, already showing signs of attaining Tom Tring's bulk, if not the sergeant's well-earned place in the detective branch of the Met. "What can I do for you?"

"I'm Miss Dalrymple, Lord John's sister-in-law."

"Bless your heart, miss, I knows that. Keeps me eyes and ears open, I do."

"Good for you, Constable. There's been a fatal accident in the churchyard. A suspicious death."

"Well now, miss, which would that be?" he asked stolidly, propping his bicycle against the wall and taking out his notebook and pencil. "Accidental or suspicious, is it?"

"*I* think it's suspicious. I ought to tell you that as you weren't at home, the Ashford police have been informed, and I gather they're sending someone out."

"Ah, Inspector Flagg, that'll be," the constable said with relief, putting his notebook away. "Well then, all that needs doing till the inspector arrives is to keep people away."

"Exactly," Daisy congratulated him, glad she was not going to have to try to stop him messing things up. "Lord John's footman is guarding the far gate."

"Arthur? Good thinking, miss. I suppose the deceased really is deceased? I see Dr. Padgett's car's here. Ah, here he comes now."

"Dead as the proverbial doornail," the doctor confirmed. "The broken neck would have killed him practically instantaneously. Also, I'm sure though I could not see, there must be massive injuries, both external and internal, which would be equally—Steady on, Miss Dalrymple!" He put his hand under her arm. "Absolutely asinine of me to talk about it, but you've held up so nobly—Here, come and sit down in the church porch."

"Do that, miss. I'll take over here, but if you wouldn't mind staying, Inspector Flagg'll be bound to want a word with you."

"I'll stay," said Daisy faintly, once again struggling with nausea. She let Dr. Padgett support her to the porch and seat her on an ancient oak bench, polished by generations of bottoms.

"Are you sure you don't want to lie down? All right,

I'll give you something to settle your head and your stomach." He started to open his black bag.

Daisy hastily stopped him. "No, thanks, I'll be fine in a minute. I'm not usually such a poor fish, but there's something singularly beastly . . ." She shuddered.

"It was quick, poor devil. Fix your mind on that. Assuming it's Professor Osborne, I take it no one has yet informed the vicar?"

"No," Daisy admitted with reluctance. She didn't want to be the one to break the news, yet she would have liked to see Mr. Osborne's reaction. If he appeared to suspect his brother had been mistaken for him, it would suggest that he had indeed discovered the Poison Pen's identity.

But Daisy didn't dare mention the possibility to Dr. Padgett. She would have to tell the police, though, and the only way to make them take her seriously was to reveal Johnnie's anonymous letters. Oh *blast!* she thought. How she wished Alec was here and in charge!

"I'd better pop over to the Vicarage," the doctor was saying. "I suppose it really is the professor? That hat . . ."

"I've seen Professor Osborne in all sorts of peculiar headgear. I'm pretty sure. I do think you'd better ask the constable if it's all right to tell the vicar," she added doubtfully. "I hope the Ashford inspector gets here soon."

"You can't imagine the vicar murdered his brother!"

"Gosh, no! It's just that you can't tell what will upset a police investigation. So you agree that it looks like murder?"

With a grim look, Dr. Padgett nodded. "I'm afraid so. I can't see how that statue could possibly have fallen without a good shove. You'll be all right now? I have to be off on my afternoon rounds as soon as I've seen the vicar. I'll have a word with Barton first."

He went to speak to the constable, leaving Daisy

more inclined to believe him innocent of this murder, no matter what his previous crimes or blunders. Surely he would have argued for an accident if he was guilty.

She was also the more convinced that the professor's death was murder, and it would be too much of a coincidence for it to be unrelated to the anonymous letters. Either the writer had meant to kill the vicar, for fear of being unmasked; or Professor Osborne was the Poison Pen, and had been found out and done in by one of his victims who didn't see the joke.

Had he discovered now for certain that Life's a Jest? His death, at least, was a thoroughly macabre jest: the atheist killed by a fallen angel.

9

The Ashford police had not yet arrived when Daisy heard women's voices from the direction of the Parish Hall, followed by the footman's determined tones. She was going to have to face Mrs. Osborne without Inspector Flagg's support.

At the same moment, Dr. Padgett returned along the churchyard path from the Vicarage.

"Osborne is out on his bicycle, making 'pastoral' visits according to the maid. She has no idea where, or I'd go after him."

"You'd better get on with your own rounds, Doctor. The WI meeting seems to be over, so Mrs. Osborne will be here any minute. She's the best person to tell the vicar."

"Mrs. Osborne?" The doctor visibly quailed. "Yes, I have patients waiting, I must go."

Without enquiring as to whether Daisy felt well enough now to cope, without so much as pausing to speak to Constable Barton—who had his back turned, looking towards the commotion—Padgett set off at a rapid stride. He vaulted into the Humber, turned in the Oakhurst drive, and buzzed away into the village.

A procession of hats of varied shape and colour appeared above the churchyard wall as the WI members turned homeward. The wall was higher on that side, the ground on the graveyard side having built up over the centuries. Every now and then a woman taller than the rest peered over the top. Once someone even hopped up and down trying to see, but by Daisy's reckoning the intervening tombstones hid the frightful sight from them. They ought to be glad.

Barton moved towards the lych-gate, his weighty tread suggesting consciousness of the majesty of the law. Daisy realized she didn't know whether the doctor had told him who had been killed, or whether he had seen the Panama hat and guessed wrong, or whether he remained in blissful ignorance. She was tempted to let him deal with the vicar's wife, but suppose he reported that her husband was dead? Besides, however inadvertently, Daisy had let the side down by not turning up for her talk. She owed an explanation.

Technically the explanation was owed to Mrs. Lomax, of course, but that wouldn't cut any ice with Mrs. Osborne.

Daisy joined the constable. "Did Dr. Padgett tell you it's Professor Osborne who was killed?" she asked hurriedly.

He received the news without surprise. "No, miss, nor I didn't enquire, seeing that's Inspector Flagg's business. But I don't say I didn't guess, what with the perfessor being mighty taken with the angel."

"Would you say most people knew of his passion for that particular monument?"

"Not to say most, miss. Not to say many, at all, at all, I told you I keeps me eyes and ears open. It's me job."

"So you did. Here comes Mrs. Osborne now. I must talk to her."

"Rather you than me, miss, and that's a fact." As Daisy moved back, not wanting her forsaken audience to see her, he addressed the procession's leaders: "Pass along, ladies, *if* you please. Nothing to see. Pass along, there, madam. Pass along, miss. Mrs. Osborne, ma'am, if you wouldn't mind stepping through for a moment."

Suddenly pale, the vicar's wife stepped through the gate he opened for her. She put a shaking hand to her throat as if incapable of speech. Hurrying forward, Daisy took her other hand and said urgently, "It's all right, it's not Mr. Osborne."

"N-not?" Mrs. Osborne said faintly.

"No. Come and sit down. I'm frightfully sorry you had such a shock."

Daisy led her to the porch and made her sit down, though already her normal high colour was returning. So was the displeasure of an organizer whose arrangements had been overset without warning.

"We waited for you for quite a quarter of an hour, Miss Dalrymple," she said severely, "before I was forced to step in with a little lecture on the importance of—"

"I do apologize," Daisy interrupted, "but I was on my way when I discovered the . . . accident. I couldn't possibly just walk on and give a talk as if nothing had happened."

"I suppose not," Mrs. Osborne conceded. "It's most unfortunate, such a thing happening in our churchyard. Have the churchwardens been informed?"

"Not yet. Nor has the vicar. Dr. Padgett went to tell him but he wasn't at home. I'm sure you'll agree it's best for you to break it to Mr. Osborne, not the police. You see, the accident victim is his brother, and I'm afraid he's dead."

Mrs. Osborne jumped up. "Good gracious, Osmund dead? Osbert will be fearfully distressed to have lost any further chance of leading him back to God before he went to his Judgement. You are right, Miss Dalrymple, I must tell him myself. You will excuse me if I hurry home at once." And she dashed off.

Wilful blindness or genuine delusion? Daisy wondered. The Reverend Osbert Osborne was the last person to lead anyone to God. He had seemed to be on affectionate terms with his brother, though, so he would undoubtedly be dreadfully upset.

She felt a sudden qualm. Perhaps she should have suggested that Mrs. Osborne identify the body. It would be simply too frightful for words if it was in fact the vicar. Could that scrap of shiny black cloth have been attached to some sort of cassock? Might Mr. Osborne have tried to cheer himself up by contemplation of his brother's favourite epitaph?

After donning an ecclesiastical garment? Bosh, Daisy admonished herself, hopefully.

A welcome distraction came in the shape of a black Model T Ford drawing up by the lych-gate. Out of the aging motor car a very tall, thin stranger unfolded himself. He wore a fawn soft hat and a droopy lounge suit in a curious shade of bronze-green, possibly the only off-the-peg suit he had been able to find that came near to fitting his gangling form. His sandy moustache also drooped. It gave his bony face a melancholy, lacklustre cast belied—as Daisy saw when she drew near—by alert, bright blue eyes.

Though his figure could not be more different from Tom Tring's, something about him reminded her of Alec's sergeant. She was not surprised when Constable Barton saluted the newcomer.

"Inspector Flagg?" she said. "I'm *very* glad you're here."

"Constable Barton, sir," the local bobby announced. "This here's the Honourable Miss Dalrymple, the lady as found the deceased. Lord John Frobisher's sister-in-law, she is, staying up at Oakhurst."

Apparently unimpressed by her pedigree, the inspector raised his hat, revealing a shock of sandy hair quite unlike Tring's shining dome. "How do you do, Miss Dalrymple." His tone was businesslike, with a marked local accent. "Chief Inspector Fletcher told me you were first on the scene."

"You've spoken to Alec?" Daisy asked in astonishment.

"I understand the chief inspector's daughter telephoned him at New Scotland Yard when she couldn't reach Barton."

"Oh dear! I told the children there had been an accident, that's all."

"Miss Fletcher didn't see the deceased?"

"No, thank heaven, nor Derek, and I told them to stay away. Did you hope they were witnesses?"

"Certainly not, ma'am. I've girls of my own. But if you told her and the boy—"

"Young Master Frobisher," put in Barton.

Flagg nodded acknowledgement. "If you informed them," he continued to Daisy, "that there'd been an accident, I'd like to know just why the chief inspector hustled me over here under the impression it might be murder?"

"If you have daughters, you know what imaginations children have," Daisy pointed out, annoyed to feel herself blushing. She had no intention of telling the inspector that Alec was more or less resigned to her falling over victims of violence wherever she went. "As it happens, I'm pretty sure it's murder, and Dr. Padgett agrees. Do you want me to explain or do you prefer to go and see for yourself?"

"Barton?"

"I haven't looked, sir. Didn't want to risk destroying evidence when you was already on your way anyways."

"All right, Miss Dalrymple," Flagg sighed, "you'd better give me a quick account of the situation."

Daisy explained about the granite angel, the Panama, the professor's habit of wearing his academic gown and whatever headgear he happened to pick up, and his custom of meditating upon that particular tomb. Her Poison Pen theories she kept to herself, at least for the moment.

Inspector Flagg drew the constable aside. Watching

them, Daisy guessed that Barton confirmed her story, and then Flagg issued some instructions. The bobby departed village-ward on his bicycle, pedalling hard, and the inspector returned to Daisy.

"I've sent for our police surgeon and my men, Miss Dalrymple, and an ambulance of course. I didn't want to bring them out on a wild goose chase. I must thank you. You seem to have coped admirably. You'll be wanting to cut along now, no doubt."

"I could do with a cup of tea and a sit-down," Daisy admitted. "Don't you need someone to . . . Oh, Arthur doesn't need to guard the other gate now, the Parish Hall is empty. Lord John's footman, Inspector. He could come over here and fend people off for you till Barton comes back or your men arrive."

Duly summoned, Arthur returned—by the roundabout route—to be thanked for his efforts to date and assigned to his new post.

"I'll buzz off now, then," said Daisy.

"Yes, I shan't keep you," Flagg assented, "though I'll need to talk to you again, and take a statement. I suppose I can reach you at Oakhurst?"

"In general, yes, but I think I'll pop along to the Vicarage now." She had no intention of waiting tamely a good quarter mile away at Oakhurst to find out what was going on. "Maybe I can make myself useful to Mrs. Osborne, especially if it turns out to be the vicar after all."

"If the reverend has come home—or the professor, of course—I wish you would let me know."

"I will, though if the professor had turned up, Mrs. Osborne would surely have come running back."

"She might be distraught, poor lady. As may Miss Belinda . . ." Flagg added with a meaning look.

Daisy smiled at him. "I'll telephone Oakhurst and let Bel know I'm all right," she promised.

At the gate from the churchyard into the Vicarage

garden, she glanced back. Inspector Flagg was picking his way across the grass, amongst the gravestones, towards the fallen angel.

She rather liked him and would not mind working with him, though naturally she would rather have Alec. There didn't seem to be any excuse for suggesting that Scotland Yard should be called in. Rotherden wasn't even anywhere near a county boundary, except that which separated Kent from the English Channel. France was as close as London, or closer.

At least Flagg appeared to take her seriously. Sooner or later she had to tell him about the anonymous letters. Johnnie was not going to be at all happy about that.

About to knock on the Vicarage door, she became aware of a buzz of voices from the open drawing-room window. Naturally every WI member who dared had dropped in to find out what was happening. Daisy almost retreated. She had no new information to offer, and Mrs. Osborne had plenty of comforters if such were needed.

But some of her suspects were bound to be in there—Miss Prothero and Mrs. Lomax for a start. Squaring her shoulders, Daisy sent up a prayer that Mrs. Osborne had passed on her apology and explanation for her non-appearance, and knocked.

Behind her, a motor-car pulled up in the street. She turned to see Brigadier Lomax heaving himself out of a Crossley touring car.

Tramping down the garden path towards her, he hailed her testily; "Miss Dalrymple, do you know what the deuce all this fuss is about? My butler says Rosa rang up from here to say I was needed urgently. Silly woman didn't say why. I got in from my afternoon constitutional just after she rang off, but the line was engaged when I telephoned back."

"There has been a fatal accident in the churchyard." Daisy watched him closely as she spoke. He had been out walking, and as a probable recipient of an anonymous letter, he was a suspect in the murder. All she detected in his face was irritable impatience. "Mrs. Osborne felt the churchwardens should be informed."

"Pah! What am I supposed to do about it? Pick up the pieces, hah?"

The question was presumably rhetorical. Before Daisy was called upon to produce a response, the door opened. "Just a moment, Doris," she said, and advised the brigadier, "There's a policeman over there, an Inspector Flagg. Perhaps you should have a word with him."

"Might as well, now I'm here," he said in an exasperated tone, and stalked off.

Daisy regretted sending him to see Flagg without a chance to warn the inspector that he was a suspect. Still, the policeman was no fool and he would have to treat everyone as suspect until he had time to start sorting things out.

Stepping across the threshold, Daisy asked the maid, "Is Mr. Osborne home yet?"

"No, miss." Doris's sullen stolidity had cracked enough to allow a gleam of excitement. "Miss, is it true what they're saying, the professor's been killed stone dead?"

An appropriate way of putting it! "I'm afraid so," Daisy said. "At least—what was the vicar wearing when he went out?"

"I duuno, miss. Same as always, I 'spect. I di'n't see neither of 'em leave. Just after lunch it was, and I had to clear the table and help Cook with the washing up. 'S going to be dull around here without the professor," she sighed. "Livened things up a bit, he did."

"I'm sure he must have. Do you think Mrs. Osborne would mind if I made a telephone call before I go in there?" Daisy gestured towards the drawing room. "My sister will be wondering where I am."

"Oh, yes, miss, might as well get the use from it. The master says it's just an unn'essary expense when most people in the parish don't have one, but the mistress says a vicar did ought to be on the telephone. All right by me, saves me legs, running with messages. Here you are, miss."

As she spoke, she led the way past the stairs to the rear of the hall, to a nook beneath the landing. A straight chair stood beside a small table bearing the telephone apparatus and a notepad and pencil. The pad looked to Daisy exactly like the paper Johnnie's letters were written on.

Unfortunately, it was a sort that anyone could buy at any Woolworth's, sold by the hundred thousands, if not millions. No help there—until she noticed the indentation of the previous message, written in capital letters.

Doris had left. Daisy took the pad out into the more brightly lit hall and slanted it to the light. With difficulty she made out the clumsy writing: KERNLE LOMAK SEZ EEL COM BAK LETTER.

So the brigadier had dropped in when the Osbornes were out, but he could not conceivably have left such an illiterate inscription. No, Doris had written down his message. Looking at the hall table, Daisy saw two or three folded sheets of paper beneath a paperweight on a silver-plated salver, the silver wearing thin in patches.

Doris as Poison Pen? She was in the right place to hear all the gossip.

But Daisy's excitement lasted scarcely a moment. The letters on the pad were heavily impressed and ill-formed, quite unlike the Poison Pen's neat block capitals. And surely no one who spelt like that could have managed to get "you're" and "you've" correct, let alone "folk" or "caught."

All the same, the police might be able to make something of it. She tore off the top sheet and tucked it into her handbag as she turned back to the telephone.

With Winifred Burden at the exchange in mind, Daisy told Violet nothing that would not already be all over the village. It was lucky her sister was singularly uninquisitive. There was just a chance she and Johnnie might be able to keep the Poison Pen business from Vi even if the murder was connected.

"How are Bel and Derek?" she asked. "Are they frightfully shocked?"

"Not a bit of it, darling. Rather disappointed not to have seen the body—at least, Derek is, the bloodthirsty little monster. They went to inspect their dam, which has suffered from the rain, I gather, and now they're playing piggy-in-the-middle with Peter. Peter would be piggy forever, of course, if Belinda didn't deliberately throw him the ball now and then. What a kind-hearted child! I'm glad she's going to be my boys' cousin, and the baby's."

"So am I," said Daisy. "I'll be back long before dinner, Vi, but first I'd like to give my statement to Inspector Flagg, so he doesn't have to come up to Oakhurst. Toodle-oo!"

As she hung up, Daisy was glad to see Doris go past from the nether regions carrying a jug of hot water. She was simply dying for a cup of tea.

Slipping into the drawing room behind the maid, she heard Mrs. Molesworth say encouragingly, "Do drink your tea, Mrs. Osborne. Strong, hot, and sweet, it's quite the best thing for shock."

"I'm sure my nerves are in tatters," moaned Miss Hendricks. "No one knows better than I what it is to have delicate nerves. Dear Mrs. Osborne is always so *strong.*"

The vicar's wife was sitting bolt upright, her lips tightly compressed, her hands gripped together in her lap. She was clearly suppressing some strong emotion, though Daisy could not tell what. Was it sick uncertainty, the fear that the body had been misidentified and she was a widow, or was she simply irritated almost beyond bearing by the women fussing about her?

"Do stop clucking like a flock of silly hens!" came Mrs. Willoughby-Jones' strident tones. "Give the woman some peace. Ah, Doris, is that more hot water you've brought? I'll have another cup."

"Oh, Miss Dalrymple!" Miss Prothero, spotting her, jumped up and advanced upon her with an avid expression. "Perhaps you can tell us what has happened? Poor Mrs. Osborne feels quite unable to give us the details."

"All we know," put in Mrs. Lomax, "is that Professor Osborne has met with a *fatal accident*."

"I can't tell you any more," Daisy prevaricated, "except that the police are investigating, as I'm sure you're aware is necessary in any sudden death. Don't you think that when the vicar comes home he's going to want peace and quiet to deal with his loss?"

"Oh, but special friends . . ." Miss Hendricks wailed, wringing her hands. "The dear vicar has done so much for all of us . . ."

"You're quite right, Miss Dalrymple," Mrs. Molesworth interrupted in her deep voice. "Mrs. Osborne, if there is anything at all I can do to help you have only to let me know. There, I'm off."

"But special friends. . ." said Miss Hendricks weakly.

"You're not one," Mrs. Willoughby-Jones informed her with brutal candour.

The remaining women all looked at each other sidelong, then one by one said subdued good-byes, with promises of assistance as needed, and drifted out. Mrs. Osborne, it appeared, had no special friends.

Daisy certainly did not count herself as a friend, even an ordinary one. She hadn't the vaguest right to stay, as Mrs. Willoughby-Jones's truculent glance in parting made plain. But she had found the body, and talked to the police, and besides, she was Lady John's sister. No one objected aloud.

Was one of them the murderer—the Poison Pen or a victim of the Poison Pen? They had all been in the vicinity.

As chairman of the WI committee, Mrs. Lomax probably could not have arrived at the meeting late without arousing comment—though Mrs. Osborne habitually usurped her functions whether she was present or not. Any of the others might have sneaked into the Parish Hall and sat down at the back unnoticed. How much force had it taken to topple the angel? Mrs. Molesworth and Mrs. Willoughby-Jones were both fairly hefty, and even Miss Prothero, though elderly, was quite vigorous. Miss Hendricks' much vaunted feebleness could be less fact than an excuse to whine, though she did look pretty sickly.

As soon as the door closed behind them, Daisy picked up Mrs. Osborne's nearly full tea-cup. "You prefer it weak, and without milk, don't you? And I expect they have put enough sugar in to make it undrinkable. Two lumps, I seem to remember."

Preparing a fresh cup to those specifications, she set it beside the vicar's wife, then poured some for herself. Mrs. Osborne drank thirstily.

"I feel as if none of this is real," she said in a remote voice. "What will Osbert do next?"

"You don't know where he went?" Daisy asked. "I'm sure the police would send someone to fetch him."

"No!" Mrs. Osborne saw Daisy's surprise at her vehemence and added with a feverish light in her eye, "Why grieve him sooner than need be? I don't know how I'm going to tell him about his brother!"

"How long has the professor been staying?"

"Since the end of June. Why?"

"Oh, I suppose I wondered how close the brothers are," Daisy invented hastily. "Mr. Osborne may well see the police before he gets here, in which case he's bound to stop and ask what is going on in his churchyard, isn't he? If not, would you like me to break the news?"

"Would you?" Mrs. Osborne begged eagerly. "You know more than I do, at all events, and to tell the truth I'm not feeling at all well. Will you forgive me if I go and lie down?"

"Of course." Daisy couldn't blame her cowardice. The vicar knew his wife had not cared for his brother, so any expression of sympathy was bound to strike a false note.

Mrs. Osborne's departure left Daisy in indisputable occupation of the drawing room until Mr. Osborne came in. She went straight to the small hinged-front desk in the far corner. Though the vicar must have a private den with a desk where he produced his sermons, if Professor Osborne had been the Poison Pen, he was quite likely to use this to write his letters. Daisy pulled out the supports and let down the front.

The first thing she saw was a box of blue Basildon Bond, the kind with folded sheets, not a pad. She poked through the pigeon-holes and little drawers, but found no other writing paper of any sort. Closing the top, she opened the top drawer below. At first glance, it was full of receipted bills, old chequebooks, and such.

There was no time for a second glance. Someone knocked on the front door. Daisy hastily shut the drawer and moved away from the corner.

She heard Doris answer the door, then the maid came in.

"It's a p'liceman, miss. Leastways, he says he is, only he's not in uniform 'cause he's a 'tective. He's asking for you. Did I ought to go up and tell the mistress?"

"No, leave her in peace until she's needed, Doris. Will you show the policeman in here, please?"

Remembering Alec's custom of making those he interrogated face the light, she took a seat with her back to the window. Not that she intended to withhold essentials from Flagg, but she didn't want him jumping to conclusions based on her expression. Doris ushered the inspector in, and Daisy invited him to sit.

"The vicar hasn't come home yet," she said.

"Oh, Mr. Osborne turned up just a few minutes ago."

"Thank heaven!" Daisy exclaimed with feeling. When Flagg gave her an enquiring look, she explained, "It would have been too frightful if it turned out to be Mrs. Osborne's husband when I'd assured her it was her brother-in-law. Where is he? Is he fearfully upset?"

"Shattered, the poor gentleman. He went into the church, to pray, I imagine. Only natural for a parson."

To pray? To *try* to pray, possibly, or just to try to look as if he was praying, to keep up appearances even in his grief, for his wife's sake.

"I think I'd better tell the maid to let Mrs. Osborne know the vicar has turned up," Daisy said, going to ring the bell. "She didn't seem to doubt that it was the professor who was killed, but she's in quite a state and it won't hurt to reassure her."

"Good idea," Flagg agreed, taking out his notebook. "It'll be half an hour or so before my men and the police surgeon get here. I've done all I can without them, so if you wouldn't mind repeating what you told me about finding the deceased . . ."

"Of course." She turned as the maid came in. "Oh Doris, Inspector Flagg says the vicar has come back and is in the church. Would you tell Mrs. Osborne right away?"

"Yes, miss. Was you wanting any more tea or'll I clear?"

Daisy looked at Flagg, who said, "I wouldn't mind a cup."

"Bring a fresh pot, please, but go to Mrs. Osborne first. Right-oh, Inspector, I'd better explain first that I was on my way to the Parish Hall to give a talk to the Women's Institute." Pleased to note that her stomach re-

mained calm, she continued with the story of her gruesome discovery and what she did next. She finished
with Dr. Padgett's reluctant concession that the angel
could not have fallen by chance. "What do you think,
Mr. Flagg? Don't you think it must have been pushed?"

"It seems that way to me," the inspector conceded, almost as reluctantly as the doctor had. "There's no sign
of mortar to attach it to the base, so its own weight
must've held it there all these years, though we've had
a gale or two in my time."

"There wasn't a breath of wind this afternoon."

"Nary a whisper. That angel looks top-heavy, with the
wings spread and all. I should think a good shove between the shoulder-blades'd topple it. We'll look for
fingerprints, of course. The polished stone should hold
'em well if there are any, but if not I expect the super
will want to bring in some sort of scientist to say how
much force it would have taken."

"And how high up," Daisy suggested, running her
suspects through her mind. None was particularly short.

"That too," Flagg agreed. "We'll either have to ex-
periment in the churchyard, or take the angel away. The
churchwarden, Brigadier Lomax, wasn't any too
pleased when he heard that, I can tell you."

"I don't suppose he was. Did you find anything useful in the way of footprints? The gravel doesn't show
much, does it?"

The inspector shook his head. "There's a couple of
deepish indentations right where the murderer would
have stood to push the angel over, but nothing remotely
identifiable. Which isn't to say I'm not grateful to you
for keeping people off, Miss Dalrymple. It's a pity more
citizens don't have the sense to guard the scenes of
crimes."

Murmuring a modest disclaimer, Daisy wondered
whether to admit her previous involvement with several

murder cases. At that moment, the maid came in with a steaming teapot.

"Did you tell Mrs. Osborne the vicar is back, Doris?" Daisy asked.

"Yes, miss. Cheered up no end, she did, when I told her the master was in church praying for his brother. She weren't too pleased to hear the p'lice is in the house, but when I said he just wanted to talk to miss, she said she s'posed there weren't no harm. Is there anything else, miss?"

"No, thank you, Doris." Daisy poured tea for Flagg and another cup for herself. "Now you've seen the vicar, Inspector," she said, "don't you agree it's possible someone could have mistaken his brother for him?"

"I shouldn't be discussing the case with you, Miss Dalrymple," said Flagg with abrupt gruffness. The interruption had dispersed whatever spell beguiled people into confiding in her, and he was now obviously annoyed with himself for succumbing. "I don't know what I was thinking of."

"But the mix-up could be the key," Daisy persisted, nerving herself to tell him about the Poison Pen. "Supposing—"

"You'd better leave the supposing to us, ma'am. Now, if you wouldn't mind just going over these times once more, make sure I've got them down right. Half past two was it the WI meeting started?"

For the present, Daisy gave in. At least she would have a chance to warn Johnnie that the existence of the anonymous letters must be revealed.

10

Leaving the Vicarage, Daisy crossed the lane to knock on Mrs. LeBeau's door. The mistress of the house opened the door herself, dressed in a glorious tea-gown of rose chiffon.

"Miss Dalrymple, do come in! I hope you have come to satisfy my vulgar curiosity? I'm all agog. It's been all I could do to restrain myself from going over to ask what has happened."

"I'll tell you, but I'm afraid you won't like the rest of my errand."

"You'd better come and sit down," said Mrs. LeBeau soberly, showing her into the drawing room, which was filled with fragrance from the vases of roses. "Sherry?"

"No, thanks." Daisy needed a clear head, and she had not eaten since lunch. She told the bare facts of Professor Osborne's demise, little more than that he had been killed by a falling tombstone.

Mrs. LeBeau made the proper shocked and sympathetic noises, without pretending to great distress. "I didn't know the professor except to bow to in passing," she explained, "and I doubt anything more than formal condolences from me would be well received at the Vicarage. I'll rely on you to tell me if you think there's anything I can do to help without giving offence. But what else did you have to tell me?"

Daisy hesitated, then came to the conclusion that

there simply wasn't an easy way to say it. "The thing is, there seems little doubt that Professor Osborne was murdered."

"I wondered whether that might be the case, since the police appear inordinately interested. Why on earth would anyone kill him? He seemed an inoffensive sort of man, if rather eccentric." She frowned. "Don't say you came to warn me there may be a homicidal maniac about?"

"Good gracious, no! At least, I don't think the police are thinking on those lines. No, the thing is, it seems to me the murder is very likely tied up somehow with the Poison Pen letters."

Mrs. LeBeau stared at her in surprise. "The letters? But how?"

"It's rather complicated, and I really ought not to explain to anyone but the police. Because I'm afraid I'm going to have to tell the police about the letters, and they're going to want to know who's been getting them."

"Must you?" Mrs. LeBeau cried. Daisy thought she paled, though it was hard to be sure because of her make-up. "Must you tell them about *me?* There are others, you said."

"The others won't be any happier than you," Daisy pointed out gently. "I can't very well pick and choose."

"No." Her shoulders slumped. "And after all, one of them— one of *us*—is your brother-in- . . . Miss Dalrymple, I'm not a suspect, am I? Surely you don't suspect me! Truly, I didn't know the man."

"I believe you," Daisy hastily assured her.

In fact, it had not dawned on her before that Mrs. LeBeau might be the murderer, with the same conceivable motive as any victim of the Poison Pen—including Johnnie. On the whole she was inclined to the theory that the murderer was the Poison Pen, found out by the vicar and killing his brother by mistake.

She was pretty sure Mrs. LeBeau had not written the

anonymous letters, including those to herself to divert suspicion. But one never could tell, Daisy thought uneasily.

"Excuse me," said Mrs. LeBeau, rising, "I believe I'll have a glass of sherry now. I feel rather in need. You won't?"

"Thank you, no." She jumped up, glad of a suitable opening to take her leave. "I must be getting back to Oakhurst, to warn Johnnie."

"I do appreciate your warning me, Miss Dalrymple, not just sending the police round to interrogate me." Mrs. LeBeau ushered Daisy out into the hall and opened the front door as she went on with a faint smile, "And I'm grateful to you for believing me. You will be careful whom else you warn, won't you? Before the police have all your information, I mean."

"Gosh, yes!" said Daisy, dismayed.

Of all the feeble-minded chumps! The inherent danger in advising suspects of her intention of blowing the gaff to the police had not occurred to her. Alec would be furious if he found out—so he mustn't. Too fearfully lucky that Mrs. LeBeau was innocent. Daisy had even contemplated ringing up Dr. Padgett. That was out.

Johnnie was all right. She *had* to trust him. But she jolly well hoped he had an alibi.

All the way up the hill, she pondered how to persuade Inspector Flagg to take her theories seriously, without setting his back up. The easiest would be to phone up Alec and ask him to convey her concerns. However, she wasn't frightfully keen on Alec finding out she had set out to investigate an anonymous-letter epidemic without his knowledge. Anyway, Flagg would resent his repeated intervention.

Her reflections were interrupted as she approached the house. Derek and Belinda burst out of the front door.

"Aunt Daisy, Aunt Daisy, Bel's daddy's coming to stay!"

"Daddy telephoned and said he was motoring down tonight and Aunt Violet said he could stay here, at Oakhurst. Isn't it spiffing?"

"Spiffing!" Daisy agreed with a laugh, wondering how Inspector Flagg would take the unofficial arrival of a superior officer from the Met. And how she was going to explain everything to Alec.

"We were watching for you from the nursery windows and when we saw you coming up the drive we came down because I have to ask you, what shall I call Bel's daddy? Bel says 'Uncle Alec,' because she calls my daddy uncle, but I don't know if it's all right to call a *detective chief inspector* from Scotland Yard uncle, even if he really nearly is."

"I'm sure it's all right, Derek, but we'll ask him, if you like. When is he arriving?" Entering the hall with a child hanging onto each arm, she suddenly felt exhausted.

"Not till after we're in bed, probably," said Derek. "He's stopping for dinner on the way."

"But he can come and say goodnight, can't he?" Belinda asked anxiously. "If I'm not asleep yet? He always does when he comes home in time."

"Yes, of course." Daisy's father would never have dreamt of turning up in the nurseries at Fairacres to bid his children goodnight. Nor would her mother, come to that, nor Violet and Johnnie. That was what nannies were for. If a bedtime kiss was the middle-class way, there was a lot to be said for it, Daisy decided.

"Will you, when you're my mummy?"

"Absolutely," Daisy promised. "But run along now, I must talk to Uncle Johnnie."

"About . . . about the dead body?" Bel's freckled face took on a pinched look.

Daisy hugged her. "Yes, darling, but there's no need

for you to have anything more to do with it. You've both been absolute angels—I don't know how I'd have coped without you. Now you can forget all about it."

"Golly," said Derek in disgust, "that would be an awful waste. Don't be such a *girl,* Bel. Come on."

As Daisy entered the drawing room, Violet looked round and Johnnie started to his feet.

"Daisy, darling," Vi exclaimed, "I'm so glad you're back. I've been worrying. And so, I may say, has your Mr. Fletcher. He's on his way."

"The children told me," Daisy said, dropping into a chair. "I can't think how Alec got away in mid week."

"He said he had just cleared up two or three cases, and he's due a couple of days off after working several weekends in a row. He asked about accommodation in the village, but of course I invited him here."

"Thanks, darling."

"Daisy," Johnnie said impatiently, "what exactly has happened? I came home to one garbled story from the children and another from Violet. Professor Osborne's dead?"

"Yes, it is the professor. I was frightfully afraid I was wrong, and it was really the vicar, but he's turned up."

"How did it happen?"

"I don't want to hear the gory details," Violet said firmly. "I'm going upstairs to write a note of condolence, and to lie down for half an hour before changing for dinner." Standing up, she stooped to kiss Johnnie's scarred cheek. "Don't get up, darling."

He caught her hand and squeezed it. "Take the stairs slowly, love. Daisy, can I get you a cocktail, or sherry?"

"A drop of vermouth with loads of soda, please, but what I'd really like is some salted almonds to nibble. I'm starving. I missed tea, but I don't want to spoil my dinner."

Her needs provided for, and Violet well out of the way, she told Johnnie about the fallen angel.

"But who on earth would do in the professor? Perhaps he was followed from Cambridge by a student he'd ploughed, or a rival academic," Johnnie speculated. "Surely no one local. He's been to stay in Rotherden before, but hardly enough to drive the neighbours to violence!"

"Unless he was the Poison Pen."

"Unless . . . Daisy, was he? You found him out already?"

"No," she admitted regretfully, "but it's a possibility. When did the first letter come?"

"I feel as if I've been getting the beastly things forever, but I suppose it's just a couple of months."

"Any before the beginning of July?"

Johnnie pondered. "I couldn't swear to it one way or the other."

"Bother!" Crunching on a handful of almonds, Daisy wished she hadn't forgotten to ask Mrs. LeBeau the same question.

"Why should you imagine Professor Osborne wrote them?" Johnnie asked. "Just because he's been murdered?"

"Not entirely. I wondered before."

"I can't see how he could have known about . . . my fall from grace."

"The Vicarage is a hot-bed of gossip, and he was the sort of man who might think it a joke to write anonymous letters. The alternative is that the vicar unmasked the Poison Pen, who meant to kill him, not his brother. They are . . . were very alike. Either way, Johnnie, you see why I have to tell the police about it."

"You *what?* Dash it, Daisy, no!"

"It's murder now, not just anonymous letters. You're a magistrate. Would you really advise me to withhold information from the police?"

"N-no, I suppose not," Johnnie said doubtfully. "But, dash it, it may have nothing whatsoever to do with it."

"Maybe, but we can't be sure. Anyway, as they investigate there's a good chance they'll find out a Poison Pen's been active in the village. Then they'll really start to dig, and it's far more likely Violet will hear about your letters than if you're frank with them and ask them to try to keep it from her."

"I think I'll have a whisky," groaned Johnnie.

"I don't see any need to tell them what the letters were about," Daisy said, trying to cheer him. He merely groaned again.

While he was at the drinks cabinet, Daisy sipped her soda-and-It and guzzled a few more almonds. She wondered how to break to him what had apparently not dawned on him: that he would inevitably become a suspect. The moment was postponed when his butler appeared.

"There's a person to see your lordship. A plain clothes policeman he says, my lord. A Detective Inspector Flagg."

Heaving a mighty sigh, Johnnie set down his glass unsipped and said resignedly, "Show him in, Mitchell."

The lanky inspector looked a trifle embarrassed to see Daisy. He gave her a brief nod, but addressed Johnnie: "I beg your pardon for disturbing you, my lord. You'll have heard about the unfortunate incident down in the churchyard, I don't doubt."

"I have," Johnnie said curtly.

"The thing of it is, sir, when my men came out from Ashford they brought a message to ring up my superintendent. Which I did, and he wants me to talk to Master Derek Frobisher and Miss Fletcher."

"The children? Why the deuce—? Sorry, Daisy."

She waved permission at him to use what language he liked.

"It's not what I like to do, sir," Flagg apologized. "I've young daughters of my own. But we always like to get more than one witness whenever possible, and we've only Miss Dalrymple's description of what happened when she found the deceased."

"Surely you don't doubt Miss Dalrymple's word!" Johnnie exploded.

"No, no, not at all, sir," the inspector said hastily, and not quite convincingly. Not, Daisy decided, as if he did actually doubt her, but as if he bore her possible untruthfulness in mind. "Nothing like that. It's just that in the stress of the moment, as you might say, specially in a nasty business like this, witnesses do get confused and forget exactly what they saw and did."

"The children told me they didn't see the body."

"And I'm glad to hear it, sir, but for that very reason they're less likely to have been upset and more likely to remember just what they did see. It's remarkable how much children notice. They might, for instance, have observed someone making off down the lane, which Miss Dalrymple naturally missed. Perhaps you'd like to telephone the super, sir?"

Going over the inspector's head might give umbrage, Daisy thought, and make him less likely to heed a plea to keep the anonymous letters from Vi. To her relief, Johnnie shook his head.

"No, I dare say I'd only hear the same from him. I'll send for them," he continued, "but I must insist on myself and Miss Dalrymple being present."

"You, sir, naturally. We try not to interview young children without a grown-up family member present. But . . ."

"Miss Fletcher has no family member in the house," Johnnie interrupted. "Unless you wish to wait until her father arrives . . ."

"Her father?" Flagg was obviously startled, dismayed, and annoyed. "You mean Detective Chief Inspector Fletcher is coming down?"

"Purely in a personal capacity, I understand. He is engaged to be married to Miss Dalrymple. She is the nearest thing to a relative Belinda has at hand."

The inspector sighed. "Very well, Miss Dalrymple stays, but please, ma'am, not a word of prompting. Otherwise I'll have to stop and give it another go when the chief inspector gets here. You won't be wanting to put the child through it twice."

"No," Daisy agreed meekly.

"I'll send for them." Johnnie moved towards the bell to summon Mitchell.

"Wait, Johnnie. Before you speak to Derek and Belinda, Inspector, you really must listen to what I have to tell you. It's important."

"Not now, please, Miss Dalrymple, I'm pushed for time. I left the police surgeon and my fellows down there, and I must go and find out what they've come up with."

"I think you ought to hear her out," said Johnnie with a grimace of resignation.

Flagg glanced at his wrist-watch. "I can't spare you more than a few minutes."

"Right-oh. Do sit down."

"Something to drink, Inspector?" offered Johnnie, with an air of postponing the dreadful moment.

"A beer would be welcome, sir, if there's one to hand."

"No, but I can send for—"

"I haven't the time to spare, sir. No matter. Be so good as to ring for the children and I'll listen while we wait for them." Impatient, he leaned forward in his chair, hands on his knees, while Johnnie rang the bell, picked up his whisky and subsided nearby. "Now, Miss Dalrymple."

No time to beat about the bush. Daisy plunged straight in. "There has been a spate of anonymous letters in Rotherden recently, Inspector. I believe the murder may be connected with them."

For a moment Flagg sat absolutely still, his shrewd blue eyes fixed on her face. Then he sat back and took out his notebook. "Anonymous letters, eh? We can't do a great deal about those unless they contain threats or blackmail."

"The ones I've read, or heard about in detail, had neither, but they were pretty foul and upsetting, and there's always the possibility they might proceed to blackmail."

"You don't reside in Rotherden, Miss Dalrymple. You are not a victim, I take it?" No, the detective was certainly no fool. Even as he asked, his gaze swung to Johnnie.

"Yes, Inspector, I've had letters," Johnnie admitted gloomily.

"Well, I shan't waste time now asking why you informed your wife's sister—or how she discovered for herself. Let me hear your ideas about the murder, if you please, ma'am."

As Daisy yet again set forth her two opposing theories, the butler came in. Johnnie told him to have the children sent down, then Daisy finished her exposition.

Flagg nodded slowly. "Sounds reasonable," he conceded, "though we may find a more straightforward motive once we start investigating. A village girl Professor Osborne's got into trouble, or something of the sort. Still, we'll bear it in mind. You'd better tell me who you reckon might have done it—who else received these letters, that is, besides Lord John."

As Johnnie absorbed the implication, his mouth opened, then shut again without utterance. He took a swig of his hitherto untouched whisky.

If Flagg was no fool, neither was he a toady. Daisy quite approved of him, on the whole, but she jolly well hoped Johnnie had a witness to his presence far from the churchyard.

"Where were you between half past two and five to three?" she asked him.

"Now, now, Miss Dalrymple," the inspector reproved, "that's for me to ask. But since it's said, my lord, perhaps you wouldn't mind answering?"

"Not at all," Johnnie said eagerly. "I was out riding all afternoon, all over the estate. I was looking—"

"Alone?"

"With Jackson, my bailiff. He thinks we ought to get a tractor, but most of my arable is under hops so we were looking—"

"You were with Mr. Jackson the entire afternoon?"

"Sorry, I tend to get a bit carried away. You're not interested in tractors, of course. Yes, Jackson was with me the whole time."

Daisy breathed again.

"I'm glad to hear it, sir, though naturally we'll be checking with him. Is he on the telephone by any chance?"

"No, but his place is just a hundred yards or so up the lane. Turn right at the gates, and Hillside Cottage is just along on your right. You can't miss it."

"Thank you, sir. I'll get on to him this evening. Please don't attempt to speak to him before I do."

"Why—?" Johnnie started with a puzzled frown, then his face cleared. "Oh, because his livelihood depends on me. Silly of me. I daresay he might be tempted to lie for me, but he doesn't need to. Inspector, there's no need to let my wife know I've been getting these letters, is there?"

"Ah, like that is it, my lord? Never fear, I'll do my best to keep her ladyship in the dark, and I can't say fairer than that." Flagg's understanding tone had a touch of amusement. Johnnie bridled, but he was hardly in a position to protest.

"Johnnie hadn't the foggiest who wrote them," said Daisy. "That's why he asked me to try to find out."

"Did he, now?" Flagg fixed her with an unwavering stare. "I've been racking my brains to imagine what motive a young lady of your standing might have for doing in a professor of Latin and Greek. After all, you are the one person we know was at the scene of the crime between the start of the WI meeting and the arrival of the footman. Now, if you had discovered Professor Osborne was the Poison Pen, you might decide on the spur of the moment to seize the chance to eliminate the threat to your sister and her husband. Mightn't you?"

11

While Daisy and Johnnie were still gaping at Inspector Flagg in stunned silence, Derek and Belinda came in. The arguments on the tip of Daisy's tongue had to be bitten back. The children must not know she was suspected of murder.

Since Johnnie appeared too flabbergasted to cope, Daisy said, in a voice she hoped sounded like a croak only to her own ears, "Bel, Derek, Inspector Flagg wants to ask you a few questions."

"I expect you have been talking about this afternoon," the inspector said to them, "but all the same, I'd like to see you two young people separately, so that you don't get mixed up with each other's answers. All right?"

They nodded solemnly.

"You first, Miss Belinda." He smiled at her as she crossed to Daisy and took her hand in a tremulous clasp, leaning on the arm of her chair. "Lord John?"

"You'd better take Derek to wait in the library, Johnnie."

Johnnie failed to insist on his gentlemanly duty to protect the ladies. The omission was probably due to his dazed state, but Daisy chose to attribute it to his recognition of her ability to defend herself and Belinda.

"Suppose I don't remember properly," Bel asked anxiously.

"All I want is what you remember, missie," said Flagg,

fatherly and reassuring. "Now, you walked down the avenue with Miss Dalrymple?"

"And Derek and Tinker Bell. That's his dog. I wanted to go and hear Aunt Daisy speak to the meeting, but she said it wouldn't be interesting, so we stopped at the gates. Aunt Daisy went across the road. Derek said, 'Let's climb the gate,' and he took off his gumboots and climbed up to the top, and then he said, 'Aunt Daisy's checking her stocking-seams are straight.'"

Daisy blushed, and Inspector Flagg said gravely, "You've got a very good memory. Comes of being a policeman's daughter, I expect. What next?"

"I took off my boots. I put them all—mine and Derek's—I put them through the gate so Tinker wouldn't run off with them. Then I climbed up. It was quite easy," Belinda assured the detective.

"And what did you see from the top?"

"I looked over to the graveyard and I saw Aunt Daisy bending over something. I said, 'What's she doing?' and Derek said, 'Something's fallen over. That great big angel, I think. You wouldn't know.' 'Cause I don't live here," she explained. "Then Aunt Daisy took her hankie out of her bag—at least, I think it was her hankie. It was something white. She put it down on the ground and came hurrying back. That's when she told us there was an accident and to ring up the doctor and the police. After that, we just put on our boots and ran home to the telephone."

"I see. How long would you say it took between Miss Dalrymple crossing the lane and Master Derek seeing her checking . . . er, hm . . . and Master Derek saying he could see her?"

"Just a minute," Belinda said earnestly. "Half a minute. His gumboots are new and a bit too big so he can grow into them, so they're easy to take off. And he climbs ever so fast. *Frightfully* fast," she corrected herself.

"And you didn't notice anyone in the lane?"

"There wasn't anyone."

"That's all then, thank you, Miss Fletcher," said Flagg. "That wasn't too bad, was it? Tell me, did Tinker Bell work out she could get at the boots if she went around the gate?"

"No," said Belinda, laughing.

The inspector stood up. "Thank you, too, Miss Dalrymple." He gave her a bland smile.

"Not at all, Inspector," Daisy said ironically, half inclined to wish she had not helped with the information about the Poison Pen. But it was true, as she had told Johnnie, that it was better to be frank with the police. Concealment only furthered their suspicions, justified or not. "I wish to speak with you when you are finished with Derek," she informed him in her most haughty manner, and was glad to see him look a trifle apprehensive.

He went off to the library.

"He's nice, isn't he?" Belinda remarked. "Aunt Daisy, was Professor Osborne really murdered?"

"I'm afraid it looks like it, darling."

"Oh well," said Belinda philosophically, "Daddy's coming and he'll soon find out who did it. I've got to go back to the nursery, now. I promised to read Peter a story before he lies down."

Daisy went to replenish her supply of nuts, thinking what a pity it was that being nervous made her eat more instead of destroying her appetite. Inspector Flagg did not leave her long on tenterhooks. He reappeared in a couple of minutes, with Johnnie at his heels.

"You'll be happy to hear, Miss Dalrymple," said the inspector, his face stolid but a gleam in his eyes, "that young Master Derek confirms Miss Belinda's account. He's quite certain the angel had fallen before . . . he climbed the gate."

"Before I had time to get anywhere near it, you mean," Daisy corrected him tartly. "I'm no more a fool than you are, Inspector."

"I'm aware of that, ma'am. That's why I didn't consider your sending for the police and the doctor to be evidence of your innocence. You would have realized . . . Still, that's all water under the bridge. You and Lord John appear to be out of the running."

"I'm glad you realize that, Inspector," Johnnie said sourly, but Daisy noted Flagg's "appear to be," and recalled Alec's reluctance to cross anyone off his little list.

"I hope you'll let bygones be bygones, ma'am."

"Being engaged to a detective," said Daisy dryly, waving him to a chair, "I accept that you were only doing your duty. I take it you want to know the other recipients of anonymous letters."

"If you please, ma'am." His meekness was undoubtedly put on, though Johnnie seemed satisfied that the upstart was cowed.

"I'm only certain of two others," Daisy said, "and I don't think Johnnie has any need to hear about them."

"No, but I shan't desert you," her brother-in-law said stoutly, and he moved to the far end of the room.

"Mrs. LeBeau got one while I was with her," Daisy told Flagg in a low voice, "and she told me she'd had several. I ought to mention that I warned her I'd be reporting them to the police."

"Did you, now? And what was her reaction?"

"Isn't that hearsay, Inspector, or something of the sort? Oh, well, she was naturally dismayed, but she didn't try to stop me. The other person I'm sure of doesn't know I know. I saw an envelope, exactly like the ones Johnnie described and Mrs. LeBeau showed me, addressed to Dr. Padgett."

"Padgett! Isn't he the doctor who first examined the body?"

"Yes. I know it's a pity," Daisy excused herself, "but I was in a bit of a state and hadn't worked things out yet. I still thought it was the vicar. Besides, Padgett was the closest doctor and I couldn't very well have told the children to try to find someone else."

"No, no," said Flagg soothingly, "you did the best you could in the circumstances. But that reminds me . . ." He glanced at his watch. "Dr. Soames, the police surgeon, will be waiting for me, and he's not a patient man. I must be off. Those you think *may* have had letters, and those, other than the professor, who you think may have written them, can wait until tomorrow. Thank you for your cooperation, ma'am, my lord."

Not waiting for the butler to be summoned to show him out, the inspector loped to the drawing room door. There he paused and, turning his head, said in a grim voice, "Be so good as to inform Detective Chief Inspector Fletcher I'd appreciate a word with him." With that, he departed.

"Whew!" Johnnie made an elaborate show of wiping his forehead, then finished his whisky in one swig. "I quite expected the fellow to haul one or the other or both of us off to prison. I'm most frightfully sorry to have put you through that, Daisy. I ought never to have asked you to investigate."

"I didn't have to accept," Daisy pointed out. "Admittedly I wasn't expecting to be suspected of murder, but nor were you, and no doubt it's good for me to be on the other side of the fence for once. I dare say Alec will say so, anyway."

"I'm afraid Flagg's not awfully pleased about Fletcher coming down."

"Oh, Alec will spin him a yarn about only coming to stop me meddling. Which is probably true, whatever he told Vi about worrying about Belinda. Gosh, look at the time. We'd better go and change for dinner."

Motoring through the Kent countryside, newly rain-washed and lit by the evening sun, Alec was conscious only of gladness. He was looking forward to four days with Daisy and Bel, and if there was a murder in the offing, it was entirely someone else's responsibility.

His host and hostess, Lord and Lady John—to call the former Frobisher was easy enough, but could he bring himself to address Daisy's sister as Violet?—he had met only briefly, at the crowded engagement party. He was accustomed to summing people up quickly, though, and had approved of what he saw. Lady John—Violet—seemed a quiet, self-contained woman, quite unlike both her spirited sister and their sharp-tongued mother, and with a charmingly friendly smile. Frobisher was a decent country squire. Though not particularly quick-witted, nor was he a red-faced, view-hallooing booby, thank heaven.

They were kind to Belinda. Alec knew Daisy was fond of both of them, and he was quite prepared to like them, too.

So as to take advantage of daylight while it lasted, he did not stop to eat until he reached Ashford. After plaice with fried potatoes and runner beans, and a pint of an excellent local beer, he returned to his Austin Seven. He almost managed to convince himself he was not tempted to call in at the police station to find out what was going on.

Temptation successfully resisted, he drove on. Though it was now full dark, Lady John's directions were clear and easy to follow. Less than half an hour later, he turned in between the iron gates of Oakhurst.

For once he was greeted by a butler to whom he was merely a guest, with no taint of Law and Order. Mitchell probably knew, in the omniscient way of butlers, that Mr. Fletcher was a policeman, but such was not his present function.

"Miss Belinda left a message, sir, asking you to go up to say goodnight, but she'll be long asleep by now."

"I'll go up anyway."

"Very good, sir. The family are taking coffee in the drawing room, sir, if you care to join them afterwards."

Mr. Fletcher cared. "You need not wait about. I'll take myself in."

"Very good, sir. I'll inform her ladyship of your arrival."

Bel was fast asleep, not stirring when he kissed her. He went down again and through the door Mitchell had pointed out.

Daisy sprang up, flew to him, and hung on to him, rather tight. As his arms closed around her, he remembered that though the murder was none of *his* business, *she* had suffered the horror of finding the body.

"Oh, Alec," she whispered, "I'm most frightfully glad you're here, darling. It was beastly, but we won't talk about it now, please, for Violet's sake."

He gave her a quick, fierce hug, then went to say his how-do-you-do's. Violet—it was quite easy after all to use her Christian name—poured him coffee. Frobisher added a glass of cognac. They talked about how the children had occupied themselves since Belinda's arrival. To Alec, the Frobishers praise of his daughter was even headier than the smooth old brandy.

After a while, the conversation somehow moved on to tractors and other modern farm machinery. Alec knew nothing of the subject, but he found Frobisher's well-considered views on the effects of mechanization interesting. It was Violet who noticed that Daisy's head was nodding.

"The poor dear has had an exhausting day of it. Come along, Daisy darling, we'll go up and leave the men to their reapers and binders and hop-pickers."

So Alec had no opportunity that evening to talk to Daisy in private. He and his host went out to the terrace to smoke their pipes, chatting casually. Frobisher did not refer to the murder except for voicing, as they parted for the night, a rather incoherent apology for Daisy's involvement.

"Oh, and," he added, "ah, Inspector Flagg hopes you can spare him a few minutes tomorrow. 'Night, Fletcher." With that, he disappeared into his bedroom.

Thus, when Alec awoke early next morning, he had no more knowledge of the business than he had gained in yesterday's two brief telephone calls, when he had spoken only to Violet and the children.

It was too early for breakfast, too early even for early morning tea, but he did not feel like staying in bed. Outside the sun shone. He bathed and dressed, and went to the nursery where breakfast was by then in progress. Belinda was delighted to see him, Derek thrilled. Peter fixed him with an unwinking stare, said "Hello," when prompted, and then returned his full attention to excavating his boiled egg.

The main thing on Belinda's and Derek's minds was what Derek was to call Alec. That settled in favour of "Uncle Alec," to everyone's satisfaction, the day's plans had to be discussed. Alec accepted an invitation to play cricket but declined one to help restore their dam, breached in the rain.

Yesterday's disquieting events seemed utterly forgotten. Much relieved, Alec went down to find his own breakfast.

A young footman directed him to a pleasant, sunny breakfast room. Frobisher was alone there, methodically disposing of a plateful of eggs, sausages, and muffins, while scanning *The Times*. On Alec's entrance, he looked up with a friendly greeting but laid aside his newspaper with scarce concealed reluctance.

"Good morning," Alec responded. "Don't let me interrupt your reading."

"Oh, well, if you don't mind. Somehow I never find time for the paper later in the day. You'll find one or two others on the sideboard there." He waved. "Help yourself, and to breakfast, of course."

"Thank you." Alec selected ham and eggs, coffee, and the *Daily Chronicle,* and seated himself at the table.

Apparently feeling obliged to make some sort of show of polite conversation, Frobisher said, "Violet doesn't come down to breakfast at the moment. She's . . . er, hm . . ." He flushed.

"Oh, is she?" Alec said hastily. Pregnant, he assumed. Funny that a farmer, who presumably discussed cows and bulls, ewes and rams, with the best of them, found it impossible to speak openly of his wife's condition.

"Looks as if Daisy's sleeping in this morning," Frobisher went on. "She's usually an early riser, but yesterday took it out of the poor girl, I'm afraid." He ducked behind his newspaper again.

Alec would have liked to ask for details of yesterday's events, but he could not proceed in the face of his host's evident disinclination. He applied himself to breakfast and the *Chronicle.* Professor Osborne's death had not yet reached the national press, he discovered.

He was still eating when Frobisher folded the *Times* and stood up.

"You'll excuse me, my dear fellow. There's a gelding out in the stables I'm a bit worried about, seems to be going lame. Make yourself at home," he said with a vague gesture encompassing house and lands, and he departed.

Not five minutes later, the footman came in, looking excited. "It's Inspector Flagg, sir, from the police. *Detective* Inspector, he said to be sure and say. Wants a word with you, he says. He questioned me yesterday, sir, acos I helped Miss Dalrymple down the church."

"Did you? Thank you . . . Arthur, isn't it? Yes, I'll see the inspector. If it won't disturb the rest of the household, you can show him in here."

Alec girded his loins for an awkward interview. The

whole situation was extremely irregular, from his original telephone call to the Ashford police, to his presence here. Local police often resented Scotland Yard's official appearance in their cases. Flagg had every excuse for resenting Alec's unofficial arrival.

"Detective Inspector Flagg, sir."

A beanpole of a man came in—a flagpole, Alec thought, wondering if the inspector suffered under that nickname. Flagg's knobby face wore a wilting moustache and a carefully noncommittal expression. His blue eyes were wary.

Standing up, Alec offered his hand. "From the Ashford C.I.D.," he observed perhaps a shade too heartily. "We spoke yesterday."

"I *am* the Ashford C.I.D., sir. We don't get much in the way of crime that a uniformed constable can't handle."

"Lucky man." Definitely too hearty. "Take a seat, Inspector. May I offer you a cup of coffee?"

"I don't mind if I do, sir."

Alec poured coffee and hot milk, passed the sugar. "Look here," he said, deciding there was no point beating about the bush, "I came down because I was worried about my daughter and Miss Dalrymple. You can sympathize with that, I'm sure. I'm on leave. I've no right to interfere in your case, and no intention of trying, I promise you."

"Ah," said Flagg ruminatively, strongly reminding Alec of Tom Tring. He stirred his coffee, sipped, and set down the cup before he spoke further: "I'm glad you said that, sir. Because if you hadn't . . . But there, you have, so I've no scruples about asking your advice on one or two points."

Honest enough to acknowledge he would have hated to be shut out completely, Alec was yet dismayed at the prospective disruption of his precious free days. "I don't see how I can help you, Flagg," he said. "I know damn all about the affair."

The inspector proceeded to enlighten him. "The deceased was . . . I'm afraid the only possible word is squashed," he said distastefully, "by a falling monument in the form of an angel. Dr. Soames, our police surgeon, says he would have died instantly of a broken neck, if not of the other massive injuries. I haven't spoken yet to Dr. Padgett, the first medico on the scene."

"I imagine Padgett will be able to narrow the time of death."

"Not by much, sir, if at all. You see, a number of women would have taken the path through the churchyard on their way to a meeting at the Parish Hall, which began at half past two. I haven't questioned any of them yet, either, but our local man confirms that. They couldn't possibly have avoided seeing the corpse if it was already there. And Miss Dalrymple says she looked at the church clock a minute or two after discovering the body, and it was then five to three. I hope you'll understand, sir, that I had to consider the possibility of Miss Dalrymple having done it."

"Great Scott!" Alec yelped. "Yes, I dare say you did. I sincerely trust you have been able to clear her by now?"

"On the children's evidence, sir," Flagg said cautiously, "and taking into account certain further information she has volunteered, I can say I consider it highly unlikely she is implicated."

"That will have to do for the present, I suppose. What information?"

"I'll come to that in a minute, if you don't mind. First you ought to know that there seems to have been at the outset some question as to whether the vicar or his brother, the professor, had been . . . ah, struck down by the angel." The inspector explained the close resemblance of the two, the question of the hat, the academic gown, and the vicar's eventual arrival, which confirmed Daisy's identification of the deceased.

"So the murderer may have caught the wrong man," Alec said thoughtfully. "It's quite certain the angel didn't fall by accident, is it?"

"It doesn't seem possible, sir, though there's tests to be done. It took four men to raise it off the body, tilting it not lifting it straight up, but the damn thing—if you'll excuse the expression—is so top-heavy it wouldn't have taken much of a push to topple it. You'll be wanting to see it."

"Not me!" Alec disclaimed. "This is your case. I don't want to get mixed up in it. Any dabs?"

Inspector Flagg quickly covered a grin with his hand, smoothing his ochre moustache. "None, sir, and the granite's polished, would have taken them a treat. Gloves, or wiped off."

"Pity. I don't imagine you've had time yet to dig for possible motives."

"No, but that's where Miss Dalrymple's information comes in. She has it all worked out."

"Oh, does she!" Alec said grimly.

"Inclined to theorize, is she?" Flagg asked, his face bland. "Well, now, she's her wits about her, no doubt of it, and I'm obliged to take her notions seriously, for the information behind 'em has been confirmed by an indisputable source. I can see you aren't aware, sir, that Lord John Frobisher invited Miss Dalrymple down here to investigate some anonymous letters he'd been getting."

"He *what?* " Wrath warred with disbelief. He must have misunderstood!

"What the Yankees call Poison Pen letters. I don't know why his lordship should have decided to consult his sister-in-law . . ." Flagg's voice made it a statement, but his eyebrows rose interrogatively.

Discomfited, Alec said, "I assume he thinks she's a

competent detective because he's heard that she got herself involved in one or two of my cases—much against my will, I need not tell you."

"Of course, sir. So Miss Dalrymple agreed to help. Her choice and very obliging, too, but I must say I'd not be best pleased to have one of my little girls mixed up in this sort of business."

"No." What the dickens did Daisy mean by bringing Belinda along?

"Still, it can't be denied Miss Dalrymple was making progress. She gave me the names of two more she knows received these letters, and there's others she suspects of getting or writing 'em. I didn't have time last night to get a list, which is another reason, besides seeing you, why I came to Oakhurst this morning."

"What's the connection with the murder?"

"Oh, didn't I explain? She's got it taped coming and going," Flagg said admiringly, and recounted Daisy's reasoning. "I told her there's more likely some commonplace motive, but the more I think about it, well, it'd be quite a coincidence. Rotherden's measure in the way of crime is mostly poaching, and now and then a bit of a barney outside the Hop-Picker after closing of a Saturday night."

"And suddenly you have both a Poison Pen and a murderer in the village," Alec mused. "No connection between them does seem a bit much to swallow."

"So we have to investigate Miss Dalrymple's theory."

"Yes. For a start, we'll—*you* will want to ask the vicar if he knows who's writing anonymous letters. If he doesn't, the Poison Pen has no known reason for killing him, or his brother in mistake for him."

"Yes, sir. I thought, while I'm up here at Oakhurst, I'd ask Lord John to tell me a bit more about those letters, give me something to go on, if you see what I mean. And I wondered if you'd be so kind as to join us, him being more likely to talk to you than to me."

"I don't know about that, Inspector." Struggling with temptation, Alec spoke quite sharply. "He hardly knows me."

"Who? Johnnie?" Daisy came in.

She looked pale and heavy-eyed, as if she had slept badly. Alec repulsed a pang of sympathy. It was her own fault for agreeing to help Frobisher. He was angry with her for getting herself into such a situation, and furious with her for involving Belinda.

A glimpse of his darkly lowering brows and Daisy was sure he and Flagg were at odds. Though her heart sank, she did her best to smile as she said, "Good morning, Inspector. Good morning, darling. Don't get up. I'm ravenous. All night I kept dreaming of angels, and they weren't the friendly guardian kind. Flaming swords and trumps of doom." She went straight to the sideboard and helped herself to sausages and bacon. Arthur had promised to bring fresh toast and tea.

Flagg returned her greeting. "I was just saying I'm hoping Lord John will give me a bit more information about the letters," he said.

"They're written in pencil," Daisy told him, "in block capitals, on cheap white notepaper. The envelopes match all round. All I know about were posted in the village and Johnnie's have been coming for a couple of months—he can't remember exactly when they started." Turning to sit down at the table, she saw that he had taken out his official notebook to record her words.

"Contents?" he asked briefly.

"Filthy. Badly spelt, but my guess is that they were written by an educated person." She explained why.

"Thank you, ma'am, that's a help, but what I really meant was what did the Poison Pen write *about?*"

"I can't tell you."

"Can't, or won't?" Alec grunted.

"Won't," Daisy said flatly. "You'll have to ask Johnnie and the others. Ah, thanks, Arthur."

"Toast in just a minute, miss," said the footman, setting down teapot and hot water jug in front of her.

Flagg asked him where Lord John was, and decided to go himself to the stables to request an interview. "I'll ask you to give me those names when you've finished your breakfast, Miss Dalrymple," he said. "Chief Inspector, I hope you'll join his lordship and me in the library shortly."

Surprised by this evidence of concord, Daisy turned to Alec. He was scowling at her, the dark, thick eyebrows still frowning. His grey eyes, so capable of freezing a recalcitrant witness, an erring subordinate, or a wretched villain to the marrow with one icicle glance, were now hotly stormy.

"How *could* you bring Belinda down here," he demanded harshly, "when you came expressly to meddle in a crime? Does her safety mean nothing to you?"

"Of course it does!" Daisy cried. "I didn't know there was going to be a murder."

"You knew about the Poison Pen's activities—*not* a desirable environment for a child. And you might have guessed it could lead to violence, especially considering your propensity for falling over bodies."

"I don't *choose* to fall over bodies. Believe me, I most sincerely wish I hadn't found this one!"

"You choose to meddle in what doesn't concern you."

"I just wanted to help Johnnie, for Vi's sake," Daisy said helplessly.

"And your sister's welfare comes before Belinda's!" he accused.

"If that's what you think," she retorted, seething with anger and hurt, "then obviously I'm not a fit mother for her, nor the right wife for you. You'd better take this back." She wrenched off her sapphire engagement ring and dropped it in the middle of the table between them.

Alec flung back his chair and strode from the room.

12

One simply didn't cry in front of the servants. Blinking hard, Daisy stared with loathing at the sparkling sapphire. All that bosh Alec had talked about it being the same colour as her eyes, when he obviously didn't really care about her at all, only about his daughter.

At the sound of footsteps behind her, she snatched the ring up.

"Your toast, miss."

"Thank you, Arthur." Her voice sounded unnaturally calm.

She could not have eaten a bite to save her life. The very thought choked her. While the footman cleared up the men's dirty plates, she swallowed a few sips of tea. As soon as he left, she jumped up, intending to run to her room and cry her heart out.

But Inspector Flagg wanted to see her again. She had promised him information. She wasn't going to withdraw her assistance just because Alec considered her an uncaring, untrustworthy busybody. If nothing else, pride would make her see it through.

Going to the drawing room, she sat down at a small writing table between the windows and took a couple of sheets of paper and an envelope from the drawer. She'd write down a list of suspects for Flagg, so that she did not forget any. But first she put the ring in the envelope, licked and sealed it, and wrote across the front—awkwardly because of the bulge of the ring—*Detective Chief Inspector Fletcher.*

Better deal with it right away, because the tears were gathering in her eyes again. Too maddening! She slipped out into the hall and put the envelope on the salver on the table.

Back at the desk, Daisy took a sheet of writing paper, fine cream bond, watermarked and imprinted with the Oakhurst address, and headed it *Poison Pen.* At the top of the second, she wrote *Victims.* That one was easier to compile. She listed Mrs. LeBeau and Dr. Padgett, then Brigadier Lomax and Mrs. Burden with a question mark each. After the brigadier's name, she put *Johnnie suspects,* in brackets. After Mrs. Burden, she put *postmistress, may be able to name others.*

She hoped Inspector Flagg wouldn't be insulted to be offered such an elementary suggestion.

Professor Osborne topped the Poison Pen list. Next came Mrs. Burden, because she was in Daisy's mind, not because she was especially likely. Miss Prothero quickly followed. Mrs. Lomax, Mrs. Willoughby-Jones, Miss Hendricks, Mr. Paramount—except that he couldn't be the murderer—and who else?

Mr. Paramount's manservant. The Vicarage maid, Doris? Improbable, but put her down, and Mrs. Osborne, too. Mrs. Molesworth? Could her cheerful kindliness hide a bitter venom?

No, Daisy thought, revolted, and crossed out Mrs. Molesworth. She must not let herself be led into casting baseless aspersions in her effort to escape her misery.

After marching out of the breakfast room, Alec barged blindly across the hall and through the first door he came to. He didn't care what room he was in, only that it was empty.

What the dickens had happened? All he'd wanted was to bring Daisy to a sense of responsibility towards Belinda. It was not much to ask. Great Scott, she was going to be Bel's mother, after all!

Or rather, she wasn't, he thought desolately, pacing.

He had had the unbelievable luck to find another woman he could love as much as Joan, and the still more incredible luck to win her—too incredible to be true. Now he had lost her. She had made it perfectly plain she no longer cared for him, if she ever had. Why should an adorable young woman with an Honourable before her name fall in love with a middle-class, middle-aged copper?

Acquitting her of deliberately making a fool of him, he supposed he ought to be glad she had discovered her true feelings before the wedding. But how could he live without her?

As he started on a third or fourth circuit of the room, he realized he was in the library. Flagg and Frobisher would arrive any moment. He couldn't stay here. In fact, he couldn't stay in the house, her sister's house. He no longer had any claim on the Frobishers' hospitality, and no professional duty obliged him to assist Flagg. He and Belinda must leave at once.

The sooner Belinda was out of here the better. Daisy had been *mad* to bring her. Heading for the stairs to find her, he began to wonder just what Frobisher had done to make himself the target of an anonymous letter writer.

Alec found his daughter sooner than he expected. She was sitting on a step half way up the first flight, sobbing her heart out. Peter sat beside her, his round face doleful, patting her knee. The dog, Tinker, was trying to lick her face, and Derek hovered over her, shifting anxiously from foot to foot.

"Bel, don't take on so," he pleaded. "They'll get it sorted out, honestly."

Cursing himself for believing for a moment that she had forgotten the murder, Alec leapt up the stairs. How could Daisy have embroiled her in such a nightmare?

"Sweetheart, it's all right, we're going home. Once we're far away, you'll forget all about it, you'll see. Come on, let's go and ask Nurse to pack your things."

Belinda glared at him with red-rimmed, tear-swollen eyes and wailed, "But I don't *want* to go! If we go, I'll maybe never see her again, and I want her to be my *mummy!*"

"Good lord!" Alec groaned. Running his hand through his hair, he looked down at her, then firmly moved the dog, sat down, and put his arm around her. Tinker licked his cheek.

Before he could gather his thoughts, Belinda said accusingly, "Derek says you quarrelled with Aunt Daisy, and you're not going to marry her."

"I wasn't eavesdropping," Derek defended himself. "I was going to ask when you'd like to play cricket and I couldn't help hearing. Aunt Daisy said 'You'd better take this back,' and then you came out—I don't think you saw me—and I peeked in and saw her blue ring on the table, which she *never* takes off. So I thought Bel ought to know," he finished in a self-righteous tone.

"Daddy, can't you tell her you're sorry?" Bel asked urgently.

Alec sighed, feeling like an absolute ass. The loss of Daisy would be far more damaging to Belinda than proximity to any number of murders, he realized. She had been too young when Joan died in the great influenza pandemic to remember much of her mother, but she remembered enough to know something was missing. Her grandmother did her best, but she was elderly and old-fashioned, with a Victorian fear of spoiling the child by too great a display of affection. No wonder Bel adored Daisy.

Almost as much as Alec did. Infuriating, yes, impulsive and sometimes imprudent in her loyalties, inclined to interfere in matters which were none of her affair, but always warmhearted . . .

"Ahem!" The butlerian cough emanated from Mitchell, who stood at the foot of the stairs, a silver salver in his hand. "A . . . hm . . . a communication for you, sir. It was on the hall table."

"I'll get it, Uncle Alec." Derek bounded down and returned to hand over an envelope.

The bulge gave away the contents. The superscription, Alec's official title in full, gave away the sender's frame of mind.

"It's Aunt Daisy's ring, isn't it," Belinda said, and bit her lip, fresh tears beginning to trickle down her freckled cheeks.

"Don't cry, sweetheart, I'll see what I can do." Alec ripped open the envelope, his heart sinking as he saw there was no note enclosed, no hint as to the best way to approach a reconciliation. "Mitchell, do you know where Miss Dalrymple is?"

"In the drawing room, I believe, sir."

Alec kissed Belinda and commended her into Derek's care. Starting down the stairs, he felt rather as if he were back in his fragile canvas and piano-wire observation plane, crossing the front line into dangerous territory.

As he set foot on the bottom step, he was hailed.

"Hullo, Fletcher," Frobisher said with a distinctly apprehensive glance back at Flagg, a pace behind. "The inspector says you're taking a hand in this ticklish business."

"Not officially." Alec cursed silently. Another thirty seconds and he'd have been with Daisy. But she wouldn't be pleased if he abandoned her brother-in-law in his hour of need. "And only if you want me."

"Well, yes, I think so." Noticing the listening children, Frobisher told them to run along, and turned back to Alec. "Yes, please do. After all, I've told Daisy everything, and you know the form, old man."

The latter phrase, Alec presumed, meant Frobisher trusted him, unlike Flagg, to comport himself as a gentleman. That was encouraging—if Daisy would take back the ring. He wanted to go to her, but instead he accompanied the others into the library.

Having made up his mind to take the bull by the horns, Frobisher—to mix a metaphor—did not beat about the bush. "Though I'm a magistrate," he said with dignity, "I don't know much about police methods in this sort of case. Flagg assures me the information I provide may help to catch a murderer. I need hardly say I'm sure you will do your utmost to keep it confidential."

"No guarantees," Alec warned, "but we certainly won't pass on anything unless it becomes absolutely necessary."

"Well, I can't see why it should. Right-ho, here goes. The fact is, I had a . . . Oh lord, I don't know what to call it. Affair, liaison—they imply too much." He explained, tersely, not naming the lady who had led him astray. Alec understood why Daisy had forgiven his brief unfaithfulness to her sister, and he wondered whether she knew the woman involved.

"May we see the letters, please?" he said. "Oh, sorry, Inspector, your call."

"If you please, sir," Flagg said to Frobisher.

"Yes, of course, I just wanted to tell you first what actually happened, so that you wouldn't assume something worse." He unlocked a drawer in his desk and handed Alec several sheets of paper.

Alec passed them to Flagg, accepting them back from the inspector one by one as he finished studying them.

"Just as Miss Dalrymple described them," grunted Flagg. "Nasty bit of work."

"Thoroughly nasty," Alec agreed shortly. How could Frobisher have let Daisy read such filth?

All the same, he had to agree with the conclusions Daisy had drawn from the letters, as reported by Flagg. She did have a certain flair for the detection business, for drawing reasonable conclusions, whether logical or intuitive, from the evidence. And that was quite apart from her extraordinary talent for drawing out confidences.

He recalled her interference in previous cases, meddlesome, certainly, but not infrequently helpful, he had to admit. If only she would submit to some sort of discipline while she exercised her abilities! It was a pity there was no worthwhile place for women in the police, let alone in the criminal investigation branch.

Folding the anonymous letters, Alec gave them back to Flagg, who picked out one, returned it to Frobisher, and tucked the rest into his inside pocket. "Here's the 'magistrate' one, sir. The rest—there's no way to connect them to you—we'll hang on to for evidence."

"If you don't need this, I'll burn it. I'm heartily glad to be rid of them," Frobisher said with obvious relief. "I'm sorry I can't remember just when I received the first."

"A pity, but thank you for your cooperation, my lord." Flagg moved towards the library door.

Alec started to follow, but Frobisher held him back.

"Not a bad chap," he said in a low voice. "I'm afraid you must think me a frightful bounder, Fletcher, what with one thing and another."

"I could wish you hadn't invited Daisy to investigate," Alec said candidly, "but we all make mistakes and lord knows I'm in no position to cast stones."

"Things were so much simpler in the trenches." Frobisher was wistful, almost nostalgic. "One knew where one was, even if it was hell. Well, I'd better burn this right away."

He turned back to the fireplace and Alec went after Flagg.

The inspector was waiting for him just outside the library door. "Not a bad chap," he said, in an unconscious echo of Frobisher's judgement of him. "I told you the bailiff cleared him of the murder. We'll get those names from Miss Dalrymple now."

Alec froze. This was his punishment for letting Frobisher believe they were soon to be related! He could not decently back out of the investigation now. Still more impossible to explain to Flagg that he and Daisy were no longer on speaking terms. What the dickens was she going to think if he went in and started talking about the Poison Pen, casually, as if she had not just kicked him out of her life?

Too late. Flagg, about to enter the drawing room, glanced back to see what was keeping Alec. Joining the inspector, he waved him first through the door.

Daisy looked round. "I have your lists, Inspector," she said brightly, before she saw Alec behind him.

The unmitigated gall of the man! Waltzing in under Flagg's auspices as if he had not hurled horrible accusations against her not an hour ago! He ought to have whisked Belinda away by now, far from Daisy's baleful influence.

She would not show him she cared. Not looking at him, she handed her two lists to Inspector Flagg, who quickly scanned them.

"Thank you, Miss Dalrymple. I'd like to ask you one or two questions."

"Of course. Do sit down," she invited with a gesture Alec might interpret to include him if he chose. He did, but took a chair farther from her than Flagg's.

"Mrs. LeBeau, now," said the inspector. "You mentioned her last night, and I had a word with Barton about her. She's the lady lives right at the bottom of the drive? The one Lord John . . . er . . . erred with, shall we say?"

"He told you? How ungentlemanly!"

"Oh no, ma'am, Lord John's too honourable a gentleman to give the lady's name. However, he did describe the circumstances, which, with what Barton told me, led to the fairly obvious conclusion you have just confirmed." He gave her his bland smile. "Mrs. LeBeau's in a good position to blackmail him, yet you haven't listed her as a possible Poison Pen."

"No," Daisy said shortly, annoyed with him for tricking her, particularly in Alec's presence. But further explanation was called for, even if it led Alec to accuse her of "taking Mrs. LeBeau under her wing," as she had others in past cases. "I realize getting letters could be camouflage for sending them, but she just isn't the sort to write such scurrilous stuff."

She felt Alec's sceptical gaze upon her, but he didn't speak.

"Is she the sort to bump off the professor," Flagg asked bluntly, "if he was the writer? She lives right across from the churchyard, with a good view of comings and goings."

Daisy hesitated. It was much easier to imagine Wanda LeBeau calmly disposing of a menace than composing vulgar letters. "I don't see how she'd ever have found out it was Professor Osborne," Daisy said. "She doesn't care for village gossip, and Mrs. Osborne strongly disapproves of her, so she wouldn't call socially at the Vicarage."

"Any more questions about the lady, sir?" Flagg asked Alec.

From the corner of her eye, Daisy saw him shake his head. Under normal circumstances he would have pressed her for every little detail she knew about a suspect, so he must be feeling awkward, she was glad to note. Why was he staying? Did he find the case so fascinating, he would even sacrifice his daughter's perceived welfare to his curiosity? If so, he had a nerve denouncing Daisy for bringing Bel with her!

"Right, Dr. Padgett next, Miss Dalrymple. He was out last night when I went to see him about his examination of the body."

Daisy told about finding the envelope in the doctor's car.

"Did he realize you'd seen it?" Alec asked sharply.

"He'd have no reason to suppose I'd have the slightest idea what was in it, Mr. Fletcher," Daisy pointed out, her tone frosty. Not for the world would she confess to her fears at the time, or later, in the churchyard.

"Brigadier Lomax?" Flagg read.

"I've no evidence, just Johnnie's guess from something the brigadier said. Which reminds me, I heard Sam Basin's mother talking about a letter he got which upset him no end. They're village people, but he's a mechanic at a garage in Ashford."

"Sam-u-el Basin," said Flagg, writing. "And Mrs. Burden? She's the village postmistress, sir, and the shopkeeper, too, if I'm not mistaken."

"I had quite a chat with her," Daisy said, "and I'm convinced she knows something. You'll see I put her on both lists. Her daughter probably hears all the gossip, too, come to think of it."

"We'll bear that in mind, ma'am. And we'll ask Mrs. Burden about other possible victims, as you suggest."

Daisy flashed a glance of triumph at Alec. The infuriating man was looking at his wrist-watch.

Flagg noticed, and consulted his own. "You're right, sir, we'd better get moving before people start going out for the day. We'll just go over this list of possible Poison Pens quickly, Miss Dalrymple, if you'd be so kind as to tell us briefly why you suspect each person. Professor

Osborne we know about. Mrs. Burden—I'll add her daughter. Miss Prothero?"

"She lives next door to Mrs. LeBeau, so could have seen Johnnie that once, and spied on Mrs. LeBeau in general. Besides, she's one of the Vicarage scandal circle, and she has a very sharp tongue."

"Vicarage scandal circle?"

"Tea and gossip with the vicar's wife. Mrs. Lomax, Miss Hendricks, Mrs. Willoughby-Jones—but she has no qualms about attacking people head on, so why write letters? Likewise, Mrs. Osborne herself. She had every chance to observe Johnnie and Mrs. LeBeau, and to hear all the Rotherden gossip, but she practically runs the village single-handed. I'd think she was too busy and too much in control already to bother with anonymous letters. And if she did, and her husband found out, I doubt she'd have anything to fear from him. Who else did I list?"

"Mr. Paramount," Flagg read.

"Oh, yes, Johnnie's disgruntled uncle, lives in the gatehouse, but far too frail to have committed the murder. I really put him and his servant down because they could have seen Johnnie at Mrs. LeBeau's gate, and the daily help actually told me she retails all the village gossip to the old man."

"Might have seen something in the graveyard yesterday afternoon, too. We'll talk to them."

"But lord knows how many other people get all the gossip from their servants," Daisy sighed. "There could be dozens of possible suspects I've never even heard of."

"I'd say you've done a pretty thorough job, considering, Miss Dalrymple. Wouldn't you agree, Chief Inspector?"

"Miss Dalrymple's gift for getting to know people constantly amazes me," Alec said in a noncommittal voice. Daisy could not quite find anything in his comment to take exception to.

"Just two more here," said Flagg. "Doris, the maid at the Vicarage."

"Cross her out. She's virtually illiterate."

"And one you've already crossed out."

"Oh, Mrs. Molesworth. She seems to frequent the Vicarage, but she's far too good-natured to write that filth. You know, Inspector, the trouble with all of them is that even if the professor avoided them, as I believe he did, they all know the vicar too well to misidentify him."

"I shouldn't worry, ma'am. You'd be surprised, I dare say, how many people are too vain to wear glasses when they need 'em. It's easily tested for. Now, sir, we'll see the vicar first, as you suggested, shall we?"

"Yes," said Alec, jumping energetically to his feet, "and, if he can't help us, Mrs. LeBeau next as she lives opposite. I think, Inspector, it would be a good idea to take Miss Dalrymple with us to see Mrs. LeBeau, as she has already won the lady's confidence."

Daisy stared at him, astounded, as Flagg said dubiously, "If you say so, sir."

"I do, assuming Mrs. LeBeau agrees. You don't need me to go with you to see Osborne, though. You drive down, so as not to waste time, and Miss Dalrymple and I will walk down to meet you."

"If you say so, sir," Flagg repeated with an air of enlightenment, "I'll be on my way."

The inspector departed, and Daisy rounded on Alec. "But you're always trying to *stop* me getting involved," she said suspiciously. "What are you up to?"

"Flagg's so keen to involve *me,* it was the only way I could think of to grab a moment to talk to you privately."

"I knew you didn't really want me to join in the interview. There's nothing to talk about." She turned her back and pretended to busy herself at the desk.

"Daisy, please, give me a chance." He sounded desperate. "How can I make you understand if you won't listen?"

"All right. But come on or Flagg might not wait for us."

She stood up as she spoke, pushing back her chair and turning. He was disconcertingly close behind her. She stumbled. He caught her in his arms. Her resistance crumbled instantly.

After all, she thought when conscious thought returned a few minutes later, what more could one ask by way of an apology?

But it wouldn't do to let him get away with anything. She gave him a last, quick kiss and said, "Come on, darling, we can talk on the way down the avenue."

"Hoist by my own petard," he said with a rueful grimace, but he followed her to the door. "I'm afraid Flagg's opinion of Scotland Yard took a nose-dive when I proposed including you in the interview with Mrs. LeBeau. Daisy, it's obvious you've taken a liking to the woman, but don't, please, let it—"

He stopped as three small figures confronted them. Belinda seized Daisy's left hand. Her face crumpled.

"You haven't put the ring back on!" she grieved.

"Only because I haven't had time," Daisy assured her as Alec hastily retrieved the torn envelope from his pocket.

He took out the ring, slipped it onto her finger, and kept hold of her hand.

"That's better," said Derek. "Now you can jolly well stop crying, Bel. Uncle Alec, when will you play cricket with us?"

"I'm not sure, old man, and I don't want to promise what I can't perform. We'll manage it sometime, but your aunt and I have to go out now."

"Walking?" Bel asked. "We'll go with you to the gates."

"Not this time, darling," said Daisy, giving her a hug. "We still have some talking to do."

"Well," Belinda said severely, "next time you squabble with Daddy, don't give him back the ring!"

Inspector Flagg's black police Ford was parked in the lane near the lych-gate. The inspector stood on the doorstep of the lodge, just inside the Oakhurst gates, talking to a small, aged man with the wrinkled face of a monkey.

As Daisy and Alec approached, they heard Flagg say, "Here's the people I'm waiting for, Mr. Popper, so I'll be thanking you for your assistance and bidding you good-day."

Mr. Popper squeaked something and popped back into the house like a startled rabbit. The door closed, but did not click shut. Daisy felt eyes upon her through the crack.

"No luck," said Flagg. "Mr. Paramount sleeps afternoons, and Popper takes his chance to nap. Ancient as the blooming hills, both of 'em." Noticing Daisy and Alec's still-linked hands, he nodded with his blandest smile.

Alec promptly dropped Daisy's hand. "Er . . . ah . . . and what about the vicar?" he asked.

"Out. Parish visits. A clergyman can't take a day off just because of a family tragedy, or so Mrs. Osborne informs me. She seems pretty shaken still, so I didn't try to find out if she'd come across any evidence which might link the professor with the letters. Are you all right, Miss Dalrymple? Sure you want to see Mrs. LeBeau with us?"

"Yes, it's not that," Daisy said as Alec turned to her with concern. She must look as pale as she felt. "I just thought, suppose the murderer for some reason suspected Professor Osborne of being the Poison Pen but was wrong?"

The men glanced at each other. "Then he—or she—might try again," said Alec.

"Specially if a new lot of letters turn up," Flagg agreed uneasily. "We'd better get a move on!"

13

Mrs. LeBeau received Daisy and the two detectives in her rose arbour. She apologized for the informality of the setting.

"I was reading out here," she said, gesturing to the Michael Arlen novel lying on the table. "I hate to waste a fine day indoors, but we can go in to the drawing room, if you prefer. I realize you're here on business, gentlemen. And you, Miss Dalrymple?"

"I'm only here if you'd like me to stay. Since I already know pretty much what you have to tell them, the chief inspector thought you might be more comfortable if I came with them."

"I don't need my hand held," said Mrs. LeBeau with a laugh, "but it was a kind thought and by all means stay."

Alec and Flagg opted to stay out in the garden, sunny but still fresh. They refused coffee, pleading haste. Daisy began to regret missing breakfast, but she too felt the increased sense of urgency caused by her latest conjecture. She didn't want to delay the men, even if they consented to wait for her—which they wouldn't. Now that she had a toe in the door, with both Alec's and the inspector's concurrence, she wasn't going to let herself be shut out of the investigation without a fight.

"All I've told them," she said, "is that you've had

anonymous letters, but they know about . . . you and
Johnnie, too." As Mrs. LeBeau's flawlessly plucked
arches drew together in surprised disapprobation, Daisy
quickly added, *"He* didn't tell them, either. They're detectives, after all."

"Have you any idea, ma'am," Flagg broke in, taking
out his notebook, "who wrote the letters?"

"Not the least notion."

"You couldn't guess from the contents? May I ask
what they said?"

Colour darkened Mrs. LeBeau's face, though she was
well made-up, perhaps in anticipation of the police visit.
"As a police officer investigating a murder," she said
tartly, "you may ask what you please, I suppose. The letters accuse me, in the vilest language, of promiscuity.
It's not true, incidentally, in the strict sense of the
word—the definition reads something like: indefinite
polyandry joined with polygyny, as among some races
of low civilization."

"Which naturally excludes the English," Daisy put in
dryly.

"Naturally. However, I'm afraid that is the reputation
I bear in the village, so anyone could have written the
letters."

"Have you tried to find out who it was?" Flagg asked,
his tone a trifle sharp to Daisy's ears.

"No. I don't much care." Glancing from the open
incredulity on Flagg's long face to Alec's polite interest, she sighed and explained. "The letters are
unpleasant, but so far there has been nothing like
blackmail or threats of exposure. If it came to that, I
might find it more comfortable to move away. I'd be
sorry to go, to leave my roses, my little house, and
some pleasant acquaintances, but nothing ties me here.
I wasn't brought up in this area; no family connec-
tions."

Inspector Flagg, who had probably spent his entire

life in Ashford and environs, looked nonplussed. Alec took over.

"Then I take it your . . . uh . . . non-family connection doesn't reside in the neighbourhood?"

Mrs. LeBeau smiled appreciation of his tact. "No, Chief Inspector. He is in London all week. I have a flat in town, and he often comes down here for weekends, alone or with friends, though he has a country house elsewhere."

"Am I right in supposing he would suffer a great deal more than you from exposure of your liaison?"

"Yes. Therefore, if the letters started to make that kind of threat, I should inform him and let him deal with it. We are . . . fond of each other, but I certainly shouldn't murder to protect him, even if I knew who wrote them. Was it Professor Osborne?"

"Sorry, I can't answer that," said Alec, truthfully if misleadingly. "May we see your letters?"

"I destroyed them." At Alec's request, she described the letters' physical appearance. As far as she could recall, the longer words were misspelt, the rest correct, as in Johnnie's. "Deliberate mistakes?" she asked.

"Another question I can't answer," Alec said, smiling. He looked at Flagg.

"Deliberate mistakes such as you yourself would make," Flagg suggested stolidly, "to divert suspicion if you wrote such letters?"

"If I did, I might, I suppose, but I assure you I've never had the least desire to express myself in that way."

"Then you won't object if we take a look through your desk?"

Mrs. LeBeau frowned. "I object in the sense that I thoroughly dislike it, but not in the sense that I refuse permission."

"I dare say we'll find there the name and address of your gentleman friend."

"Certainly not. I keep nothing with his full name on it.""

"Then I'll ask you to oblige me with the information now." Flagg's pencil poised over his notebook.

"That's one *I* can't answer," Mrs. LeBeau said adamantly, "or won't, rather. His position is extremely sensitive. You must allow ladies the same sense of honour you expect of gentlemen."

As Flagg opened his mouth to insist, Alec intervened. "I think we can manage without for the present, Inspector." He met Flagg's annoyed gaze with a slight shake of the head. "But I must warn you, ma'am, we may ask again at a later date."

"And require an answer," said Flagg, tight-lipped. "Where were you between two and three-thirty yesterday afternoon, Mrs. LeBeau?"

"Until about three, out here, cutting off spent blooms. They stop flowering if one doesn't."

"Alone?"

"Yes," Mrs. LeBeau said soberly. "My gardener only comes mornings. But shortly after three, my maid called me in to take a telephone call. I was talking to a friend for the next half hour or so. I'll willingly give you her name and address."

But the professor was dead by five to three. The Merry Widow had no alibi.

On the way out, Flagg asked the maid, Alice, whether she had seen her mistress in the garden between two and three. She had not, being busy with some mending upstairs at the front—too busy, also, to have looked out into the lane or the churchyard opposite. On the other hand, having no cause to speak to Mrs. LeBeau before the telephone rang at three, Alice had not searched and failed to find her in the garden. Nor were cheap white envelopes and writing paper unearthed in the desk.

"Pity," grunted the inspector as he and Alec and

Daisy went out to the lane. "We might have nabbed her."

"Why don't you like her?" Daisy asked, settling on her curls the straw hat Mrs. LeBeau had insisted on lending to cover her bare head. She hadn't been thinking about hats when she and Alec left Oakhurst.

"I don't hold with that sort of carrying-on." Glancing back, Flagg added sourly, "The wages of sin is a nice house in the country and a flat in London."

"Actually, she inherited money from her husband," Daisy informed him. "And I bet you didn't turn up your nose at Johnnie because—"

"Daisy!" Alec warned. "Flagg, I owe you an apology. I had the impression that her lover is very likely a genuinely important man, and in my view his name won't help us, at least as yet. However, it's your case, and if you want to send me to Jericho, I'll go quietly."

"You can't say fairer than that." Flagg pondered for a moment. "No, on the whole I'll be glad of your assistance, sir. Do you want to make it official?"

"Heaven forbid!" said Alec. Daisy guessed he had in mind the Metropolitan Police Assistant Commissioner for Crime whose hair—according to Alec—stood on end at the thought of Daisy mixed up in a case. "Unless it seems a good idea later on," Alec qualified his response. "Who do you want to see next?"

"Dr. Padgett, I think, sir, before Mrs. Burden. Miss Dalrymple's certain he had at least one letter, and it's about time I got his report on his inspection of the body. Also, it's his surgery hours, so we'll find him at home. He lives down the bottom of the green. We'll drive so as not to waste time. I'll run you up to the house first, Miss Dalrymple," he added, crossing the lane to the Ford.

"Thank you, Inspector, but I'll drop in at the Vicarage to see if there's anything I can do to help." As he stooped to crank the engine, she added innocently, "If you're quite sure you don't need the rest of my information about the doctor and Mrs. Burden, and the other people on the lists?"

Alec raised laughing grey eyes to heaven, but forbore to intervene. Flagg cranked the engine to life, then straightened with a sigh. He glanced from Daisy, who smiled sweetly, to Alec and back.

Sighing again, he opened the car door and said, "All right, hop in."

Daisy hopped.

On the way, she pointed out the dwellings of Miss Prothero, Sam Basin, and Mrs. Molesworth. Turning right down the near side of the village green, Flagg asked impatiently, "But what about Dr. Padgett? What's this vital information I need before talking to him?"

"Actually, I was thinking more of Mrs. Burden," Daisy admitted. "The doctor is a charming gentleman, with a practice which includes the best people—best meaning superior in birth and fortune, not necessarily in character, of course. My sister says he also does a great deal of panel work, though."

"Sounds like an exemplary character," said Alec, ironically.

"Been getting anonymous letters," Flagg pointed out. "Maybe he's a wife-beater or a secret toper."

"Or he wasn't always so exemplary," Daisy suggested. "A doctor's in a delicate position. If he loses his patients' trust, he loses his livelihood."

The Ford stopped opposite the duck pond on the lower corner of the green, in front of a large Georgian house veiled with neatly trimmed Virginia creeper. A gleaming brass plate on one brick gatepost announced Old Well House; a second, on the other post, gave the doctor's name and surgery hours.

"You'll wait here, Daisy," Alec decreed in his no-nonsense voice. "You're the only one who can swear to Padgett's having received a letter, and I don't want him to have the least inkling of where we got our information."

Though Daisy felt quite safe now that he was here, the memory of her former fears stopped the protest on her tongue. She even tilted her hat forward and turned away her head, feigning fascination with a pair of white ducks and a plump grey goose on the pond, while Alec and Flagg walked up the short drive.

They were back in a couple of minutes. "Padgett's been called out to an emergency," said Alec, getting back into the car.

Flagg cranked again. "Tell us about Mrs. Burden, Miss Dalrymple," he invited when he took his place behind the wheel.

As they drove around the bottom of the green, past the station road and the Hop-Picker, and up the other side, Daisy described her chat with the postmistress. She became more and more convinced the woman was hiding something. "It could be that she felt she ought not to have talked about Post Office business, but she got jolly nervous and cut me off pretty sharply in the end."

"You led her on to say more than she meant to," said Flagg with a hint of admiration, "and quite neatly."

"She must hear loads of gossip in the shop," Daisy pointed out, "so she'd have the material to write the letters. I should think she must be well enough educated to write correctly, or she couldn't run the business, but I don't know that it would occur to her to deliberately spell wrong."

"No, that's rather a sophisticated touch," Alec agreed.

"And the way she talked wasn't really as if she'd written them herself. So more likely she's been getting them. Either that, or her daughter has, unless she suspects her daughter wrote them. Winifred's the sulky, grudge-against-the-world sort who might, and she runs the telephone exchange so she must hear all sorts of things, if she listens in."

"As most of 'em do," said Flagg cynically. "Amazing what folks'll say on the telephone, knowing perfectly well there's a pair of ears in the circuit."

"All very true," Alec said dryly, "but could either of them have left the shop for long enough to murder Professor Osborne? When's early closing?"

"Today," said Daisy, vexed with herself for missing the obvious. "The exchange doesn't close down, of course."

Flagg was unruffled. "Well, that's as may be, and two suspects the fewer's all to the good. But Mrs. Burden told you she'd noticed those envelopes, and with any luck she'll remember at least some of the people they were addressed to." He drew up in front of the shop.

"Shall I come in?" Daisy asked, dying to but not wanting to press her luck. "Unlike Mrs. LeBeau, Mrs. Burden didn't unbosom herself to me. She isn't exactly going to fall on my neck."

Inspector Flagg regarded her, his face bland but for the twinkle in his eye, very reminiscent of the way Tom Tring generally looked at her. Daisy decided he was beginning to get her measure.

"What do you reckon, sir?" he said to Alec. "It seems to me, Mrs. Burden will deny everything, likely as not, unless we have Miss Dalrymple on hand to remind her of what she said about the envelopes."

"As you choose, Inspector," Alec said with a wry smile. "But Daisy, you stay out of things unless you're needed."

"Yes, Chief," said Daisy.

They went into the shop. Mrs. Burden was at the Post Office counter, registering a letter for a stout, smart matron she addressed as Mrs. Lympne. Daisy recognized her from a previous visit, when she and her husband had dined at Oakhurst. Not wanting to get caught in a chat, Daisy went to the other counter and started looking through the box of picture postcards. She glanced round as someone else stepped up to the counter.

"Mrs. Gresham, how do you do! I've been hoping to see you, to apologize for not turning up at the meeting."

The farmer's wife smiled at her. "From what I hear, you have every excuse in the world, Miss Dalrymple. I'm sorry, though. I was looking forward to hearing your talk. Another time, perhaps."

"Win, come and lend a hand," Mrs. Burden called just then. Daisy looked back to see Mrs. Lympne's back departing and Alec and Flagg standing at the Post Office counter.

Winifred slouched through from the exchange. "Who's first?" she enquired uninterestedly.

"Help Mrs. Gresham," Daisy said. "I haven't made up my mind yet."

"I'll take a box of puppy worming pills, please."

"Mu-um, where're the worming pills?"

But Mum was leading the detectives into the storeroom at the back. Regretfully Daisy decided she had better wait until called.

"They're over there, down near the bottom." Mrs. Gresham leaned forward and pointed at the shelves behind the counter. "The white box with 'Padgett's' in blue and a picture of a dog."

Winifred crouched with a grunt, rose with a groan, and slapped a small box on the counter. "Tenpence ha'penny."

The picture looked just like Tinker Bell. An idea occurred to Daisy. "You have puppies?" she asked.

"Five, in need of homes." Mrs. Gresham handed over a shilling and dropped her penny ha'penny change in her purse. "I don't know what Ellie found to mate with but they're no good as farm dogs. My Amos is too soft-hearted to drown them, I'm glad to say."

"No promises," said Daisy, "but if Alec—my fiancé—agrees, I'll bring my stepdaughter-to-be to see them."

"Miss Dalrymple!" Flagg stood at the store-room door. "If you wouldn't mind stepping this way?"

Daisy most certainly wouldn't mind. She said a hurried good-bye to Mrs. Gresham, and followed the inspector into a small room even more crammed with goods of every size, shape, and description than the shop. Just inside the door, Mrs. Burden sat on a cardboard box labelled BOURNEVILLE COCOA, stacked on another marked COLMAN'S MUSTARD. Looking frightened but stubborn, she let out a little gasp when she saw Daisy.

Alec, leaning against the nearest shelves, towered over her. "Mrs. Burden seems to have had a lapse of memory, Miss Dalrymple," he said. "I hope you can jog it for us."

Daisy sat down on a box of Lifebuoy soap. "You talk to so many people every day, Mrs. Burden," she said encouragingly, "you can't possibly remember every conversation. We were chatting about how badly written addresses often are. You mentioned as an example those in pencil, which are hard to read even when they're written in capitals. And you said they're infrequent, but that recently—"

"Oh *those* letters!" Mrs. Burden seized on the excuse to get out of the corner she had painted herself into with her flat denial of all knowledge. "What about them?"

"We want to know," said Flagg, "who they were addressed to."

"I don't know that I ought . . ."

"We can get a warrant."

"Oh no!" The shopkeeper looked as if she might faint.

"Not an arrest warrant," Daisy said quickly, "just some sort of official permission for you to tell the police."

"That's right, ma'am, but it'd waste time, and there's a murderer on the loose."

Though hardly reassured by this announcement, Mrs. Burden pulled herself together. "I'm sure I don't want to obstruct the police. Let me think. Well, there was Lord John for one, I'm sorry to say, miss. And that Mrs. Willoughby-Jones who thinks she's so superior, always carping at other people. Mrs. LeBeau, Miss Prothero that's her next-door neighbour, Miss Hendricks . . . Let me see. Oh, Brigadier Lomax and that writer he let his cottage to. And the doctor, I'm sorry to say. That's all that comes to mind just now, but I think there's more."

"Yourself?" said Flagg.

"No!"

Flagg glanced at Alec, who shook his head slightly and asked, "Have you any idea who might have written the letters, ma'am?"

"The amount of gossip in this village," said Mrs. Burden bitterly, "it could've been anyone."

So she *did* get one, Daisy thought, while the inspector asked when the first lot of letters had been posted. That question, she realized, everyone had forgotten to pose to Mrs. LeBeau.

"First I noticed was the middle of July. You'll have to let me go now," Mrs. Burden insisted as the bell in the shop rang. "I've customers to be seen to."

"Just one more question, for now. Where were you yesterday afternoon between two o'clock and half past three?"

"Here, where d'you think?" She pushed past him, calling, "I'll be right with you!"

"Should we talk to the girl?" Flagg asked Alec.

"Not now, I think. Mrs. Burden has given us plenty to be getting on with. We can always come back later. Let's try the doctor again. His nurse thought he wouldn't be gone long."

They went out through the shop. Mrs. Burden, busy with a customer, did not so much as glance their way.

In the car, Daisy said, "I'm sure she got a letter, and whoever wrote it, she blames it on Mrs. Willoughby-Jones."

"Oh, undoubtedly," Alec agreed, "but I see no need to press the poor woman about it unless we get no lead elsewhere. What can you tell us about Mrs. Willoughby-Jones?"

"She's one of the Vicarage tea-and-scandal set." Daisy described the forthright termagant. "Whatever she found out about Mrs. Burden, she would have taxed her with it to her face, and tattled to the rest of the old cats."

Flagg stopped the Ford outside Old Well House again. This time Dr. Padgett's Humber stood in the drive. "Caught him," said the inspector with satisfaction. "You coming in, Miss Dalrymple? Now we have another source of information about his letters, you're quite safe, wouldn't you say, sir?"

"I dare say, but there's no good reason to give for her presence."

"I'll think of something. Miss Dalrymple's got insight, sir, and I'd give a deal to hear what she makes of his story."

Daisy did her best to look modest.

Alec resignedly assented, and they went into the doctor's waiting room. The sole occupant, a shabby, weatherbeaten old man bent with rheumatics, glared at them. "We'll wait our turn," Flagg soothed him. From the inner room came a baby's wail.

Ten minutes later, Padgett was free. If he was surprised to see Daisy, he did not show it. He was all charm to her, man to man with Alec—introduced as both her fiancé and a Scotland Yard detective—and gravely professional with Flagg, as he ushered them through to the private side of the house, into an elegant, expensively furnished drawing room. The voices of small children came from the garden beyond the open windows.

"I need your medical report on the murdered gentleman, sir," Flagg opened, "but first we'd like to make sure your recollection of your movements in the graveyard chimes with Miss Dalrymple's."

Padgett smiled at Daisy. "Miss Dalrymple was most particular that I must be careful not to destroy any clues." He described circling between the tombstones, crouching by the professor's head, returning by the same route. Then, before she could stop him, he divulged her sudden faintness and his supporting her to the church porch.

"Daisy, you never told me!" Alec exploded.

"You couldn't expect me to admit to being such a frightful drip," she retorted. "Anyway, it was only for a moment. Dr. Padgett offered to go to the Vicarage to tell the vicar—"

"So you were quite certain of the identity of the deceased, sir?"

"Not absolutely, no," Padgett said, "but if I'd found the vicar at home it would have become obvious. I told Barton I was going, went, found Osborne out, and returned to Miss Dalrymple. I had my rounds to do, so I couldn't wait for your arrival, Inspector."

No word of his dash to escape Mrs. Osborne, Daisy noted.

He gave his medical report next. Daisy tried not to listen to the details, giving her attention to a magnificent, green-eyed, silver Persian which strolled in just then. Going straight to Padgett, it leapt into his lap, and he fondled its ears as he spoke. The main part of his evidence was that when he examined the body, at about twenty past three, Professor Osborne had been dead for at least half an hour but not more than an hour.

"That agrees with our other information, sir," said Flagg. "You'll understand that I have to ask where you were between two and three o'clock yesterday. Just routine."

"I left Lower Foxwood Farm at five past two. I noticed particularly because I was reckoning how long a nap I'd have time for, having been up half the night. I must have got home by twenty-five past at the latest— I spoke to our parlourmaid, Nancy, she might know. Went straight upstairs, took off my shoes and jacket, and slept like a log till the call came through from young Master Derek just after three."

Thirty-five minutes to dash up to the church, bump off the professor, and dash home again. He would have to have set up a meeting. If he had murder in mind, why such a public place? No, the murderer surely came upon Professor Osborne by chance, Daisy thought, as Flagg recorded Padgett's answer without comment.

"But of course I had no conceivable motive," the doctor finished. "I don't suppose I'd exchanged more than a couple of dozen words with the chap in my life."

"We've reason to think the murder may be connected with a spate of anonymous letters," Flagg said deliberately. "And we know you to be one of the victims of the Poison Pen."

Padgett paled. The cat meowed indignantly, as if his caressing hand had abruptly tweaked its ear. "I don't know what you're talking about," he blustered, apologetically smoothing the offended feline's fur.

He liked cats but disliked dogs. Daisy had a sudden vision of his avoiding Tinker Bell's friendly lick. Tinker . . . so like the dog on the packet of pills Mrs.

Gresham bought . . . the words on the packet . . . "Padgett's Patent Puppy Worming Pills," said Daisy. "'Gentle but thorough.'"

Alec and Flagg stared at her as if she had run mad, but the doctor slumped with a groan.

Dr. Robert Padgett, M.D., was sole heir to the Padgett puppy-wormer fortune. The pills had paid for a public school education, medical training, and the purchase of a profitable practice. They also paid for the ambitious young man to move in fashionable circles. There he had met and fallen wildly in love with Miss Henrietta Bevis, third daughter of a County family with more pride than money.

Puppy worming pills—of all the nauseating ways to make a fortune. Unmentionable in polite company! Hetta refused to marry him unless he swore to cut himself off from all social intercourse with his plebeian, *nouveau riche* parents. (The purse-strings, naturally, were not to be severed.)

"There's enough from them to live on in comfort, but I always wanted to be a doctor," Padgett said, adding even more defensively, "I go to see them regularly. Hetta won't let the children see them. In fact, they don't know that set of grandparents is still alive."

"If they're such a secret," Alec said, stony-faced, "who in the village might have found out? You've told nobody?"

"Just one . . . My parents are getting older, you see. They desperately want to know their grandchildren. One evening at the Lomaxes, I must have had a glass too much of the brigadier's excellent port and I found myself asking the vicar's advice. Of course I should have known what a man of God would say . . . But I couldn't bring myself to hurt Hetta so. She would be devastated."

"Could anyone have overheard you?" Flagg asked neutrally.

Padgett shook his head. "Lomax was practically comatose. The ladies were playing whist, and Lympne was watching over his wife's shoulder, giving her bad advice. Yet I can't believe Osborne would have told anyone! He's a clergyman, and a good fellow, to boot."

Alec and Flagg exchanged a glance. Flagg wound up the interview with a warning that the doctor would be called at the inquest in Ashford next day. They left him sunk in gloom and went out to the car.

"The Reverend told his wife," said Flagg.

"You'd think one uxorious man would recognize another," Daisy observed, thinking of Osborne's reluctance to upset his wife.

"Daisy, how the dickens did you know about the puppy pills?" Alec demanded.

"It was the cat," Daisy told him smugly, if obscurely. Not prepared to admit to hitting the bull's-eye with a shot in the murkiest dark, she reverted to the inspector's comment. "All the same, I'm surprised the vicar told Mrs. Osborne, and even a bit surprised she'd spread the story. I rather had the impression she's more of a collector of gossip than a disher-out. Yet I really can't see her as the Poison Pen. Too busy trying quite openly to run people's lives."

She enlarged upon the subject while Flagg drove up to the Vicarage. Neither he nor Alec uttered a protest when she got out of the car and went with them to the front door. Alec *looked* a protest, but after saying so often that it was Flagg's case, he could not very well object.

Flagg asked for Mr. Osborne. While Doris went to inform him of their arrival, Daisy whispered, "Remember he just lost his brother. They seemed pretty fond of each other."

Flagg nodded.

The maid returned and showed them to the vicar's study at the back of the house. Osborne rose, turning from his desk, on which lay several unopened books, a blank sheet of foolscap, and a capped fountain pen. He looked dreadful, his round cheeks sunken, his eyes red-rimmed. "Have you found out who did it?" he asked.

"We're making progress, sir. We've a question or two about anonymous letters."

The vicar crumpled, dropping into his chair. "I wondered if there could be a connection," he said dully, burying his face in his hands. "I must have been mad to do it. Had I guessed they might lead to Ozzy's death, I'd never have written the damn things!"

14

While Daisy, Alec, and Flagg gaped at the vicar, all equally stunned, Mrs. Osborne burst into the room. "What's going on here?" she demanded stridently.

Flagg turned to her. "Police, ma'am. We have a few questions to put to Mr. Osborne."

"He's not to be disturbed. Can't you see he's writing his sermon?"

The vicar looked up at her. Uxorious was the wrong word, Daisy saw. He didn't love his wife, didn't even like her. As he had said, he was bound to her by the vows pronounced before a Deity he had ceased to believe in. Faith was gone, yet the standards set by that faith remained.

"My dear," he said, his voice shaking, "I have just confessed to writing anonymous letters. Naturally these gentlemen expect an explanation."

"Nonsense, Osbert! I'm sure they don't believe you for an instant. I certainly don't. You're obviously protecting someone. Who is it? That Gresham woman?"

"Mrs. Osborne," said Flagg, "I'm afraid I must ask you to leave."

Alec caught Daisy's eye and, scarcely perceptibly, gestured with his head first towards Mrs. Osborne, and then to the door. Reluctant as she was to miss anything, she had to agree it was up to her to remove and soothe the frantic woman. Gently she took her arm.

Mrs. Osborne shook her off. "What are you doing here?" she cried. "What business is it of yours? Leave me alone!"

"Let her stay, Inspector," said her husband tiredly. "Please. Adelaide has a right to hear what I have to say. And I should like Miss Dalrymple to remain. She will understand."

With a furious glance at Daisy, Mrs. Osborne opened her mouth. Flagg beat her to it. "You may stay, ma'am, if you will keep quiet. Otherwise I shall be forced to send for the constable."

The fight went out of the vicar's wife. She slumped into a chair. Daisy took another, and the two detectives followed suit.

"Sir?" queried Flagg.

Osborne rubbed his eyes. "It started in the trenches," he said in a monotone. "Was either of you . . . ?"

"Reserved occupation," Flagg said.

"R.F.C.," said Alec, "up above in my canvas kite, well out of the way."

"It was hell. A hell on earth, and not reserved for the wicked. How could I go on believing in a loving god? You see, Adelaide, it is no new, ill-considered notion."

Her usual ruddy colouring blanched, Mrs. Osborne jumped up. "But, Osbert . . ."

Alec turned his piercing gaze on her, and she subsided again. "Go on, Mr. Osborne."

"No loving god, no reward in heaven, no afterlife." He spoke in a sort of chant, as if he had rehearsed the words a thousand times. "No punishment in hell, hereafter. *I saw the prosperity of the wicked, flourishing like a green bay-tree.* There is no justice! They pay no heed to my sermons. Why should they, fearing no hell? *Vengeance is mine, saith the Lord,* but there is no lord. I felt I must . . ." He faltered.

"Exact vengeance yourself," Daisy said softly.

"Make the sinners suffer, and renounce their sins!

Pride goeth before destruction, but why was my brother destroyed for my pride?" the vicar cried, agonized.

"We can't be sure . . ." Flagg started.

"Don't be ridiculous, Osbert! I'm convinced it was a tramp. I dare say he was begging, and Osmund refused to give him anything and very likely laughed in his face."

"Life's a jest," said Osborne somberly. "Ozzy grasped that, but I cannot."

"Fiddlesticks! Life is a serious—"

"If you please, madam!" said Flagg.

"If you please, ma'am," echoed Doris, coming in, "Mrs. Lympne's here to see you."

"I think you'd better go and see the lady, Mrs. Osborne," Alec advised, quite forcefully.

"Do!" burst from Flagg.

Mrs. Osborne scowled at them, but then, with a backward admonitory glare at her husband, she swept out. The inspector breathed a silent but visible sigh of relief.

"Are you going to arrest me?" Osborne asked humbly.

"Well, now, sir, from what we've heard so far, there's not been any question of threats, let alone demanding money for your silence."

"Good gracious, no! I had no thought of personal profit, and exposing people's misdeeds could only hurt the innocent. That was not my purpose."

"And you won't go and do it again, will you, sir?"

"Need you ask? I'll be leaving the village soon, anyway, leaving the ministry, leaving the Church. I can't bear . . ."

"Yes, sir, that's between you and your bishop and your lady wife. Now, I'm sure you'll be wanting to cooperate with the police in finding the villain who killed your brother. I'll ask you to give me a list of the people you wrote to."

"If it will help."

"And what you wrote about," Flagg added.

At that, the vicar straightened. "I can't do that, Inspector. As a clergyman, I hear—"

"But you won't be a clergyman much longer, will you?" Flagg said with surprising gentleness. "And I suspect you heard most of this nasty stuff via gossip, not confessions."

"A hint of the subject will serve," said Alec. "No need to go into details."

Osborne bowed his head but said stubbornly, "No, I can't. I'll give you their names, but nothing more."

Daisy kept very still and quiet. If the vicar chose to confess in her presence, that was one thing. For her to stay and hear who had earned his condemnation was most improper. Fortunately both Alec and Flagg were intent upon Osborne.

"We know all about Dr. Padgett," said the inspector, consulting his notebook, "and Lord John Frobisher, and Mrs. LeBeau. What about Brigadier Lomax, Mrs. Burden, Samuel Basin?"

"All three," the vicar groaned, "and Mrs. Lomax, too. Lomax actually hit her! I could scarcely credit it, but the evidence . . . Then there's the Willoughby-Joneses."

He continued the list which included, along with several people Daisy did not know, Mr. Paramount (whose bitterness hurt Lady John as well as himself he said), Mrs. Molesworth, Miss Hendricks, and Miss Prothero. As he named the last, indignation again overcame his reticence.

Miss Prothero, it seemed, had a sister living in poverty whom she refused to help. Daisy could just imagine her confiding to Mrs. Osborne the transgressions which justified her harshness. Mrs. Osborne would have told her husband, feeling that as Mabel Prothero's spiritual guide he ought to know.

"And then there's Piers Catterick," finished the vicar.

"I dare say you are familiar with the reputation of his books. I need hardly say more."

Flagg had obviously never heard of Catterick. Alec looked as if the name was vaguely familiar. They both glanced at Daisy, who nodded slightly. No need to ask the vicar to elaborate.

"That's the lot?" asked Flagg.

"Yes, yes! I don't know how I could have done such a thing. I was under a sort of horrible compulsion—inexplicable. Tell me, do you . . . do you think someone found out I wrote the letters and . . . killed Ozzy in mistake for me?"

"It's a possibility we have to consider, sir," Flagg said, at his most stolid. As Osborne closed his eyes and swallowed painfully, the inspector raised his eyebrows at Alec, who shook his head. "That will be all for now, sir, but we may well have more questions for you. I must warn you that if any further letters are sent, there will be official repercussions. Nor can I promise that word of your part in the affair will not get about as we interview these people. And it's bound to come out if that particular theory of the professor's death is correct."

"I understand," said Osborne hollowly. "I must write to the bishop."

He turned to his desk, but Daisy, glancing back as she left the room, saw him staring blankly at the wall, making no move to start a letter.

Closing the study door behind him, Flagg said in a low voice, "Phew, there's a turn-up for the books, if you like! An atheist clergyman writing Poison Pen letters! Yet I can't but feel sorry for the poor chap. We'll want to talk to his wife at some point, but if you agree, sir, I think we'll start with the brigadier."

Alec agreed. Of one mind—to evade Mrs. Osborne, whose voice floated from the drawing room along with the fragrance of coffee—they all crept quietly towards the front door. On the way, they passed the telephone nook and Daisy recalled the sheet of paper she had torn from the pad and put in her handbag.

Once they were safely out of the house, she was about to mention it when Alec said, "I should like to take a dekko at the scene of the crime, Flagg. You've found nothing helpful there, I take it?"

"No fag-ends, no dabs, no handy footprints," said the inspector, leading the way down the path to the churchyard. "But we did get the angel set up on its perch again last evening, and gave it a shove between the shoulder-blades, and over it went, easy as pie, just like Miss Dalrymple suggested. Wouldn't take a lot of strength, but no chance it fell off its own bat. You wouldn't have to be that tall, either, to push it."

"Your police surgeon agrees with Dr. Padgett's evidence?"

"Yes, sir. Dr. Soames hasn't done the autopsy yet, but he reckons the professor died instantly of a broken neck, never mind the rest. Of course, arriving later, he can't be as precise about the time of death, but we've Miss Dalrymple's evidence for that." Opening the gate, he stood aside to let the others pass. "You won't want to come much farther, I expect, Miss Dalrymple," he said kindly.

"Not all the way, but I'll come as far as the church porch. I don't imagine you've had a chance to follow up your other theories, Mr. Flagg?"

"Just what Constable Barton's told me. Professor Osborne wasn't involved with any local girl, and there's been no unaccounted for strangers about. I cabled the Cambridge police, too, to find out if he'd got across anyone there, in the town or the university. They weren't any too pleased at having to enquire at his college. I'm waiting for their answer."

"Johnnie wondered if it could be a student who'd

failed his exams, or a rival professor he had done down in some way."

"Let's hope not. I don't want to have to run up there to tackle a bunch of highbrows. If it comes to that," said the inspector with a sidelong look at Alec, "I'll get my super to call in the Yard, officially."

"Thanks for nothing! I'd rather tackle the House of Lords. All right, you wait here, Daisy. We shan't be long."

Daisy was glad of the shade in the porch, for the sun still shone brightly and the day was growing muggy. She was dying of hunger, the smell of Mrs. Osborne's coffee having reanimated her appetite, forgotten in the shock of the vicar's revelation. They might have been sharing that coffee—and perhaps a biscuit or two—had Flagg not decided to go to Brigadier Lomax next.

That message from the brigadier impressed on the Vicarage telephone pad, what had it said? Daisy had left her handbag up at Oakhurst along with her hat. She couldn't remember Doris's extraordinary spelling, but the gist was that Brigadier Lomax would return later.

She told the others about it as soon as they came back. "It *must* have been written that afternoon," she said as they went through the lych-gate into the lane. "It was the most recent message, and the Vicarage must get quite a lot, don't you think? Brigadier Lomax said he was out walking when they called him from the Vicarage about the professor. He's a churchwarden," she explained to Alec.

"And a right fuss he made about us experimenting with that angel," grunted Flagg, and he bent to crank the car.

Daisy jumped in quick, before anyone could stop her. "Do you agree about the angel's toppleability, darling?" she asked Alec.

"I take Flagg's word for that. I wanted to see how

likely it is that someone who knew the vicar pretty well could take his brother for him. After all, however alike, they weren't identical twins, or someone would have mentioned it, and the professor was wearing his academic gown as well as the vicar's hat."

"And?" Daisy asked as the inspector climbed in.

"Just possible. Someone walking fast along the path would have caught glimpses, between those tall tombstones, of him standing there. Suppose he—for simplicity's sake—was so angry with the vicar he deliberately averted his head so as not to have to speak to him, he might have noticed nothing but the hat and a general impression of black garb. And then, coming to the angel, a sudden impulse, a shove, and Bob's your uncle."

"The trouble is," said Daisy . . .

"The trouble is," said Flagg, "I don't know where the Lomaxes live."

"Somewhere down that way." Daisy waved. "But I'm not sure."

"We'll have to stop off at Barton's. Sorry, Miss Dalrymple, you were saying?"

"The professor was the one who was always contemplating that epitaph."

"John Gay," said Alec. "Early eighteenth century poet and playwright." Flagg gave him a blank look, stopped the car, and left the motor running while he went into the village police house. "Sorry, love," Alec went on, "I'd been trying to think who wrote the original. Incidentally, what does this chap Catterick write?"

Daisy knew her face was turning pink. "Steamy novels of rural passion, which just manage to skirt the Censor's rules."

"But that's no secret," Alec pointed out. "The question is, how many people would have been aware of the professor's habit of brooding over that rhyme?"

"Probably not many," Daisy said slowly. "I just happened to come across him. From the lane you wouldn't see him unless you particularly looked, and then you wouldn't see enough to identify him. And really, you'd expect to see the vicar meditating in a churchyard, wouldn't you? Not a professor, even if you didn't know he was an atheist. Alec, I've thought of something else, which could cut the number of suspects. Why would anyone not going to the Parish Hall take that path in the first place?"

"Good question!" Alec jumped out of the car and strode into the police house.

Left alone, Daisy was tempted to dash into the shop next door to buy something—anything!—edible. But she was not sure she wanted to face Mrs. Burden, and the men came out before she had decided.

"No luck," said Alec. "There's a well-used footpath down the side of the hall which goes on through the wood behind."

"Cambridge rang up," said Flagg, setting off across the top of the green and down the lane beyond. "No luck there as yet. Tell us about the Lomaxes."

Daisy described the brigadier and his mousy wife. "Feeble or not, Mrs. Lomax is one of the Vicarage tea-and-scandal set," she said, "as ready as the rest to believe ill of anyone. She went to the Women's Institute meeting, I'm sure. In fact, she's chairman of the committee, though Mrs. Osborne flagrantly usurps her position."

"Everyone'd notice if she wasn't on time, then," said Flagg. "She's unlikely to be our murderer. All the same, I wonder if she has any secrets she's desperate to hide, or if Mr. Osborne was just after her for gossiping. Ah, here we are." He turned right between gateless brick gateposts. A sign read LOWER DENE HALL.

Beyond a narrow belt of woodland, they came to a halt before a pleasant manor house, considerably smaller than Oakhurst despite its grandiose name.

"Daisy," Alec said cautiously, handing her out of the Ford, "how about you seeing if you can get anything useful from Mrs. Lomax, while we see the brigadier?"

She saw through his ploy at once: He didn't want her sitting in on the interview with the brigadier. The wife was a diversionary tactic, a sop to Cerberus. However, at least he had not tried to give her orders. Besides, Daisy felt she might very well find out something useful from Mrs. Lomax, especially with neither her husband nor the detectives present to intimidate her.

Still more pressing was the likelihood of being offered coffee. It wasn't too late for elevenses.

"What a good idea, darling," she said. "She has one thing to hide, at least. She wouldn't want people to know her husband mistreats her, and to keep that secret she might conceal other information."

"Don't try interrogating her, though," Alec warned. "That's a job for us."

"Well, don't you interrogate the brigadier in his gunroom." Daisy retorted. "Do be careful, won't you?"

"Miss Dalrymple!" Mrs. Lomax came round the corner of the house, bearing a trug of roses. "How kind of you to call. But I'm afraid the young people have gone to the seaside for the day." She looked doubtfully at the two men.

Daisy was in a quandary, whether to introduce Alec as her fiancé or as Detective Chief Inspector Fletcher of Scotland Yard. In the end she did both, and added Detective Inspector Flagg. "I'm afraid they have come on business," she said.

"Oh yes, the poor professor, and in the churchyard of all places. Maurice will be anxious to hear your news. He takes his churchwarden duties very seriously. Do come in."

She led them into an untidy hall, with fishing rods

and tennis racquets leaning against the wall and a blotchy yellow croquet ball nested in a crumpled pink silk scarf on the table. Ringing for a servant, she ordered the parlourmaid who appeared to show the gentlemen to the brigadier's study and fetch her master.

"And then bring coffee to the drawing room, Annie. I was just coming in for my morning coffee, Miss Dalrymple. You will join me, won't you?"

"Yes, thank you. I missed breakfast."

"Oh dear! Bring cake and biscuits, Annie. And put these flowers in water, please. I'll arrange them later. Oh, and oh dear," Mrs. Lomax dithered, "coffee for you gentlemen?"

Alec and Flagg politely accepted, and followed the maid, while Daisy and Mrs. Lomax went into the drawing room.

Well dusted and polished, it was as disorderly as the hall. Magazines lay open; a half played game of backgammon awaited the return of the players; the lid of the gramophone was up and several records lay scattered on the table beside it. Daisy thought it looked comfortably lived in. Remembering the rigid tidiness of the sitting room in Alec's house, she wondered if it was always cleared in honour of her visits or if Mrs. Fletcher insisted on neatness at all times.

"Such a horrible thing to happen," Mrs. Lomax babbled on. "Mrs. Osborne was severely affected, I fear. She didn't take to her brother-in-law, you know, though naturally she never said a word against him. The poor dear vicar must be simply shattered. I believe they were quite fond of each other. It was a tramp, I suppose?"

"I'm sure the police have a number of theories. You didn't see anyone lurking about when you went to the Parish Hall?"

"Not a soul. I was a little early yesterday. The chairman should be there to greet members, don't you think? I find it rather a responsibility, though Mrs. Osborne says I make too much of it. She has such a *strong* character," the brigadier's wife said resentfully, "she doesn't quite sympathize with us weaker vessels, doesn't understand that what we need is *support*."

The vicar's wife must have taken over the chairman's cherished prerogatives at the meeting, as Daisy had foreseen. She said sympathetically, "Mrs. Osborne is quite managing, isn't she? Of course, a country vicar's wife has great scope for her organizing talents. People like Alec, who have lived all their lives in London, are surprised at how busy village life can be. Always something going on. Take this Poison Pen, for instance."

"P-poison Pen?" Mrs. Lomax squeaked.

"You didn't know about the anonymous letters people have been getting?" Daisy hoped she wasn't overdoing the amazement. "I thought everyone knew."

"Oh yes, those, of *course* I know about those."

Doubtless Mrs. Lomax would have claimed knowledge even if she had never heard of such a thing. As the maid came in with a nicely filled tray just then, Daisy waited to pursue the subject until she had been provided with a cup of coffee and a large slice of cherry cake.

Then she said, "Isn't it extraordinary how practically everyone seems to have received anonymous letters? Of course, you wouldn't be a target for the Poison Pen."

"Oh, but I am!" Mrs. Lomax was determined not to be left out. "Such *horrible* things, all about malice and uncharitableness, and keeping my tongue from evil-speaking and slandering. I'm sure I wouldn't dream of telling lies about anyone, but when one's friends tell one things, one can't cover one's ears, can one? So *rude* it would look!"

"I suppose Miss Prothero's letters must have said much the same as yours, condemning you both for a little harmless gossip."

"I expect so." Mrs. Lomax would surely have mentioned Miss Prothero's sister if she had known. Daisy congratulated herself: She had never seen Mrs. Osborne as a broadcaster of scandal, whatever her faults. "I wonder," Mrs. Lomax went on, "if Miss Hendricks's letters mentioned her little trouble."

"I wonder!" Daisy hid her hope behind her coffee cup.

"It was so long ago, that lucky miscarriage, but her health hasn't been the same since, she claims. If she wasn't always complaining, she'd never have let it out. And then she convinced herself we hadn't understood— of course, we never mentioned it to *her*," Mrs. Lomax added self-righteously. "Who else, now," she mused. "Mrs. Willoughby-Jones—so quarrelsome and unkind—and her husband tells shocking untruths about the houses he sells."

"Mr. Willoughby-Jones is a house agent?"

"Yes. There was something shady about a new factory in Ashford, too, I don't know the details, but perhaps the . . . Poison Pen, was it? . . . perhaps she knows. She probably knows about Mrs. Burden, too."

"Mrs. Burden?" Daisy prodded, though the shopkeeper was an unlikely suspect and had already given what help she could.

"My dear, have you not heard? (Do have another slice of cake, or a biscuit, and let me refill your cup.) Mrs. Willoughby-Jones's cook needed some cheese for a savoury and the piece she had was mouldy, so she sent the housemaid to the village shop for quarter of a pound of Cheddar."

"It came up short?" Daisy guessed.

"Half an ounce! The cook weighed it before making her recipe, because Mrs. Willoughby-Jones had once complained about her skimping the cheese in a Welsh rarebit—I'm sure I don't know how she keeps her servants. Mrs. Willoughby-Jones couldn't prove Mrs.

Burden had given light weight on purpose, but she gave her a piece of her mind anyway." Mrs. Lomax maundered on about how both the women had deserved to receive upsetting letters.

At last Daisy managed to slip in another question. "Have you any idea who wrote them?"

"Gracious, no. It must be a regular churchgoer, don't you think? 'Uncharitableness' and the rest come from the prayer book. But such an unchristian thing to do, upsetting everyone!"

"I expect the brigadier was pretty angry," Daisy suggested.

Mrs. Lomax looked frightened. "Oh, he doesn't know I . . . Oh, you mean about *his* letters. He hasn't mentioned them to me, of course, but I'm sure he must be terribly angry. You don't think he has found out who wrote them, do you? Oh, Miss Dalrymple, it wasn't *Professor Osborne,* was it?"

"Gosh, what do you . . .?"

"No, no, it couldn't have been. He was never seen in church even though his brother's the vicar. In any case, Maurice would have shot . . . would have horsewhipped him, not . . . he wouldn't, would he?"

"Surely not," Daisy said soothingly. So Mrs. Lomax considered her husband capable of doing away with the Poison Pen?

15

A lot of rubbish about temperance," blustered Brigadier Lomax, sloshing another dollop of whisky into his coffee cup. A trifle glassy eyed, he still had control over his tongue. His hand shook a little as he waved the decanter. "Sure you won't join me?"

Alec once more declined, as did Flagg. "What else did the letters say, sir?" the inspector asked.

"Else? Else? What the devil do you mean, *else?* Isn't that enough, damning a chap for enjoying a nip now and then?"

The brigadier clearly hoped to keep dark his violence towards his wife, assuming that was what Osborne had started to say. Was it a secret he'd kill to keep? The same question was going through the inspector's mind, Alec guessed, as Flagg gave him a quick but meaningful glance.

Pressed, Lomax was liable to 'clam up,' in the graphic American phrase. To Alec's relief, Flagg changed his tack.

"You'll understand, sir, that I have to ask everyone where they were between the hours of two and three thirty yesterday."

"Out and about." Far more relieved than Alec by the turn of the questioning, Lomax not only refrained from taking offence but did not query Flagg's *everyone.* "I generally take a gun along on my daily constitutional, take a few potshots at vermin. Yesterday I trotted along to the Vicarage, on church business, but Osborne was out."

"What time did you stop at the Vicarage, sir?"

"Must have been about quarter past. Left here at two. Walked with my wife, on her way to the Parish Hall."

"And then?"

"Took a turn around the green. Got home to find a message from my wife. Motored back to the church— you were there."

Flagg consulted his notebook. "That's as far as you walked, sir? Just round the green and back here?"

"I don't walk as fast as I used to," Lomax said testily.

"Still, not much more than a mile in over an hour."

"If you must know, I stopped to have a word with Jellaby, the landlord at the Hop-Picker." And, no doubt, to drink a dram out of licensing hours, which would explain the brigadier's reticence. "Promised Rosa I'd speak to him about a couple staying there she swears are living in sin, just because they're friends of Catterick's. Of course, Jellaby can't do anything about it if they are."

"What time would it be you stopped at the inn, sir?"

"Good gad, I don't spend all my time looking at my watch! Ask Jellaby."

"Oh, we'll do that all right, sir. Did you see anyone else on your walk?"

"Look here, my man, what is all this about?" the brigadier demanded belligerently. The whisky had steadied his hands, Alec noted, a sign of a confirmed toper. "Are you suggesting I did for Osborne's brother? Hardly knew the fellow."

"There seems to be a connection with the anonymous letters, sir. We'll be asking everyone who received them the same questions."

"Then don't miss the Basin boy! Told me he couldn't work on my Crossley any more because he'd got a nasty letter about it."

"About your motor-car, sir?" the inspector said, puzzled.

"About the private work he's been doing on his employer's time." Lomax had the grace to look abashed. "Charged a bit less than Wyndham's rates, don't you know. Dare say I shouldn't have mentioned it to the padre, but I gave him a lift and he commented on how smooth the engine was running. Of course he disapproved, though I must say I'd never have thought he'd pass it on." He brightened: "On the other hand, my motor isn't the only one Sam Basin's repaired on the side."

"Well, it's no business of ours unless Mr. Wyndham calls us in. Unless you want to report Basin, sir?" Flagg asked blandly.

"Good gad, no!" The brigadier obviously regretted having let that particular cat out of the bag. He poured himself another splash of whisky. "In any case, Basin would be at the garage at the times you're interested in. Catterick's another kettle of fish. Saw him come out of the shop and turn up the street towards the church, just as I turned down the side of the green."

"Is that so? And you think he received Poison Pen letters?"

"Complained to me, as though I could do anything about it! Not part of a landlord's duties, damn it! He rents my old gardener's cottage. Can't get a live-in man nowadays for love nor money. Have to make do with a jobbing gardener from the village. Shocking the way servants—"

"Mr. Catterick, sir?" Flagg prompted.

"Gnashing his teeth, he was. Said it ruined his concentration. Doesn't take much concentration to write that sort of rubbish, if you ask me. Not that I read it, mind you. So you think Professor Osborne found out who's been writing those damn' letters, do you?"

As a leap in illogic, that was a record-breaker. Flagg

appeared flummoxed. Alec said, "We have to follow up all possibilities, Brigadier. Have you any notion who wrote them?"

"Some damn' frustrated spinster. You can tell by the spelling. They didn't bother with all this damn' rubbish about educating women in the good old days. Women's Institute, pah! Just gives 'em ideas above their abilities and makes it difficult to keep 'em in order. Whisky?"

"No, thank you, sir," said Flagg, rising. "Thank you for your help. We'll keep your suggestions in mind, and we may want to ask you a few more questions at a later date."

"Any time, any time." Lomax waved the decanter in such an expansive gesture it would have slopped over had the level of Scotch not fallen by several inches. "Happy to be of assistance. All for Law and Order. Do come again, my dear fellows."

Outside the door, Alec and Flagg exchanged a glance. Flagg shook his head. "Amazing how he can still control his tongue."

"Even with his brain out of gear. He's unlikely, I think."

"So do I, but I shan't cross him off yet."

"A man after my own heart," said Alec. "Do you want to see Mrs. Lomax?"

"Not till I've heard what Miss Dalrymple has to say. She's a proper wonder," Flagg said in a congratulatory tone.

"Daisy's sometimes quite a help," Alec admitted with caution. "She has a way of getting people to confide in her. But don't fall into the trap—like my young detective constable—of thinking she must always be right."

"Oh, I take everything with a pinch of salt, sir. It goes with the job, doesn't it? But she's done me well on this case so far, and I hope she'll stick with it." He gave Alec a sideways look.

Alec sighed. "I couldn't keep her out of it if I tried.

Lomax has something there. The modern young woman is not the biddable creature her foremothers supposedly were. It's a good job she didn't hear the brigadier ranting; I'm not at all sure she could have held her tongue."

"Let's hope she's got something out of his missus. How do we hale her out of there without getting caught up . . . ?"

Spotting a bell-pull, Alec rang for the parlourmaid. He told her to tell Daisy they were ready to leave and would wait for her outside, and Flagg asked how to find the gardener's cottage.

"Not that this writer bloke sounds like our man," he said, following Alec through the front door, "but we might as well see him while we're here. Then I must ring up Ashford and have a man check on Sam Basin at Wyndham's Garage. And then, before we go chasing around any more, I want to sit down and talk things out, if that's all right with you."

"It sounds like an excellent plan," Alec approved. "Add lunch, and I'm with you. Any luck, love?" he asked as Daisy joined them.

They briefly exchanged news on the way to Piers Catterick's cottage, round the side of the house and through the row of elms and the shrubbery which concealed one building from the other. From the open upstairs window of the one-up, one-down dwelling came a tuneless whistle and the rapid patter of typewriter keys. Flagg knocked.

The sounds continued. The inspector knocked again, harder, and stood back from the door to shout, "Mr. Catterick!"

A long, pale face, adorned with long, unkempt hair and distorted with anger, appeared at the window. "What the bloody hell is it? I'm busy!"

"Police, sir. Detective Inspector Flagg."

"What do you want? I'm in the middle of a crucial scene." Disconcerted, Flagg said lamely, "Just to know

where you were between two and half past three yesterday, sir."

Still more disconcertingly, Catterick shouted with
laughter.

"In the police station," he said, "talking to the bobby."

"Sir?"

"A professional consultation, Flagg, on a little matter
of murder." The writer giggled. "Don't look so startled,
this one's fictional. I wanted to pick the good Barton's
brains. Oh, if you want the full narrative: I lunched at
the Hop-Picker with my friends, Mr. and Mrs. Edgbaston, who are staying there. Afterwards, must have been
a bit after two, we walked up to the shop to buy smokes
and a few odds and ends, and Jillie had the brilliant notion of consulting the copper next door."

Flagg had out his notebook. "How long would that
have taken, sir?" he asked, stolid demeanour restored.

"Oh, fifteen or twenty minutes. He wasn't a great
deal of help. I say, Inspector, you could probably give
me the straight dope on investigating murder. Hold on
a mo, I'll be right down."

"Not just now, sir! I have a real murder on my hands.
If you want to come into the station in Ashford once this
is out of the way, we'll see what we can do. Where did
you go from the village police house?"

"Back here for a cup of coffee. The stuff at the inn is
foul. The Edgbastons stayed till five-ish, when inspira-
tion once more overtook me. I do my best work
mornings and evenings. Can't I come with you and
watch?"

"Eh? No, no, I'm afraid that's out of the question, sir."

"Oh, right-ho, hurry up and catch your murderer,
then, and I'll come and see you in Ashford." Catterick
disappeared. A moment later the tuneless whistle and
the rattle of the keys started up again.

Shaking his head, Flagg returned his notebook to his

pocket. "Barton can check with the Edgbastons," he said acidly.

"Great Scott," Alec murmured to Daisy, "I'm glad you don't write steamy novels of rural sex, darling."

"No, but I might start writing murder mysteries."

Alec groaned.

They drove to the police house. Flagg sent Barton to the Hop-Picker to see the Edgbastons, and telephoned the Ashford station to send a man to Wyckham's Garage. Then Daisy phoned her sister.

"Alec and I won't be back for lunch, darling. Mrs. Barton has made us mountains of sandwiches."

"Mrs. Barton the Bobby?" Violet asked. "Darling, what *are* you up to?"

"Helping the police with their enquiries," Daisy explained, "and I don't mean they're about to arrest us. Vi, Alec says please tell Derek he swears he'll be back in time for a game of cricket, but we can't be sure when. Toodle-oo, darling."

"But Daisy—"

But Daisy pressed the hook and hung up. She wasn't going to get involved in explanations with Vi when a discussion of the case was at hand. Not to mention sandwiches.

Mrs. Barton, a young woman who bade fair to rival her hefty husband in figure, brought a glass of orange squash and two mugs of beer into the front parlour which served as Rotherden's police station. Beaming at their enthusiastic thanks, she bobbed a curtsy—she had been in service with the Lympnes before marrying—and left them to their business.

Daisy reached for a ham-and-cheese and said, "Does the county constabulary reimburse the Bartons for this?"

Mouth full of cheese-and-pickle, Flagg shook his head. Alec fished his wallet from his pocket, and half-a-crown from his wallet. "Will that do?" he asked.

Daisy nodded, her mouth being full by now. But for the odd crunch, silence reigned for several minutes.

Flagg's appetite being as meagre as his frame, he finished first. He set down his empty mug, wiped his drooping moustache with his handkerchief, and said portentously, "I've been thinking." In response to Daisy and Alec's raised eyebrows, he continued, "You remember, sir, what Brigadier Lomax said about Professor Osborne having found out who wrote the letters?"

"But we know the vicar wrote them," said Daisy. "Oh gosh, you don't honestly think he killed his brother?"

"Do you, Miss Dalrymple? If the professor discovered the vicar was the Poison Pen, would he have spread the word? Could Mr. Osborne have relied on him to keep quiet about it? Or would he have killed his own brother to protect himself?"

"Daisy hardly knew them," Alec protested.

"Better than either of us, sir."

"I'm afraid," Daisy said slowly, "the professor would have thought it a very good joke, possibly worth sharing. And though I don't believe Mr. Osborne would have killed to protect *himself* for his family's sake he just might . . . No, I can't believe it!"

"Just because he's a vicar?" Flagg asked shrewdly. "He's an avowed atheist, remember."

"It seemed to me it was a relief to him to avow it openly, and a relief to confess to writing the letters. We didn't have the slightest suspicion it was him till he told us. At least I didn't." Her querying look won rather sheepish shakes of the head from both men. "Even though I knew he'd lost his faith."

"Daisy, you knew?" Alec demanded, at the same moment as Flagg exclaimed, "You never told us!"

"I didn't have much chance," Daisy said guiltily. "We were always rushing somewhere and talking about someone else. Besides, he told me in confidence, and it didn't seem relevant."

"How many times have I told you that you can't judge what may or may not turn out to be relevant?"

"Dozens, darling. But one can't just go around spilling people's inmost secrets on the off chance."

"In a murder investigation one can," Alec said grimly. "What else did Osborne tell you?"

Daisy cast her mind back to that rainy afternoon when the Reverend Osbert Osborne had walked with her up the Oakhurst drive. Only three days ago!

"He's been offered a position at Canterbury Cathedral. Mrs. Osborne can't decide whether she'd rather be a small fish at the heart of the Church or a big fish in Rotherden, but he can't accept because he'd be unable to hide his atheism—he'd managed it till then, for her sake and their children's. It was becoming more and more of a strain, though. He hated the hypocrisy. What he really wants to do is teach in the East End, or one of the big industrial cities, but Mrs. Osborne is used to a comfortable life . . ."

"Why on earth did he tell *you* all this?" Flagg enquired, bemused.

"He said I looked sympathetic." Daisy frowned at Alec, daring him to mention her "guileless blue eyes." "He was desperate to talk to someone, and his brother didn't understand because his atheism had a logical basis, whereas he—the vicar—had revolted against religion on purely emotional grounds."

"So he was desperate," Alec said thoughtfully, "and his brother was unsympathetic."

"But killing his brother would leave him with exactly the same problems," Daisy pointed out, "with the guilt and danger of murder added, whereas being exposed as the Poison Pen would solve the worst, or what he perceived as the worst. You know, it wouldn't surprise me if he wrote those letters hoping to be caught. Unconsciously, at least," she added defensively when they stared at her.

"It's possible," Alec admitted, "but that just adds to the proof that he's been in a highly unstable frame of mind."

"Suicidal?" said Flagg, and the two detectives rose as one.

"You're not coming, Daisy," said Alec, as they strode out.

Daisy made no move to follow. She refused to believe the kindly gentleman who had rescued Derek from the Oakhurst gate had killed his brother. On the other hand, he had no dearth of other reasons for killing himself. If he had been driven to that point, she did not want to be one of those who found his body.

She wasn't going to bow out of the investigation, though. Finishing her orange squash, she carried plates and glasses out to Mrs. Barton, thanked her again, and asked, "Where does Miss Hendricks live?"

"Third house on the left going down the green, miss. Or is it the fourth? Mafeking, she calls it. There's a silver birch in the front garden."

"Thanks, I'll find it."

Mafeking, Daisy thought as she walked across the corner of the green. Had Miss Hendricks lost her secret lover in the Boer War? Was she what Daisy might have become if she had not found Alec?

Daisy had not been pregnant when Michael drove his Quaker ambulance over a landmine, but all the same, there but for the grace of God . . .

With more sympathy for the discontented, querulous woman than she had expected to feel, Daisy approached her garden gate.

Constable Barton puffed up the hill from the inn on his bicycle and came to a halt beside Daisy. "Mr. and Mrs. Edgbaston swear Mr. Catterick was with them," he said, "from ten to one till round about five. Reckon he's out of it, miss."

"Sounds like it," she agreed, and told him the detectives had returned to the Vicarage. Then she went on to knock on Miss Hendricks's door.

She had not readied an excuse for calling, but Miss Hendricks did not require one. Opening the door herself she invited Daisy into a tiny hall, and thence into a small sitting room overcrowded with furniture and knick-knacks. The furniture was good, though. Her circumstances might not be easy, but they were more comfortable than her complaints suggested.

"I've seen you motoring about with the detectives, Miss Dalrymple," she said. "The chief inspector is your fiancé, I hear."

"Yes, actually. They have been interviewing people. Mostly those who received those horrid anonymous letters."

"I suppose I'm not important enough for a Scotland Yard detective to come himself," said Miss Hendricks resentfully.

"Oh, I'm not here officially. They didn't want me along on their present errand," Daisy explained with a rueful moue. "I expect they'll want to talk to you later. It must have been a beastly shock when someone started raking up that old trouble."

"Old trouble?" snapped Miss Hendricks. "What old trouble?"

"Sorry! Someone said . . . But they must have been mistaken."

"Who was it? Mrs. Lomax? She's a fine one to talk, with a husband who drinks like a fish and knocks her about."

"You know about that?"

"No quantity of powder altogether hides a black eye," Miss Hendricks informed Daisy with a sort of spiteful satisfaction. "Or was it Miss Prothero? That letter-writer has a nerve, lambasting me for malice and evil-speaking when Mabel Prothero is a ten times worse backbiter than anyone else! Or did she write them?" she asked eagerly.

"I believe not."

"No, I'm sure it's Mrs. Willoughby-Jones. She doesn't care whom she hurts. It wouldn't surprise me if she's written to her own husband, taking him to task for his dishonesty—except that he makes a very good thing of it, so she would suffer if he stopped. I wonder . . ."

"Gosh, is that the time?" With feigned dismay, Daisy stared at the dainty, flowered porcelain clock on the mantelpiece. She was pretty certain Miss Hendricks hadn't the faintest idea the vicar was the Poison Pen. "I must be getting back, in case they're looking for me."

Disappointed, Miss Hendricks showed her out. "You can tell the chief inspector there's no truth in that story," she said, adding complainingly, "It's dreadful the things people say about people."

"Isn't it?" said Daisy.

Miss Prothero was next on her mental list. To get there she had to pass Mrs. Molesworth's cottage, so she decided to drop in for the sake of thoroughness, although she did not suspect that peaceable, good-natured lady of angel-shoving.

The tiny row-cottage had no front garden and no entrance hall. Stepping from the street into the only downstairs room, Daisy saw that it hadn't much in the way of furniture, either. Everything was shabby but colourful and comfortable. Stairs to the upper room started in one back corner; beneath them a door led to the kitchen in the rear. Through this Mrs. Molesworth vanished with a cheerful: "Tea! Shan't be a minute, it's on the boil."

Daisy went to look at a photograph in an ornate silver frame, which stood on a bookcase crammed with cheap editions of Dickens, Hardy, Trollope and the like. The plump, pretty bride in the photo was obviously Mrs. Molesworth, wearing an elaborate Victorian wedding dress and pearls, and beaming in a most unVictorian way. The solemn young man at her side was togged out in morning coat and grey topper, a gardenia in his buttonhole.

"Choccy biccies," said Mrs. Molesworth, bringing in a tray. "I try to save them for visitors. Chocolate is my downfall, I'm afraid."

Manfully resisting temptation, Daisy waved away the chocolate biscuits. "Thanks, but I've just had lunch. Do please regard me as an excuse, and indulge. I'd love a cup of tea, though. Would you mind frightfully if I asked you a few questions about the anonymous letters?"

The stream of amber liquid pouring from the teapot in Mrs. Molesworth's steady hand flowed smoothly on. "Not at all," she said. "I only received one. These days, I dare say, even a churchman can't work up much enthusiasm for damning the deadly sin of gluttony." She passed Daisy's cup, took a biscuit and crunched with unapologetic enjoyment.

"So you guessed the vicar was the Poison Pen?"

Mrs. Molesworth laughed. "I couldn't think of anyone else who might regard overeating as worse than a venial weakness. Except the doctor, of course, but he'd write about heart disease, not the body as a temple for the Holy Ghost."

"Did you speak to Mr. Osborne about it?" Daisy asked.

"Good Lord, no. The poor man has troubles enough, even before his brother met such an unpleasant end. The letter did me no harm—unlike others, I suspect."

"Some people are very upset," Daisy admitted, "and afraid their secrets will come out."

"No secrets here!" Mrs. Molesworth glanced down at her substantial self, which shook again with laughter. "I carry the evidence of my failing for all to see."

"One thing you may be able to tell me: Is there anything, besides her evident . . . er . . . failings, which the vicar might have written about to Miss Prothero? I'm not asking for details," she added quickly, "just whether you know of something."

Mrs. Molesworth shook her head. "If Mabel Prothero has a skeleton in her cupboard, she's a great deal cleverer at keeping the cupboard closed than most people. But I don't want to suggest she has something to hide. I expect her only failings are . . . er . . . the evident ones."

"Believing the worst of people and talking about it," said Daisy. "Thank you, Mrs. Molesworth. I don't expect the police will want to see you, but they may. I'm not official, you see."

"Presuming on your fiancé's position?" Mrs. Molesworth's limpid brown eyes twinkled. "Be careful, my dear, curiosity killed the cat."

"My chief failing is all too evident," said Daisy, laughing.

A frown creased her forehead, however, as she stood on Mrs. Molesworth's doorstep, gazing across the street at Miss Prothero's ugly bungalow. Apparently the vicar was the only person in the village who knew about the poverty-stricken sister, except, possibly, for Mrs. Osborne. Miss Prothero could easily have guessed that he was the Poison Pen.

On the other hand, meanness towards an indigent relative didn't seem a secret worth killing to keep. It was like Dr. Padgett's worming pills, uncomfortable but not disastrous.

Perhaps whatever the sister had done to earn Miss Prothero's enmity was the real secret. A well-bred lady of her vintage might feel herself utterly disgraced by— Daisy gave her imagination free rein—a sister who ran off to be a model in a Parisian *atelier,* for example; or who married a man drummed out of his regiment, blackballed at his club, perhaps actually convicted of a crime.

Daisy could practically hear Miss Prothero's sharp voice: "She made her bed. Now she must lie in it."

But murder? Was the old lady even physically capable of pushing over several hundredweight of granite, however top-heavy?

Still staring at the bungalow, Daisy saw a lace curtain twitch. She was dying to go over and talk to Miss Prothero, to study her with an eye to her height and strength. But Alec would be furious if she called alone on someone she strongly suspected of murder.

She didn't want to quarrel with him again, not so soon, though making up was very sweet. And curiosity killed the cat, Mrs. Molesworth had warned her. Yet her besetting sin tugged her towards that twitching curtain.

Daisy dithered.

16

Alec was too well brought up to yell after Daisy, when he came out of the police house, glanced to his right, and spotted her crossing the street from the row of cottages. He was too conscious of the necessary dignity of a Scotland Yard Detective Chief Inspector to race after her. He merely set off at a very fast stride, muttering, "What the dickens is she up to now?"

Inspector Flagg had no such inhibitions. Catching up with Alec, he shouted, "Hi, Miss Dalrymple!"

Daisy looked round, stopping with her hand on the gate of the bungalow next door to Mrs. LeBeau's house. It was one of the houses she had pointed out earlier, Alec remembered.

"Miss Prothero's?"

"That's the name, sir. Do you think Miss Dalrymple's found out something about her?"

"If she hasn't, she's trying to," Alec said tersely.

"The vicar doesn't care for the way she treats her penniless sister. Nice place she has." As they approached, Flagg regarded the city-park-like garden with approval for its gaudy precision, mingled with disapproval for its owner's living in comfort while her sister starved.

"Oh, Alec, and Mr. Flagg, I'm so glad you've come," Daisy said softly.

Her smile of welcome set Alec's heart somersaulting,

but he made his face and voice stern. "What are you up to, Daisy?"

"Hush! She's watching from behind the curtains. The windows are open, she'll hear you."

"We'd better go back to Barton's," Flagg whispered. "You can tell us there."

"She'd think it was frightfully fishy if we all arrived at her gate and then dashed off again. All I've discovered is that she seems to be the only person whose secret is known only to the vicar. By the way, I take it you didn't find him trying to kill himself?"

"No," said Flagg, "and he's given us an alibi. He was visiting the old chap whose seizure kept Dr. Padgett up the night before. Barton's gone to check."

Alec broke in impatiently. "So you think Miss Prothero has a good motive for the murder, Daisy? And you were going to question her on your own? Sometimes I wonder if you're stark, staring mad!"

"I wasn't going to *question* her," said Daisy, injured. "I've been jolly careful not even to mention the murder, let alone ask for alibis or anything like that. Just gossiping about the letters, which everyone's dying to talk about. But we can't stand here arguing with her watching. Since you're here, let's go in." She opened the gate and started up the path.

Alec and Flagg looked at each other, shrugged, and followed.

A neat young maid opened the door, and showed them into a sitting room full of highly glazed chintzes in flowery patterns. The wallpaper was flowered, too. At first sight, Miss Prothero fitted well into this daintily old-fashioned setting, so at odds with the modern exterior of the bungalow. She took Alec by surprise. He hadn't expected the hard-hearted, malicious scandalmonger of report to look like the epitome of a sweet old dear, with softly waved white hair, bright eyes, pink cheeks.

She was not, however, either short or frail-looking. Alec reckoned that under the impetus of strong emotion she might have been able to topple the angel.

From a rocking chair, a large tabby with a tattered ear fixed the intruders with a disdainful stare, and flexed sharp claws.

Unprepared for this interview, Flagg came straight to the point. "We have reason to believe, ma'am, that you have received one or more anonymous letters. Do you know who wrote them?"

"I suppose Mrs. Burden gave you a list of people," said Miss Prothero censoriously. "Really, the woman is quite unreliable! She is a civil servant, and she has no business disclosing what passes through her hands. I've a very good mind to write to the Post Office."

"Have you any idea who wrote the anonymous letters, ma'am?" Flagg reiterated patiently.

"Mrs. Osborne, I assume," Miss Prothero announced with apparently sincere resentment. "She must have a finger in every pie, and she expects people always to conduct themselves according to her notions. There was a certain matter raised in the letters—I have no intention of telling you what—which I was once persuaded unwisely to confide in her. No one else knows of it."

"What makes you sure she has not told anyone?" Flagg asked, his frequently expressive face at its most phlegmatic.

"I cannot be sure, of course, but Mrs. Osborne has never been inclined to pass on gossip, however avidly she listens to it. She likes to know everything about everyone. No doubt it is part of her desire to control. I imagine the letters have the same purpose."

"You don't think she even passes on what she hears to her husband?"

Alec saw Daisy frown. He guessed she had second thoughts about Miss Prothero's guilt, in view of her vehement denunciation of Mrs. Osborne as the Poison

Pen. If she had not killed Professor Osborne in mistake for his brother, it was unnecessary and a pity to let the arch-gossip know of the vicar's misconduct.

For the old lady had at once seen the implications of Flagg's question. Already sitting back-board straight, she became rigid, her face flushed. "Do you mean to tell me," she demanded with surprised disgust, "the vicar wrote the letters? Disgraceful! I shall most certainly write to the bishop."

Taken aback, Flagg hesitated.

Alec took over. "The inspector made no such statement, ma'am. He merely asked whether, in your opinion, Mrs. Osborne might inform her husband of matters pertaining to his parishioners. I take it you consider it possible. Would you be so kind as to tell us where you were between two o'clock and half past three yesterday?"

"Two and half past three? But the professor was killed between half past two and a quarter to three," said Miss Prothero.

Flagg pounced. "How do you know?"

"My dear man, it's perfectly obvious. At least, it must have been before five to three, at any rate, though I am disposed to set it earlier. I myself passed through the churchyard at two minutes before the half hour—when one lives so close to the Parish Hall, one is liable to set out at the last moment. At that time the angel was in its accustomed place. At five to three, Miss Dalrymple must have been approaching the hall if she intended to arrive on time." Miss Prothero inclined her head regally in Daisy's direction. "As I am sure she did, being a well-bred young lady, unlike so many these days."

Alec might have quarreled with this description, but Daisy accepted the encomium with an equally regal inclination of the head.

Miss Prothero continued. "Naturally one cannot conceive of Miss Dalrymple murdering Professor Osborne.

She found him already dead. Therefore he died before five to three."

"But why did you say quarter to?" Flagg burst out.

"Because," said Miss Prothero gloatingly, "that is when Mrs. Osborne arrived at the Parish Hall, and Mrs. Osborne loathed the man!"

"Yes, I knew she didn't like him," Daisy admitted sheepishly.

They had returned to the police house to discuss Miss Prothero's revelation, not quite trusting that lady's veracity when she so clearly revelled in her story. As Daisy informed them on the way, the old cat had cast utterly unsupported aspersions on the married status of Catterick's visiting friends, Mr. and Mrs. Edgbaston.

"The first day I was here," Daisy continued, "Mrs. Osborne came to tea at Oakhurst and mentioned that she couldn't bear her brother-in-law's dreadful jokes. She also complained that the brothers held such learned discussions, she couldn't understand a word."

"Neither's exactly what you might call sufficient motive for murder," Flagg said doubtfully.

"Ah, but then I found out about the professor being an atheist, and the vicar himself told me it was since his brother arrived that his wife had begun to suspect he was too. If you follow me."

"I do," said Alec, frowning. "You think Mrs. Osborne suspected the professor of leading the vicar astray? In that case, she would fear him, fear the loss of her position and everything that goes with it. Motive enough. We don't have to prove motive, but there's no gainsaying it influences the jury—and the judge—if we can provide one."

Mrs. Barton bustled in with a tray with a vast teapot flanked by a vast Dundee cake and a plate of jam tarts.

No wonder Constable Barton, sitting quietly in the corner listening, was such a fine figure of an officer!

"Don't let me interrupt," said his wife genially. "I'll leave you to pour, miss, if that's all right." She departed.

Pouring, Daisy said, "The trouble was, once we knew Mr. Osborne was the Poison Pen, I was sure the murderer had aimed at him. It was fixed in my mind that the vicar was the intended victim, and I didn't know of any motive for Mrs. Osborne to bump off her husband."

"Rather the opposite," said Flagg.

"Exactly." Daisy gave him a grateful smile. "Also, I'd assumed Mrs. Osborne ran the WI meeting. Mrs. Lomax, who's the chairman was bemoaning her officiousness, but now I come to think of it, she carried on about needing support, not about being superseded."

"You didn't ask whether anyone had arrived late?" Alec enquired, a trifle sceptically.

"No, darling, because I knew you'd be livid if I started asking that sort of question."

"I would," he had the grace to admit.

Daisy sighed. "Oh dear, I've really made a bit of a mess of things, haven't I? I've thoroughly misled you about a connection between the letters and the murder." She nibbled a jam tart, though she had resolved not to touch another bite for hours.

"There could have been a connection," Flagg consoled her. "In a way there is, seeing both are connected with his being an atheist. Anyway, we'd have found out about Mrs. Osborne arriving late as soon as we got around to questioning the women."

"You just got to them before us," Alec said dryly.

"That's assuming," Flagg continued, "Miss Prothero's telling the truth, not making it up just to cause trouble."

"Ask the missus," Barton put in, and blushed when everyone turned to him. "She went to the meeting, sir."

"Ask her," said the inspector, with a long-suffering look.

The constable returned in a moment, shaking his head. "The door being at the back, sir, only them on the platform 'd see when anyone come in. Mrs. Osborne wasn't up there with the committee at the beginning, but that's not to say she weren't in the hall."

"I never thought of that," Daisy groaned. "Miss Prothero's on the committee."

"So she'd be on the platform, I expect," said Flagg.

"For everyone to see, and with a good view of the door."

"Who else . . . ?"

"Mrs. Molesworth isn't a committee member, but she might know something." Daisy jumped up, abandoning the remains of her tart. "She won't spread false rumours. Living just two doors from the Vicarage, she could even have walked to the hall with Mrs. Osborne, if Miss Prothero's story is untrue."

Rising with his hand outstretched, Alec protested, "Daisy. . ."

"It's quite all right, truly, darling. I shan't need my hand held. I've already talked to Mrs. Molesworth, and it won't take a minute." Eager to redeem her errors, she hurried out.

Mrs. Molesworth was about to pop over to the church to freshen the flowers, but she invited Daisy in. "More questions?" she asked cheerfully.

"One or two, I'm afraid. Did you by any chance walk with anyone to the Parish Hall?"

"I wondered why you hadn't asked me for an alibi." Mrs. Molesworth was amused. "As it happens, Miss Prothero and I met at the lych-gate and walked through the churchyard together." Sobering, she added, "I'm quite certain we should have noticed had the angel fallen by then."

"Did you see anyone else? In front, or behind you?"

"I didn't look back. We were often the last to arrive, living so close."

"Mrs. Osborne lives closer," Daisy pointed out.

"Mrs. Osborne likes to arrive early," said Mrs. Molesworth dryly, "to make sure things run as she feels they should."

"She was already in the Parish Hall when you got there?" Daisy enquired with bated breath. If so, she was innocent, of course. So was Miss Prothero, though, of murder if not malice. Where were they to look next?

But Mrs. Molesworth hesitated.

"If you feel that telling me makes it gossiping, Inspector Flagg can come and ask you officially. A man's been killed, remember."

"Murder," murmured Mrs. Molesworth. The persistent twinkle had entirely vanished from her eyes. "Though the mills of God grind fine, yet they grind exceeding slow. Justice must be seen to be done. The truth is, Miss Dalrymple, I didn't see Mrs. Osborne when I reached the hall. That is not to say she wasn't there. It's not as if I saw her arrive late."

Daisy was beginning to think Mrs. Molesworth must once have suffered acutely from being the butt of gossip, to hate it so devoutly. "What did you see?" she asked.

"You're determined to pin me down, aren't you? I saw Mrs. Lomax running the meeting, reasonably competently, for perhaps a quarter of an hour. I saw her then stumble and lose her way, whereupon Mrs. Osborne went up to the dais and took over. She—Mrs. Osborne—seemed agitated. I assumed, because she had given Mrs. Lomax her head and watched her lose it. That's all I can tell you. I must go and get on with the flowers."

Her assumption could be right, Daisy thought as they stepped from the cottage into the street. Maybe Mrs. Osborne had watched from the back the whole time. Miss Prothero might deny noticing her, but *someone* was bound to have seen her.

Inspector Flagg would have to get a list of members and question each one. But Doris, the Vicarage maid, could well know when her mistress left the house, Daisy realized. What was more, though the girl might turn sullen if faced by the police, she was quite likely to open up to Daisy.

"I'll walk with you," she said to Mrs. Molesworth.

They parted in the churchyard. Daisy turned down the path to the Vicarage, through the gate, then right to the tradesmen's entrance at the back, instead of left to the front door.

The kitchen door stood open. Daisy stuck her head around, to the astonishment and dismay of Doris and the cook.

"Oh miss," cried Doris, "y'ought to've come to the front."

"I just want a quick word with you, Doris, and I didn't want to disturb people. I won't come in and get in your way. Can you step out here for a moment?"

Her plump face avid with curiosity, Doris joined her. "What is it, miss? Not another murder?"

"Gosh, no! One's plenty. Can you remember what you were doing at half past two yesterday?"

"Ooh, miss," Doris squealed, "you don't think I done it?"

"No, no," Daisy said impatiently. "It's what the police call a routine question for elimination purposes."

Cowed by the polysyllables, Doris said, "Hunting for Mrs. Osborne's gloves, I was. You see, Miss Gwen rang up just on twenty-five past, and I picked up the telephone and called the mistress and she told me to fetch clean gloves from her drawer while she was on the telephone but I couldn't find 'em anywheres. And Miss Gwen went on talking till after half past and madam was angry as anything 'cause she was already late and I hadn't got her gloves for her and she had to go and find some herself. She couldn't find 'em either," the maid added resentfully, "after giving me what-for and all. Not for ages, anyways. She was ever so late to the meeting."

So that was that, Daisy thought, suddenly tired.

"Miss Dalrymple!" Mrs. Osborne's voice came from behind her. She swung round, as Doris bolted into the kitchen, closing the door. The vicar's wife looked haggard. In one hand she wielded a colourful bunch of pompon dahlias like a shield, in the other a pair of sharp-pointed garden scissors.

"Oh, hullo," said Daisy, heart in mouth, trying to keep her gaze from the scissors. If Mrs. Osborne had killed her brother-in-law, as now seemed more than likely, it had been on impulse, and without thought for the inevitable discovery.

"Really, Miss Dalrymple," she snapped, "I know modern manners are lax, but to come sneaking around to the kitchen . . ."

"I didn't want to disturb you, in the circumstances," said Daisy truthfully, hoping she wasn't gabbling, searching desperately for an excuse. The one she found seemed to her pretty lame. "I lost a hankie and I wondered whether Doris had found it here."

Mrs. Osborne snorted, and the scissors lowered marginally. "That girl can't find the nose on her face. Or if she did find your handkerchief, no doubt she put it away somewhere and forgot all about it. So difficult to find competent servants these days! You should have come to me."

"Sorry!" Now how to extricate herself? "I'd better go and see if I dropped it at Mrs. LeBeau's. It's one my sister embroidered with daisies for me, you see," she invented wildly. That treasured handkerchief had frayed to the point where her nurse threw it out a good fifteen years ago.

"A pity to lose it. I shall keep an eye out for it."

"Thank you." Conveniently, the church clock chimed. "Oh gosh, is it four already? I must run."

Daisy managed not to run literally, until she rounded the corner of the house. Then she took to her heels.

At the gate to the street she paused to glance back. The Vicarage looked just as it always had, a large, ugly Victorian house, displaying no signs of the emotional turmoil within. Daisy turned her back on it with a shiver and pulled the gate to behind her.

On Mrs. Molesworth's doorstep stood Alec, his hand raised to the knocker, his dark eyebrows a thunderous line.

"Alec!" Untrammeled by a middle-class upbringing, Daisy called out as she ran to him.

"Daisy, where have you been? Mrs. Molesworth's, you said, but no one's home. Not the Vicarage, you unmitigated little idiot?"

Safe in his comforting arms, she explained, "I went to talk to Doris, the maid. I'm not a complete idiot, I went round the back way specially to avoid Mrs. Osborne. How could I guess a murderess would be out in the garden picking flowers?" Suppress the scissors, she thought. He didn't need to know about those. "Would you believe she chatted quite calmly about incompetent servants and lost hankies?"

"I take it what the maid told you supported the theory of her guilt."

"She left the house very late for the meeting. Mrs. Molesworth said she arrived on the dais at about quarter to."

"It wouldn't take more than a moment to push over the statue. She might not even have spoken to the professor first."

"But is that enough evidence?" Daisy asked.

"Flagg rang up Mrs. Lomax. She saw Mrs. Osborne enter the hall and lost her place in what she was saying. It was two forty-seven. She particularly noted the time, as she meant to point out that since she had managed quite well for over a quarter of an hour she could have managed the whole thing. Flagg's satisfied with her confirmation of Miss Prothero's story, though the maid's evidence will help. It's more than enough to tax her with in hopes of a confession, and I agree with Flagg that she's unlikely to hold out."

"Where is Mr. Flagg?"

"He drove up to the house to get a warrant, Frobisher being a Justice of the Peace. And you're going to follow him, Daisy."

She yielded without a struggle. She had no desire whatsoever to be present at the arrest.

Daisy was half way to the stairs when Inspector Flagg came into the front hall from the library. Tucking a folded paper into the inside breast pocket of his bronze-green suit jacket, he said with satisfaction, "Signed, sealed, and to be delivered. You've seen Mr. Fletcher, I expect, Miss Dalrymple?"

"Yes, he told me what Mrs. Lomax said." She reported her conversations with Mrs. Molesworth and Doris.

"Excellent." He rubbed his bony hands. "Extra confirmation never hurts. To think all this—Poison Pen letters and murder—came about because the vicar turned atheist!"

"Not really," Daisy protested. "He wrote the letters because he couldn't escape his religious instincts and training. He felt obliged to try to set the world to rights. As for the murder, if you ask me, she'd never have done it if it hadn't been for the professor's constant jokes."

"Well, that's as may be," said Flagg peaceably. "You may have gone off in the wrong direction a bit to begin with, but I must say in the end you and Mr. Fletcher have been more help than a dozen slow-witted constables going door to door. It's a feather in my cap to have the whole thing wrapped up before the inquest tomorrow. The coroner and my super'll both be happy."

The complacent inspector went off, leaving Daisy to reflect on the fact that even murder is not an unmixed tragedy.

Johnnie came out of the library, also looking pleased with himself. "So you have found the Poison Pen and the murderer all in one," he greeted Daisy.

"Inspector Flagg told you so?"

"He applied to me for a warrant for the arrest of Mrs. Osborne for murder. He said the police didn't intend to prosecute over the letters. Stands to reason, when they have a so much graver charge against her, and of course I don't want any publicity about them. Jolly hard cheese for poor Osborne, I'm afraid. I'll have to see what we can do for the family."

Daisy decided he didn't need to know that the vicar had been the Poison Pen. He would find out soon enough that Mr. Osborne was leaving the Church, but now the defection might be blamed on his wife's crime. If no one but the bishop was aware that he had lost his faith, it would be one less burden for the family to bear, she hoped.

Johnnie seized her hand. "I say, Daisy, I'm dashed glad I asked you to investigate. You sorted it all out in no time. I'll give you a recommendation as a sleuth any day."

"No, thanks! If you think I actually *enjoy* stumbling over bodies or seeing families cast into chaos, you can think again." Which was true enough in itself, though it dodged the issue of her zest for investigation. "I'm a writer," she said firmly.

"Well, thanks anyway, old dear." He dropped a peck on her cheek, and blushed. "You coming out for tea on the terrace?"

"I'll join you in a bit. I need a wash and brush-up."

When Daisy went down, the children were on the terrace with Violet and Johnnie, so there was no talk of the murder. Alec arrived soon after, and was besieged with requests to redeem his pledge to play cricket.

"You promised, Daddy."

"Please, Uncle Alec!"

"Can I play too?" asked Peter.

"Of course," said Belinda as Derek said, "No."

"Of course he can," said Vi.

"All right. Us three against Uncle Alec."

Alec groaned. "You'll join us, won't you, Frobisher? And you're not escaping, Daisy."

Johnnie agreed, and Daisy let herself be persuaded, since a cooling breeze had come up.

"But let Uncle Alec have his tea first," Violet said firmly.

The three children, Johnnie, and the dog went off to set up the wickets, Tinker Bell carrying one of the stumps. Daisy broke it to her sister that the vicar's wife had been arrested for murder.

"Oh dear," said Vi, a shadow crossing her serene face. "I must see what I can arrange to take care of Mr. Osborne. She is the very person one would ask to organize assistance if it were not—Oh dear! I wonder whether he will want to bring the children home? Excuse me, please, Alec. Daisy will pour you more tea." She went indoors to the telephone.

Full of Mrs. Barton's tea, Alec rejected a second cup. He and Daisy strolled after the others.

"You went with Mr. Flagg to arrest her?" Daisy asked.

"Yes. It was one of the most difficult ones. She ranted and raved, half hysterical. I rang up and asked Padgett to come round, both to calm her and to stand by Osborne. He's hard hit, poor fellow."

"I'm glad I wasn't there," Daisy acknowledged.

"You got it right in the end, you know," Alec said somberly. "She thought the professor was responsible for the vicar's apostasy. Since she said so before three police officers, you won't have to testify."

Not having considered the possibility, Daisy was aghast and relieved at the same moment.

Alec went on, "She seemed almost to believe the angel struck him down without human agency, or at least that she was the instrument of God. There's bound to be a plea of insanity." He cheered up. "A game of cricket is just what I need. Where are our cricketers?"

"Beyond the trees," said Daisy, "out of sight of the house. Too many broken windows."

He laughed. "Now there's a crime I could put my heart into investigating!"

EPILOGUE

The yellow Austin Chummy buzzed down the drive, paused between the tall gates, then turned left towards Ashford and London. Daisy sat beside Alec in the front. In the back were two excited children—Derek was going to stay with Belinda for a few days, to visit museums and the zoo—and a puppy named Nana.

"There's one thing I've been meaning to ask you, love," said Alec. "How on earth did you discover about Dr. Padgett and the worming pills?"

"Padgett's Patent Puppy Worming Pills," Daisy chanted. "I happened to see a box in the shop just before we went to talk to him. Sheer chance, followed by a wild guess."

Alec sighed. "There's a place for chance and guesses in solving crime," he conceded with reluctance.

"Daddy," said Bel in an ominous voice, "Derek thinks Nana's going to be sick."

Slowing, Alec drew in to the side of the lane and stopped. With an even deeper sigh, he turned to Daisy and asked plaintively, "Why do I let you talk me into these things? I must be mad!"

Please turn the page for an exciting sneak peek of
Carola Dunn's Daisy Dalrymple mystery
RATTLE HIS BONES
now available at bookstores everywhere.

Mr. Steadman ushered Daisy into the Dinosaur Gallery. Over half its length was taken up by the Diplodocus, eighty-five feet from nose to the whiplash tip of its tail, thirteen feet high, with its tiny head perched at the end of a long, slender neck.

"I'd like to take the Diplodocus," Daisy said, "but it's so huge I don't think I could do it justice. Besides, it's American, isn't it?"

"The Iguanodon is home grown," said Steadman with a smile, smoothing back his thinning hair. "Do you want to try that? It's smaller, of course, but still quite dramatic."

About to agree, Daisy heard the gallery's commissionaire say sharply, "No running, *if* you please!" She looked round to see Derek and Belinda approaching at a sort of compromise between a run and a walk.

Derek skidded to a halt, eyes only for the Diplodocus. "Crikey!" he said, scanning it from end to end. "Crikey! Is it real?"

"Course it is, isn't it, Aunt Daisy?" Belinda said scornfully. "Everything here is real."

"You'd better ask Mr. Steadman here," Daisy advised. "He's the museum's dinosaur man. My nephew, Derek, Mr. Steadman, and . . ." She could hardly introduce Bel to the curator as her future stepdaughter, particularly as he was now looking rather disgruntled. She shouldn't have troubled him with the children. "And Belinda," she finished.

"Please, sir, is it *real?*"

"In a sense, it's real, Master Derek. Miss Belinda is correct in that we don't have imaginary animals in the museum. Creatures like this did exist millions of years ago. But I'm afraid this particular skeleton is a model made from casts of the real bones."

"Oh," said Derek, disappointed. Steadman grimaced. Daisy gathered his disgruntlement was with the plaster model, not the children. "Oh well," said Derek, "it's still spiffing, isn't it, Bel? You can see what it was like, even if it's not quite real."

"You mustn't mind," Bel said kindly to Steadman. "Did you lose the bones?"

"No, no! The Diplodocus was found in America, and the Americans sent casts to various museums all over the world. Shall I tell you a secret?"

"Yes," breathed Derek. "Please!"

"Promise not to tell?" They both nodded, wide-eyed. Stooping to their height, Steadman whispered, "They used the wrong feet by mistake. The front feet of this model are really the back feet of a Camarasaurus!"

"Really and truly?"

"Really and truly."

Derek dragged Belinda off to study the erroneous feet. Daisy and Steadman went over to the Iguanodon, a heavily built beast about twenty-five feet long. It stood more upright than the Diplodocus, perhaps twelve or fourteen feet tall, its forelimbs more like arms than legs, with huge claws on the thumbs. It would be a bit easier to fit into the viewfinder Daisy agreed.

While she prepared to take the photograph, she asked several questions about the creature, and then said, "Wasn't the Iguanodon the one Dr. Smith Woodward said was discovered by a woman?"

"That's right. At least, Mrs. Mantell found the teeth."

"And there was someone else—Ann something?"

"Mary Anning, a highly talented fossil hunter of the last century. I believe she unearthed the first complete ichthyosaur and plesiosaur both. Mummery could tell you more about that."

Bother, thought Daisy. The female aspect sounded like a good idea to widen the appeal of her article, but it would mean applying to Mummery, whom she didn't much care for.

"Are many dinosaurs found in England?"

"A few. The best hunting-grounds are elsewhere, however, chiefly Africa and the American West." He glanced discontentedly around his collection. "The American museums and universities bag all the best."

"Even the African ones?"

"They have the money to send out their own expeditions, as well as to buy the best from independent finders. Our trustees have been debating setting up an expedition since 1918. Smith Woodward is pushing for it, but five years and still no decision! The poor old fellow will die of old age before it happens. But I don't want to bore you. Is there anything else I can tell you?"

"What else would you suggest I photograph?"

"Megalosaurus," he said promptly. "It's English, and actually the first dinosaur genus ever named or described in detail, just a century ago. We haven't a complete skeleton, but a photograph of its head showing the dentition would be worthwhile, I believe."

Dentition—dentist—teeth, Daisy worked out. Latin was another subject the girls at her school had not been subjected to, but French *dent,* a tooth, helped.

Derek had already found the Megalosaurus skull and was gazing with bloodthirsty awe at its vicious, carnivorous grin. Steadman explained to him the functions of the various types of teeth in far more gruesome detail than Daisy considered necessary. Belinda had already gone off in disgust to look at some innocuous fossil fish on the other side of the gallery.

Apparently the description of a dinosaur meal, even as it destroyed Daisy's usually hearty appetite, had aroused Derek's. Having politely thanked Mr. Steadman, he reminded her that they were to have lunch in the refreshment room.

After lunch, the children decided to go with Daisy to the Mineralogy Gallery. From the cafeteria on the first floor, a glassed-in room with a view to the Central Hall on one side and the North Hall on the other, they walked past the giraffes and okapis.

Derek had recently seen live giraffes at the zoo, near Belinda's home in St. John's Wood. He was more interested in hanging over the arched and pillared balustrade to see the people walking below.

"Come along," said Daisy crossly, grabbing the back of his jacket, her temper ruffled by the prospect of her interview with the unpleasant Pettigrew. "What am I to say to your mother if you fall and break all your bones to bits?"

"There's lots of people here," Derek pointed out, "who spend all their time sticking bones back together."

"Not always right," Belinda reminded him. "S'pose they stuck dinosaur feet on you?"

This struck both of them as the height of wit. Guffawing, Derek started to walk as he imagined a dinosaur might. Daisy shushed them and thrust them still giggling into the Mineralogy Gallery, while she went on to Pettigrew's office.

Over his door, the architect's whim had placed a terra cotta medallion of a strutting buck. Its combative stance reminded Daisy all too clearly of the Keeper.

However, Dr. Pettigrew greeted her courteously and answered her questions painstakingly, if with a heavy patience which suggested ill-disguised scorn for her ignorance. She finished by asking about the rock samples strewn on the work-bench under one window.

"Just some bits and pieces I picked up in Cornwall, on my summer holiday. Nothing of great value," he added, but he rose from his desk chair and went over to the table.

"Isn't that gold?" Daisy enquired, following, as a yellow gleam caught her eye.

"No, I'm afraid not. There is a little gold in Cornwall, but that's just iron pyrites. Often known as fool's gold."

Daisy laughed. "I see why. And the others? What are those green crystals?"

"Polished up nicely, hasn't it? That's torbernite, a phosphate of copper and uranium. These blue crystals are azurite, a copper ore. Both copper and uranium are mined in Cornwall. It's an area rich in useful minerals, zinc, lead, arsenic, wolfram, and tin, of course, which the Phoenicians came to trade for. This is its ore, cassiterite. Then there are the building stones, granite, sandstone, and slate; and mica; and the pigments ochre and umber. Useful stuff," he repeated insistently, "not like those ancient, crumbling bones downstairs which absorb so much money and effort."

Fearing a tirade, Daisy hastily finished scribbling shorthand hieroglyphics and said, "I'd better be getting along. I left two children in the gallery. Thank you for all your help."

"Children? Maybe they would like a piece of pyrites each. Here—no, I'll come along."

They found Belinda and Derek entranced by the display of opals. Pettigrew actually unlocked the case and allowed each of them to hold one of the iridescent stones while he lectured them on the subject. Though he was rather condescending, it was kind of him, Daisy thought. She decided Ol' Stony was not so stony-hearted as he was painted, in spite of his rudeness to

Smith Woodward—unless the story of his brutality to the one-legged commissionaire was true.

She looked around. Between the rectangular pillars embossed, oddly enough, with sea creatures, she caught glimpses of a commissionaire's uniform. The youngish man patrolling the aisles appeared to have a full complement of limbs. Of course, she couldn't tell whether he was deaf, and even if he was, it would not prove Sergeant Hamm's tale.

Pettigrew locked away the opals and gave the children the two small chunks of fool's gold. He was starting to explain them, when the sound of the commissionaire's footsteps nearby made him look round.

He frowned irritably. Then he looked beyond the approaching commissionaire and broke into a furious scowl. Abruptly deserting Daisy and the children, he stormed off towards a figure bending over one of the cases.

"There's that damn fellow again. Hi, you!" he shouted. "What have you come back for?"

All over the gallery heads turned—except the undoubtedly deaf commissionaire's. The object of Pettigrew's ire straightened and swung round. Daisy saw that he was a slim young man, whose longish fair hair, parted in the middle and carefully slicked down on top, matched a sweeping cavalry moustache.

The most notable aspect of his appearance, however, was his dress. His uniform would not have disgraced a foreign grandee in a Gilbert and Sullivan production, the Duke of Plaza-Toro, perhaps, or Prince Hilarion. The pale blue tunic with crimson facings was lavishly frogged and laced with gold, and bore the ribbons, stars, and sunbursts of at least a dozen orders. A crimson sash topped cream breeches, which descended into knee-boots with gold tassels.

The plumed helmet and ceremonial sword required by such a costume were absent. Daisy wondered whether he had left them in the cloakroom or had balked at wearing them in public.

On the other hand, he could hardly appear in public with a bowler, a soft felt, a topper, or a cloth cap to crown that get-up!

"What's that uniform, Aunt Daisy?" asked Derek, who had a vast collection of lead soldiers at home.

Daisy's confession of ignorance was drowned.

"I told you there's nothing doing!" Pettigrew's angry voice rang from end to end of the eighty-yard-long gallery.

The stranger's was not as loud but reached Daisy and the children. *"Dieser Rubin*—dis ruby—belong mine family," he said in a determined tone, his solid, obstinate jaw jutting.

"Oh, a foreigner," said Derek dismissively.

"Used to belong, *used* to belong," corrected Pettigrew. "It's mine now—the museum's."

"I ask for it to return."

"You haven't a hope in hell!"

"I ask de king, mine cousin."

"Your sixteenth cousin fifteen times removed," Pettigrew snorted. "In any case, the old queen gave it to the British Museum. You're out of luck. Get out of my gallery."

"Here is public place, *nicht wahr?* " the young man demanded sullenly. "I may at mine ruby look."

The Keeper glared but gave in. "I've got my eye on you," he threatened, then retreated to bellow at the commissionaire to keep an eye on the interloper. There, too, he was defeated. Daisy saw him writing down instructions.

"May we go and look at his ruby?" Belinda asked. "It must be extra special."

Half the people in the gallery had the same notion, but she and Derek got there first. The gaudy stranger looked somewhat disconcerted when they bobbed up on either side of him.

Daisy apologized. "We could not help overhearing," she said, enunciating clearly in deference to his foreignness. Close to, he seemed very young, not much more than twenty, she guessed. He had a long nose, and brown eyes set a trifle too close together, spoiling an otherwise handsome face. "The children are eager to see your . . . the ruby."

He pointed dramatically. "Dere it is, de largest here and de last hope of mine contry."

Between the children's heads as they pressed forward, Daisy glimpsed several rubies of varying sizes and shades of red.

"It's not as big as the opals," said Belinda, disappointed, "and not as pretty either."

"Your country?" Daisy enquired quickly.

"Excuse, please!" Recollecting his manners, the young man took a pace backwards, clicked his heels, and bowed. With a glance around at the people with pricked ears politely but unconvincingly studying the contents of nearby cases, he lowered his voice. "I am Rudolf Maximilian, Grand Duke of Transcarpathia, at your service, *gnädige Frau.*"

"*Fräulein,*" Daisy corrected, that being about the only word of German she knew. It was not at all proper to introduce herself to a strange gentleman met in a public place—her mother would have fainted at the thought—but Daisy was now dying of curiosity. In order to hold her own with a Grand Duke, she used the courtesy title she usually omitted. His stiff expression relaxed a little as she said, "I am the Honourable Daisy Dalrymple. How do you do? I'm afraid I'm not very sure where Transcarpathia is."

"Mine country is betveen Moldavia and Transylvania and Bukovina," he informed her, leaving her little the wiser. "Now is mine country not existing. De Russians have take it. Instead of Grand Duke is Red Commissar. Mine family is exile, penniless, and mine pee-ople suffer under de Russian boot. Wizzout dis ruby can I for them nodink."

The splendid uniform was threadbare, Daisy noticed, the cuffs frayed, the gold braid unravelling. Given his youth, either the Grand Duke Rudolf possessed no other clothes, or he had inherited the outfit from his father.

"How exactly does the ruby come to be in the Natural History Museum?" she asked.

"Mine *Grossvater* has de ruby to Qveen Victoria presented. You understand, in dose days vas de family rich. Dey visit to England and make gift to cousin of magnificent precious gem. But now ve have need, cousin vould give back, *nicht wahr?*"

Daisy rather doubted that most cousins would be so generous. The museum's trustees were even less likely to oblige. However, she said soothingly, "I am sure King George will sympathize and do what he can for you."

With a despairing gesture towards Pettigrew's back as the Keeper stalked out of the gallery, the Grand Duke groaned, *"Dieser viehische, schreiende Kerl* vill everysink spoil."

"Please, sir, what's . . . what you just said?" Derek queried. He and Belinda had long since stopped admiring the ruby—which, however large and precious, just sat there—in favour of listening to Rudolf Maximilian's story.

"And what will you do if you get it back?" asked Belinda.

To fend off a translation, which she suspected was better not delved into, Daisy seconded Bel's question. "Yes, what would you do?"

"I use to raise an army of loyalists, naturally. Mit mine pee-ople behind me, ve zrow out de Red Army and make peaceful again."

Though not much of a newspaper reader, Daisy knew

the Red Army had proved virtually impossible to throw out once having steamrollered in. The Transcarpathian loyalists were more likely to be slaughtered wholesale than to succeed. That an entire army of loyalists could be raised on the proceeds of even the most valuable jewel was another dubious proposition. Transcarpathia must be somewhere in eastern Europe. The common people of that part of the world were Slav peasants little better than serfs, with no reason to feel loyalty towards their German-speaking rulers. Unless the Grand Dukes' reign had been singularly benevolent, Rudolf Maximilian was probably headed for bitter disappointment even if he recovered the ruby.

Which was unlikely—but disillusioning the ardent young man was none of Daisy's business, and she still had business to be done.

"Enough chatter, children," she said. "Come along, time is passing and I want to take a photograph of the Melbourne meteorite with you two on each side to show how enormous it is. I wish you the best of luck, sir."

Instead of shaking the hand she held out to him, Grand Duke Rudolf bowed over it, heels clicking, and raised it to his lips. "I sank for your much sympazy, *gnädiges Fräulein,*" he said. "You lift to me de courage. I fight on!"

Bel and Derek were much more excited by the Grand Duke's story than by the three-and-a-half-ton meteorite. They wove a wonderful tale about a wicked sorcerer called the Red Commissar and a magic ruby with the power to raise an army overnight. Pettigrew's place in the narrative was a source of much argument. Derek had him as an ogre who had stolen the jewel, while Belinda insisted he was not an ogre, because he had been nice to them, letting them hold the opals and giving them fool's gold.

"Not real gold," Derek pointed out. "It'll prob'ly turn

into dead leaves overnight. I bet he's in league with the Red Commissar, and he's just trying to buy us off."

They were still elaborating their make-believe when Daisy put them onto a bus back to St. John's Wood—inside. Though the rain had stopped, the skies had darkened ominously. As she walked home through South Kensington and Chelsea, the photographic equipment and her notebook seemed to grow heavier and heavier. It wasn't far to Mulberry Place, but she had been tramping around the museum for hours. Hard floors and city pavements were much more tiring than fields and woods.

When she reached the "bijou residence" she shared with Lucy Fotheringay, she went straight through the house and down to Lucy's mews studio. Lucy, tall, dark, smart, and fashionably flat fore and aft, was just seeing a client out of the alley door. Turning, she asked, "How did it go, darling?"

"Not too bad," said Daisy, plopping down on the nearest chair, "except for my poor feet. The children were good and everyone was frightfully helpful."

"I mean the photos," Lucy said impatiently.

"I can't tell, darling, till you develop them for me. Be an angel and do them right away."

"Tomorrow," Lucy promised. "Binkie's taking me to see *The Prisoner of Zenda* tonight."

Daisy burst into gales of laughter. "I've just met him!" she gasped.

"Who? Ramon Novarro? Where? Not at your stuffy old museum!"

"Not Ramon, a Ruritanian prince." She told Lucy about the Grand Duke Rudolf Maximilian.

"Darling, how too, too romantic!" Lucy, who prided herself on her hard-headed practicality, was at heart far more of a sentimentalist than Daisy, as witness her choice of films. Her amber eyes glowed. "And how sad. Is he good-looking?"

"Not as handsome as Ramon Novarro, and much too young for you, darling. A good five years younger than us, at a guess."

"And no money," said Lucy mournfully.

"Even less than Binkie, I should think, and no job."

"Darling, grand dukes simply don't take *jobs,* like mere mortals. Especially reigning grand dukes."

"He hasn't got anything to reign over," Daisy pointed out.

Lucy sighed.

As good as her word, she developed the plates next morning. They were all absolutely hopeless.

"Never mind, darling," she consoled Daisy. "I'm going down to Haverhill this weekend for Grandfather's birthday— can't miss it, it's his eightieth, the old sweetie—but next week I'll go to the museum with you and get some good shots."

While Lucy was toasting the start of the Earl of Haverhill's ninth decade, Daisy joined the Fletchers for Sunday dinner, her nephew having by then gone home to Kent. Mrs. Fletcher actually unbent enough to commend Derek as nice-mannered child.

"Spoilt, though," she added hastily, as if horrified to find herself praising anything associated with Daisy, "but what can you expect, his father being a lord."

Daisy, Alec, and Belinda escaped for the afternoon by taking Bel's new puppy, Nana, for a walk on Primrose Hill.

During Lucy's absence, Daisy also typed up her notes and started to get her article into its final shape. The quantity of excess information reminded her of her idea for a more scientific article. She popped into the nearest W. H. Smith's and found several suitable magazines, surreptitiously scribbling down their addresses and editors' names without buying anything but the *Daily Chronicle*. Letters of enquiry went out by the second post on Monday.

Soon after Daisy's article and Lucy's splendid photographs set sail across the Atlantic, two magazines replied, expressing their total lack of interest. A third wanted the complete text before deciding, and a fourth requested resubmission at a later date, as the next fifteen issues were already filled. Slightly disappointed, Daisy went off to Shropshire to do the research for the next article in her series on minor stately homes for *Town and Country*.

Much as she might wish to, she could hardly visit that part of the world without staying a night or two with her mother, at the Fairacres Dower House. She found the Dowager Lady Dalrymple as disapproving as ever of Alec's middle-class background and distasteful profession, yet making plans for an elaborate—and expensive—wedding in St. George's, Hanover Square.

"Who is to pay for this, Mother?" Daisy asked, exasperated.

"I dare say your cousin Edgar can be brought to understand his obligation, since he so cruelly exiled us from hearth and home."

"Mother, you know Edgar had no choice but to succeed to the title," Daisy could not help saying for the thousandth time, "and he offered us a home."

"As though I should accept that man's charity! A schoolmaster, so underbred, and the way Geraldine puts on airs is quite shocking." Lady Dalrymple counterattacked: "When are you and Mr. Fletcher going to set the date? I disapprove of long engagements, and the church must be booked months in advance."

Daisy at once started to think about registry offices. She also wondered, rather dolefully, whether Alec could get a guaranteed leave of absence from the Metropolitan Police to be married, or if a sudden complex case might tear him from the altar—or the registry office equivalent. Frightful thought!

Her mother always had a depressing effect on her spirits but she revived as soon as she left Fairacres. Her recovery was completed when she reached Mulberry Place. On the table in the tiny hall, an extravagantly vast bouquet of chrysanthemums awaited her, and Alec's card with a note saying simply, "Missing you."

Beside the vase was a heap of letters, accumulated during her absence. Daisy flipped through them, recognizing the handwriting of her sister, two friends, a cousin. Then a business-size, typewritten envelope. Another rejection, no doubt.

But it wasn't. *Dilettanti* magazine wanted her article, as long as she could let them have it by the end of September. If so, would she please telephone as soon as possible to confirm.

"Lucy?" she called up the stairs. No response.

Only three weeks! Still, it was not like starting from scratch. She already had a good start on the research, and she had made the acquaintance of all the people she would need to interview. Reaching for the telephone she and Lucy had had installed just a month ago, Daisy confirmed.

She was dying to share the news with someone who would appreciate it, but she always tried to avoid phoning Alec at the Yard, and he was often out of his office anyway. Mrs. Potter, the charwoman who "did" for Daisy and Lucy and took a deep, admiring interest in their work, had already gone home. Daisy rang through to Lucy on the studio extension, but there was no answer.

Three weeks—she had better get cracking. She telephoned the Natural History Museum and made appointments to see the Keepers of Zoology and Botany in the morning.

That done, she dropped her hat on the table, her coat on the chair, and leaving luggage strewn about the hall, hurried to the tiny back parlour which was her study. She already had a rough draft of the stately home article, typed on the portable machine on semi-permanent loan from her *Town and Country* editor (How her mother had moaned at the evidence of her daughter's occupation!). It wouldn't take long to finish it up on the massive, ancient Underwood typewriter which sat incongruously on the elegant Regency writing table from Fairacres.

The Underwood saw a great deal of her that week. Each day she returned from the museum with reams of notes and typed long into the evening. The museum's business was far more complicated than she had realized.

In the private offices, studies, and work rooms where she was now introduced, the preparation of specimens for display was a minor aspect of the work in progress. From all over the world, unknown plants and creatures were sent to be classified. Daisy had never previously heard of Linnaeus, but she was soon as familiar with his system as with the map of the London underground. The museum staff produced not only minute descriptions but painstaking drawings and even paintings of each specimen.

That was in the Zoology and Botany Departments, where specimens normally arrived with all their parts intact. In the Geology Department, imagination played a greater part. As Mummery had explained to her, few fossils were found complete; the missing bits had to be guessed at. At least, it looked like guesswork to Daisy, though Mummery insisted it was educated deduction.

His position was undermined by the iconoclastic Ruddlestone, Curator of Fossil Invertebrates, a jolly North-country-man who rivalled Alec's sergeant, Tom Tring, in size and baldness.

"Guesswork is more like it, though we have advanced a bit since Waterhouse Hawkins," Ruddlestone admitted to Daisy.

"Waterhouse Hawkins?"

"He built life-size concrete dinosaurs for the Crystal Palace exhibition of 1851, all as bulky and firmly four-footed as elephants or hippos. Believe it or not, he gave a dinner party inside one half-completed model. Then there were the Americans, Cope and Marsh: bitter enemies, brilliant in many ways, but Cope stuck the skull of an Elasmosaurus on the end of its tail! Marsh never let him forget it." Ruddlestone roared with laughter.

"Mr. Steadman told me his Diplodocus has the wrong feet."

"Poor Steadman, it rankles badly that his prize exhibit is made of plaster of Paris. A load of real bones the Americans sent over during the War was sunk by a German submarine. A great loss, whatever that ass Pettigrew said." The curator was no longer amused.

"What did he say?" Daisy asked, though she had a good idea.

"That the loss of mere fossils was trivial. In his view, a cargo of munitions would have been a great loss. But munitions can be replaced and fossils cannot! I'm afraid affairs like the controversy over Dr. Smith Woodward's Piltdown skull play into the hands of ignoramuses like Pettigrew." Ruddlestone cheered up. "But it illustrates what I was telling you: They can't all be right, so someone's 'educated deductions' have to have gone far astray!"

Later that afternoon, shortly before the museum closed, Daisy asked Smith Woodward about the Piltdown Man controversy.

He took her to see it again, but this time he contemplated it in silence for a minute, before sighing, "It really is very troublesome. Fossil fish are really my field, you know. I believe I may say I am accounted something of an authority on fossil fish. Do let me show you my Arthrodire."

He had been so kind that Daisy let him off the hook. She could always ask someone else about Piltdown. He limped at her side across the gallery, and they entered the hall leading to the fossil reptiles, with the dinosaur gallery beyond, wherein the fishes occupied their modest place.

Somewhere in front of them a voice rose in triumph and contempt, the words indistinguishable. The bellow that followed held a note of surprised agony, like that of a wounded bull. Then came a tremendous crash.

With a gasp, Smith Woodward stopped, rooted to the ground. Daisy ran through the arch ahead.

Sprawled on his back, immobile amidst a litter of smashed Pareiasaurus bones, lay Pettigrew. Across Ol' Stony's white shirtfront and pale grey waistcoat seeped a crimson stain.

ABOUT THE AUTHOR

Born and raised in England, Carola Dunn now lives in Eugene, Oregon. Her next Daisy Dalrymple mystery, FALL OF A PHILANDERER, will be published by Kensington Publishing in November 2006. You can visit her website at: www.geocities.com/CarolaDunn